Harry Mac

RUSSELL ELDRIDGE

ALLEN&UNWIN

SYDNEY · MELBOURNE · AUCKLAND · LONDON

First published in 2015

Allen & Unwin
83 Alexander Street
Crows Nest NSW 2065
Australia
Phone: (61 2) 8425 0100
Email: info@allenandunwin.com
Web: www.allenandunwin.com

Cataloguing-in-Publication details are available
from the National Library of Australia
www.trove.nla.gov.au

ISBN 978 1 76011 320 9

Set in 11/17 pt Sabon by Post Pre-Press Group, Australia
Printed and bound in Australia by Griffin Press

10 9 8 7 6 5 4 3 2 1

Harry Mac

For my parents, Stan Eldridge and Maureen Eldridge,
and for Brenda

This is a work of fiction set against a background of historical events. For the sake of the story, I have altered or condensed some timelines, such as the period Nelson Mandela was on the run, and the start of the South African Border War.

For more information on some of the events and historical characters in this book, please see the Historical Notes.

'...behaviour is not just a matter of choices between pragmatic courses...it is also driven by irrationalities, inconsistencies, and the urge to make incompletely articulated gestures.'

—Martin Langford, *The Casual Deletions*

1

WHEN DAD GOT TENSE HE SMELT LIKE A RHINO, A BIG
suffocating smell you wanted to get away from. And when Haas
Cockroft asked him to help assassinate the prime minister, you could
smell rhino all the way down the corridor of our house.

I'll tell you later how I know what a rhino smells like, but mostly
you need to know what happened about Haas's plan, because it
changed everything.

I can't help feeling the lane where we lived had something to do
with it all. As though these families had been put there for a reason,
a sort of test, and so what one person did became all our business,
like Karel de Wet's sad smile and shake of the head if Dad mowed
the lawn on Sunday. At the same time, the lane felt thick with secrets,
and it was so still, like everyone was holding their breath a lot of the
time. It was worst in summer, when the gardens and lilli pilli hedges
and jacarandas hummed.

The lane was at the edge of town, curving down to a wall of
khaki grass, dull green thorn trees and a locked gate. Beyond the

gate a red dirt path sneaked into the trees, leading to the *spruit* which flowed along the bottom of the valley.

On the town side, the lane joined the big road, which belonged to somewhere else; noisier, the light harsher.

When you came home from the big road, the lane closed around you like a sofa.

The corner house, the *spookhuis*, was where Mr van Deventer put plastic bags over the heads of Gillian and her little brother, whose name I never knew, before shooting Mrs van Deventer and then himself. It had happened a while before and the For Sale sign was starting to fade and the agent hadn't mowed all summer. The little bottles of coloured water with feathers in them to keep out the natives were still there, tied to the gate post, and nearly every time I walked past (it was better if I rode my bike because it was over quickly, even though it hurt my bad leg to pedal fast) I thought the same thing: how can a whole family be there one day—Gillian riding home from school on her old black bicycle, not looking at anyone— and the next day just not be there? Not moved to Durban or Joburg; just not there. Not anywhere. So when I walked past I couldn't look in case maybe they hadn't completely gone away. I didn't tell anyone this, not even Millie, who was trying to hold me to a promise for a midnight visit to the *spookhuis*. Anyway we didn't talk much about it in the lane because the *spookhuis*'s front door faced away from us towards the big road.

That's what it was like in the lane. We were all jammed in there but you didn't have to see things if you didn't want to.

But I couldn't avoid what Haas said to my father that night.

I overheard them because I was fetching Laika, who'd jumped off the bed at the sound of raised voices. She stopped growling when she recognised Haas and started scooting her bum along the corridor towards the light from the lounge. Haas had been drinking and he spoke in a careful, thick way. Dad wasn't saying anything but I could smell rhino, so I grabbed Laika in the dark and started back to my bedroom. Then Haas's voice took on a new tone I'd never heard from him, sort of pushy, so I stopped and listened. Laika wriggled a bit then went to sleep in my arms.

'What I'm saying is we can't just sit around on our arses, Harry Mac. The Group believes that if we don't do something—and do it now—it'll be too late. The Dutchmen call us the enemy and disband our regiments, so let's take it to them. Look at what they did to my arm. My nose. That's the sort of scum we're dealing with. And don't think you're safe behind your new desk. How much longer do you think the Nats will allow you to keep attacking them, hey? Come on, man! What did you fight for?'

Uh-oh. You don't speak to Harry Mac like that, not unless you want him to knock your bloody block off. I gripped Laika and she whimpered.

Dad's voice, also careful, but not from drink: 'It's late. Why are you here, Haas?'

'Because The Group needs your support. Steady the boys' nerves.'

'Their nerves?'

Something was placed on the dining table. It made a crunchy metal sound, like rugby boots on concrete. I heard Dad suck in his breath. 'Get that thing out of my house.'

'It's untraceable, Harry Mac. As soon as Verwoerd sits down, I'll pull the lights and—I won't say his name—will roll it on to the stage under the bastard's chair.'

The smell was overpowering. 'Get that out of here. And get this straight: you told me nothing.'

'I take it you're in?'

There was a scrape of chairs, and I hurried back to my room.

I lay staring into the dark, the sheet stuck to my back in the still air. Outside, the crickets were silent, and the black car had long since crunched slowly up the lane on its night patrol. Next door, Haas's son Titch had put away his weights for the night, turned off his radio and flicked the garage light. Across the lane, the *Bosmoedertjie* was having an army nightmare. There was a strangled sob and then silence. The stillness was complete, and the lane reached unseen arms through the window and closed around me, crushing my chest. I kicked at the sheets, reached up and yanked aside the curtain, light from the streetlamp flooding across my face as I gulped at the thick air. I leant on the windowsill, panting, scared and excited. They needed Harry Mac to steady their nerves: my dad. If I told Millie she would toss her hair and say 'cool', but then snort and add that Haas didn't have the guts.

I knew what they were talking about because Dad's paper had reported the prime minister's planned visit to our town. The government wasn't popular in Pietermaritzburg and so they kept the date of his visit secret; most people thought it would be after we became a republic and after the election the Nats were certain to win. Dad wrote in a leader that Verwoerd was coming to 'gloat in the camp of the defeated'.

Dad knew the prime minister, and they didn't like each other. The rest of the Cabinet didn't think much of Dad either. I suppose it was him calling them mad dogs in his leaders that did it. At the cocktail party for the recent opening of parliament an old Afrikaner newspaper colleague from Dad's days on the Rand had come over, looking, as Dad told it, 'like a policeman delivering bad news'. The man had said, 'Harry Mac, *ou maat*, no offence, but I've been asked by the justice minister to let you know *jou boek is vol.*'

With Mom digging her nails into his elbow, Dad had bellowed, 'Tell the old Nazi that if my book is full, I'm only just starting to write his.'

I didn't like it when Mom and Dad told us this story. I saw this huge grey building full of government officials writing up complaints in little books, one for each person in the country. And when they'd filled one—wham! Now Dad was threatening to write a book of his own. Was this how he was going to fill it—with Haas and The Group?

Dad was a terrifying man and not just because of his size. Men seemed to shrink around him, and I could see that some of them hated it. I mentioned it to Millie's dad, Sol, and he gave one of his talks to us, about 'charisma'; how people who had it could inspire both respect and fear, 'and fear is a bedfellow of hate'.

The tightness in my chest had eased and I pushed off the windowsill. The movement sent a twinge up my leg and I rubbed it. Everyone in the house called it my bad leg. Sometimes they talked about *the* bad leg, as though it was another member of the family, like a drunk uncle or something. They could have it. I closed the curtain, lay back and pulled up the sheet, but my eyes wouldn't close.

Dad had said to Haas, 'You told me nothing'. But whether he liked it or not, he was now part of the secret. And when Haas said Dad was 'in', Dad hadn't actually said no. I wondered whether the government's threats had angered him enough to tip him over the edge. An angry Harry Mac wasn't nice.

I slipped towards sleep remembering Dad lifting a man out of his car after I'd ridden my bicycle into the side of it. It had been my fault; I'd turned too fast into the lane and the man had no chance to stop. I wasn't hurt, but Dad, who had been gardening with Mom, walked straight through the bougainvillea hedge carrying a spade, wrenched open the car door and lifted the driver out with one hand, roaring, while Mom and I screamed at him to put the man down. She had to take the man inside and give him a cup of tea, while keeping her eyes away from his wet trousers. When Dad had settled down, he checked I was all right then knocked my bloody block off. The bad leg got no special treatment that time.

That was Harry Mac. My Dad. And I was locked in a deadly secret with him and Haas Cockroft.

2

MOM DROVE DAD TO WORK EVERY DAY SO SHE COULD have the car, but next morning they left early and I couldn't see whether he had his angry face on.

School was a write-off. I only half listened to the student history teacher who talked about the US–Russia arms race and how President Kennedy was telling people to build their own bomb shelters. The student teacher, who had a beard and a leather jacket, got excited, drew a mushroom cloud on the blackboard and waved a pamphlet from America showing what to do in a nuclear attack. The pamphlet had a drawing of a man lying in a gutter with a bucket over his head. It was the sort of story I'd love to tell Dad, just to watch the big furrow between his eyebrows go smooth and his eyes widen as he started to laugh. I'd have to save the story until I knew whether he was in with Haas or not.

As I approached the lane on my bike after school, I had the feeling of something heavy hanging over me, and by the time I turned off the big road I was struggling to breathe. Normally I would freewheel past my house and up Millie's drive, but today I grabbed the brakes and the bike skidded on the gravel. I managed to stay on and wobbled to a stop just before her gate. Now I knew why I couldn't breathe. I didn't want to face Millie.

'Nice driving, Fangio.' Her voice was dry and a bit suspicious.

Too late. I got off and leant my bike against the fence and watched her cross the lawn towards me, rubbing her hands.

'Flex your twiddlers, Tom-Tom, I'm gonna whup you.'

Millie was odd in several ways. For a start, she had no neck. From behind, if she wore her long curly brown hair down, you didn't notice anything. But when she turned she looked like those weightlifters who hunch their shoulders and clasp their hands to make their muscles bulge. And like those weightlifters, she was astonishingly strong, as the first boy who called her 'neckless' found out.

Our after-school game was to kneel on the lawn facing each other, palms together, fingers locked, and try to push each other back while talking about the day we'd had. I'd have to brace myself because Millie would usually start, launching into a story about the moronic teachers at the private school her mother had forced her to go to. The game was her idea and she never tired of winning, but it didn't bother me. I was a better swimmer.

Today, we'd just started when Millie flicked my hands away, sat back on her heels and said, 'Okay, what's buzzin', cousin?' That was another odd thing about Millie. She had an uncle in America who wrote letters laced with slang, and Millie loved it.

But now I was getting the third odd thing: the frog mouth. Millie had a wide mouth, I mean really wide, and when she smiled it was the most beautiful thing you've ever seen. But her mouth could form other shapes, and this one was annoyed. She waited, but I couldn't talk to her about it.

'Is Sol home?'

'You know he's at work.'

I nodded and got to my feet. I had thought that Sol, who could explain anything, would be the one. But now I was glad he wasn't home, because what if he was involved? He was Dad's closest—maybe only—friend.

I fetched my bike and pushed it back up the lane to my house. I could feel Millie watching me all the way; knew the frog mouth would be a tight line across her face. I couldn't have handled it if she'd said what they were planning was cool. By now, no part of me thought it was cool.

•

When Mom and Dad got home, it was worse than I'd imagined.

I was sitting at the table on the verandah with my homework untouched, waiting for our station wagon to turn in the gate, and watching Haas Cockroft next door watering his garden near our fence, the late sun flashing off the gold watch that he said helped him sell more cars. I didn't greet Haas but kept a close eye on him anyway, looking for signs he was up to something. His arm was in a sling and his nose was puffy and he didn't move from the one spot, the garden hose trained on the petunia bed. Mrs Cockroft would give him hell for that. In the garage behind him, Springbok Radio was on full blast, but you could still hear Titch grunting as he heaved the weights over his head. I think Haas and I were both waiting for my dad. I was angry with Haas. Angry with his watery eyes and powdery pink face and pinched lips like he was trying to hold in a vomit (Mom said it was caused by the booze; you saw it on a lot of the men at the MOTH Shellhole). Angry that Haas needed my father to 'steady the boys' nerves'. *His* bloody nerves. Dad and Haas got along okay on a surface sort of level but Dad always regarded Haas and the 'Empire Set', as he called them, as a joke; down at the

Shellhole, moaning about the disbanding of the country's English regiments and scheming a return to the empire. Dad didn't care for their cause but the government was their common enemy. I'd once asked Dad why Mr Cockroft was called Haas, the Afrikaans word for hare. Dad had thrown his head back, shoulders shaking. 'Ah, boykie. At the Shellhole, Haas will tell anyone who listens that it's because he was the regimental running champion.' But those who'd been in the desert with Haas knew different. Dad told me their battalion had been in foxholes with only their rifles when the Panzers rumbled out of the sandstorms. 'You could feel the ground shake, and your knees with it,' he recalled, but the men just cracked up when they saw Private Wilbur Cockroft dodging and leaping from hole to hole trying to get away. He was 'Haas' from then on. Haas kept running and leaping so fast that while Dad and the rest of the battalion were swallowed up by the Germans, Haas caught up with one of the last Allied trucks out of Tobruk.

It wasn't until Harry Mac came back from the POW camp after the war that he saw Wilbur Cockroft again. He had kept the name Haas and built his own stories around it. Mom said that Haas always resented Dad because he knew the true desert story. She told me Haas had sold us this house—his dead father's—and boasted of unloading the ramshackle dump at a good price. He had watched over the years as my parents fixed the old house—'making a silk purse from a sow's ear' Mom said. So when Dad and Mom turned to the garden and started planting trees, Haas chopped down the sixty-year-old jacaranda on the boundary that gave shade to both gardens. Well, you can imagine what Mrs Cockroft said when she realised you could now see straight from our verandah into their bedroom.

Now, as the yellow wagon turned into our drive, Haas edged nearer the fence. But the car had barely stopped when Dad got out, left the door open and walked to the house, ignoring Haas, who had cleared his throat and stepped into the flooded petunias. Dad didn't even glance at me. And in his hand was a full-size bottle wrapped in a paper bag.

This was bad. A half bottle was usual, but the big one was dangerous. If it was whisky we had a chance, but gin meant he didn't care about the taste. I looked back towards the car. Haas had stepped onto his lawn, the hose whipping across the grass while he swore and wiped his shoes. Mom took a long time to leave the car and walked slowly up the steps, head down and her hair a blonde curtain across her face. She flicked a look at me and went straight to the kitchen. She'd been crying and the back of her dress was dark with sweat. I felt sick. It meant Dad had gone into a silence.

The way it was in our family, when Mom was in the room I felt warm. Normal. Nothing was missing. When my older brother Little Harry was around, which wasn't much these days, he was like all my school friends' big brothers: moody, sneery and 'casually violent' as Millie put it. But he couldn't hit me too hard because of you-know-what: '*Ag!*' Mom would say. 'Don't hurt him. Think of the bad leg.' I used it against him whenever I could, particularly when Mom was around. Now, when Dad came into a room, anything could happen. Exciting and scary at the same time. Like being around a huge animal that maybe should be tied up. You see, Dad had three states (that's another Millie word—'states'): angry with the world, angry with his family, happy about everything. The worst was the middle one, because it came from nowhere. He would start on Little Harry and then take it to Mom. Sometimes I'd get a swipe along the way, but mostly the bad leg saved me from the worst of it. When the rage was spent, a heavy silence settled on the house and nothing would make Dad speak. It could last for days.

And I had to fix it. That's why I watched and listened. To everything. At door cracks, below windows, anywhere. Head off the silence or fix it. When he was in a good mood, Dad sometimes called me *Wagter*, the watcher.

He couldn't go into a silence without an argument first—or a rant, really, because he was the only one who spoke. It would start in the early evening, around dinner time, about four drinks in. But today, it seemed he'd got the rant out of the way in the car home and gone straight to a silence.

Maybe Mom had to take it all this time because Little Harry was away camping at the beach with his friends, having their last holiday before the army.

I went into the kitchen to check on Mom, but only Essie was there, cooking her dinner. Before I could speak, Essie rolled her eyes towards the lounge, gathered her food and walked out the back door to her *kaya*, shaking her head and saying, '*Hai, hai, hai!*'

I found Mom in her chair waiting for Dad, sipping from a glass she'd filled from the flagon of Drostein in the fridge. Her face looked broken. 'Oh, Tom.'

I hugged her and sat on the couch and we waited for the footsteps down the hall. He came in like any other day, shirtless, barefoot and wearing his big khaki shorts. I looked at the condensing glass in his hand. Gin.

I decided to try my story. 'Dad, we had this student teacher today . . .'

He dipped a finger in the glass, drew a cold line across his forehead, turned and walked out of the room.

And that's the way it went.

3

THERE'D BEEN MORE SILENCES SINCE DAD HAD BECOME editor a few months before, and I wanted to find out why the government made him so angry. I decided to ask Sol. He knew everything, and if he didn't know he made up a good story. Like Millie, really. Where Harry Mac was a rhino stomping everything in his path, Sol Lieberman was a giraffe, moving in slow motion, looking over the top of everything. He was lanky and rubbery, with a long nose, thick lips and a deep chuckle. He loved to talk as much as Dad but he talked philosophy. At least that's what it sounded like. He never spoke about anything directly, but gave these little talks—sometimes not so little—and Millie would roll her eyes and make a strangled sound.

I thought I would tell Sol about Dad's mood and watch closely to see how he reacted; I had to be careful in case Sol was involved with the plot.

So next afternoon, when Millie and I had finished playing, I hung around on the Liebermans' verandah, waiting for a chance to talk to Sol, who had a day off from the mental hospital.

'Harry Mac is a bit like Samson, you see,' said Sol, gulping at a mug of ginger beer, kicking off his shoes and settling into the verandah chair.

Here we go.

'Oh, no! Not Biblesville, Sol,' said Millie, getting up and walking inside.

'*Feh!*' Sol waved dismissively and turned back to me. 'Harold MacGregor has supernatural strength but he doesn't understand that the jawbone of an ass has limitations.'

I didn't have a clue what he was on about. This was the sort of stuff that drove Millie crazy, but I didn't mind because he said things other adults didn't, and at least he talked to me. 'Dr Lieberman, please.'

'Sorry, Tomka, sorry.' He leant across to the folded newspaper on the verandah table and tapped it with the back of his fingers. 'Your father is angry. Ve-ery angry,' he said, lifting it up and flicking through the pages. He put on his glasses and read, chuckling as he tried to imitate Harry Mac's booming voice: '*Nearly fifty years ago a British statesman remarked that "the lamps are going out all over Europe; we shall not see them lit again in our lifetime". That remark presaged the start of the Great War. It is apt now to recall it, for the aftermath of that cataclysm spawned a breed of monsters who find their reincarnation in the degenerate confederation of Nazi sympathisers that is plunging South Africa into its own age of darkness.*' He looked over his glasses and wiggled his eyebrows.

I wondered who, apart from the men writing complaints in his book, read Dad's leaders. I hardly understood a word.

'Yes, Dr Lieberman, but Dad gets angry about a lot of things. Why's it got worse? Is he right? Why does he call them Nazis? Why—'

'Ay ay ay! One at a time.'

He leant back and propped his stockinged feet on the railing.

Sol never took his socks off, even at the beach, where he wore them under sandals. Mom said it was a European thing, and she spoke in that hushed way like when she told us the grocer Mr Doda visited Mecca because he was a Mohammedan.

Sol took off his glasses and pinched the flesh between his eyes. 'A bit florid. A bit melodramatic. But yes, he's right.'

He sighed, heaved himself to his feet and went inside.

I stayed on the verandah, puzzling over Samson and the Nazis. The lane below us was in deep blue shadow, but the sun still burnt yellow on the ridge opposite where the Hesketh Motor Racing Circuit caretaker's horses kept the grass down. Beyond the ridge, Table Mountain floated in the heat haze rising from the Valley of a Thousand Hills. Back in the lane, a couple of doors up from the Liebermans, the *Bosmoedertjie* was being wheeled back inside, his father's soothing voice cutting across the sobbing moans. A shouted command made me look down. Titch Cockroft was practising shot-put in the vacant lot across the lane and the family's garden boy was running around with a wheelbarrow. Titch had worked out that his Olympic training would get a boost if he used bricks—he could get a lot more throws in and a good workout at the same time. The trouble was bricks only weighed half a shot-put, so he reckoned to get the same effect he had to throw two in quick succession. When he told us this Millie had said, 'Don't be thick. Doesn't work like that.' Millie was good at maths. So now he balanced two bricks behind his ear and threw them together. When they landed, they bounced all over the place and every now and then he would shout for Phineas, hiding in the long kikuyu a safe distance away, to come out with the wheelbarrow and collect them all.

I heard Sol's low laugh behind me. He had returned with a full bottle of ginger beer from which he refilled our glasses while watching the Olympic build-up in the vacant lot. 'Poor Titch.' He raised his glass. 'Here's to Titch and Tokyo '64.'

'Dr Lieberman, is it okay to kill a bad person?'

The words hung there, ugly and hard in the soft evening light, and the smile faded from Sol's lips. He gave a funny little coughing laugh.

'Jesus, Tom, such questions.' Sol sometimes laid on his German accent to make you laugh, and so it became 'kvestions'. Millie said it was corny, but I think it was to give himself time to think, because just before he did it Sol's eyes would slide away.

He dabbed with a handkerchief at his shirtfront where he'd spluttered ginger beer, and watched as Sandra Lieberman drove into the yard, gathered her tennis gear from the back seat and walked into the house, flicking her hair. I stood up and Sol lifted a hand to his wife as she passed and she nodded to both of us without smiling. Millie had come back out and didn't look at her mother. Sol sighed and closed his eyes again.

He turned to me, 'So who do you want to kill, Tom?'

'Me? No, not me—' I clamped my mouth shut, biting the inside of my bottom lip. I'd nearly said it.

Sol was quiet for a long time as the lane closed down for the day. Titch had finished his training program, at least until after dinner, and the last golden light was slipping off the top of Table Mountain. The shadow would be reaching all the way to the coast, and Durban would already be dark. I wondered if I should get home in case Dad was ready to end the silence. Sol's voice jolted me back.

'Tom, let me tell you a little story.' The funny accent was gone. He shook himself down in the chair as a growl sounded in Millie's throat.

'Short version, Sol. It's late. And cut the dramatics.' But she stayed.

'When I was about your brother's age, just finishing school, my country passed some laws. People were classified into different races and one of the groups lost their citizenship. They couldn't do certain jobs, go to the same schools, and so on. Sound familiar?'

I didn't know whether he wanted me to answer him, so I shrugged.

'But of course we all know the story of the Nazis and the Jews and what that led to. Now!' He held up a finger as though to stop me from interrupting him, and drank some more ginger beer, his eyes holding mine over the rim of the glass. He cleared his throat and tapped the paper again.

'Now we're getting closer to why Harry Mac is so angry, and, I might say, fearful. You see, at the same time the Nazis were on the rise there was another country where a political party hated the Jews and wanted to bring in similar laws.'

He opened his arms, palms up, and shrugged. 'That was here.' His words were blunt, his rubbery face hard. 'The Jews, the Africans, the Indians and the English-speakers,' he said, ticking them off on his fingers, 'the Nats hate them all, and they are now running the country. They are the ones telling your father his book is full.'

How did Sol know the full book story? Dad must've told him. It was the sort of story he enjoyed telling. Sol finished his drink, got up, clapped me on the shoulder and went inside. I turned and looked at Millie. She had a frog mouth on, but in the gloom of the verandah I couldn't read it. And Sol hadn't answered my question.

•

There was only one light burning when I got home. Mom sat at the kitchen table in front of a glass of Drostein and a crumpled tissue while Essie bustled about, keeping an eye on her and clanging pots and pans like the silence was a bad spirit you could drive away. Dad sat on the verandah with the lights off listening to Charlie Kunz on the piano and drinking gin from a tall glass.

Mom and I had dinner together at the kitchen table but she just pushed her food around, and although she put a plate out for him in the dining room, Dad stayed outside. Mom didn't say anything until I had nearly finished eating and then she spoke in a small voice, 'Maybe it would be better if I went away.'

I put down my knife and fork and dragged my chair closer. I never knew whether she meant it or just wanted us to feel sorry for her. Either way, I panicked.

'Don't be stupid, Mom, it's not your fault.'

'Isn't it? Then why doesn't he talk to me?'

'He doesn't talk to me either.'

I looked at her, and even with her eyes red and swollen and the bit of snot running out of her nose, she was beautiful. How could Dad not see she was the most wonderful thing we had in our lives? Outside of the silences, Mom was always laughing, and sometimes when she moved she would do this little twirl. She'd been a dance teacher and that's how she met Dad, who came back from the war and wanted to 'knock off some rough edges'. So she taught him to foxtrot and waltz and things went on from there.

Mom loved to sing too, but she had a terrible voice. She'd recently been to the bioscope with a girlfriend to see *Breakfast at Tiffany's* and she'd cried for the rest of the day. Dad bought her the record of 'Moon River' and she would put it on and waltz around the lounge while he watched with his forehead smooth, looking like his soldier picture. Even Little Harry would sit down and watch without making any remarks. If Mom tried to sing along, Laika would start howling and everyone would crack up. To see Dad and Little Harry in the same room laughing was something, I can tell you.

I cleared the dishes, kissed Mom goodnight and went to my room to listen to the radio Little Harry had given me a few months before. It was just after he'd got his call-up papers when he'd called me into his room one night. I'd found him lying on his back with the lights out, shining a torch up at our Airfix dogfight hanging from the ceiling and potting them with his peashooter. He didn't seem to care whether he hit a Messerschmitt or a Spitfire. I went to the dressing table and scratched around for the other peashooter. 'Can I have a go?'

'Shut up. Listen.'

The radio glowed on the bedside table and was making an off-station hissing, crackling noise. He shifted across on the bed and I sat with my ear near the radio. A man was talking—or, rather, spit-shouting, like when they replayed Hitler on Movietone News. I couldn't follow but the man was angrier than Dad. One word kept repeating.

'What's "azania"?'

Little Harry took aim, clipped a Heinkel on its tail and sent it spinning in the cone of torchlight.

'They're waiting out there to kill us.'

He reached behind me, yanked the radio out by the lead and swung it onto my lap. 'Piss off.'

So it became my radio.

I hadn't looked for the hate station again but tonight I turned the dial, searching for the scratch and bark. I didn't find it so I listened to *No Place to Hide* without remembering any of it and then the news came on. The excited newsreader said the Springboks were the best team in the world after a grand slam tour of Britain on top of winning the All Blacks series, and an exciting new player named Frik du Preez had been discovered. In other news, the Panga Man had struck again and police were warning couples not to park in isolated areas at night. Next was Verwoerd speaking English in his smiley voice, saying he wanted all races to be happy and to 'fulfil their own destiny as good neighbours' under his government's new plans. The newsreader then said that the state of emergency had calmed the country, and he crossed to the Minister for Justice, B.J. Vorster, who growled, 'Everything is normal.' Actually, maybe Dad's leader had been right. Vorster did sound like a grumpy dog. The news ended with an unconfirmed sighting of a Russian submarine off the Wild Coast. Vorster came on again and vowed to remain vigilant in the face of communist threats 'both internal and external'. He said we lived in the most peaceful and wealthy country in Africa and, with the help of God, his government would keep it that way.

I turned off the radio and the light. Vorster was the one who'd told Dad his book was full. But the voices were reassuring and I relaxed. Verwoerd sounded like my Uncle Ian. What if Sol was just bitter because he had to leave Germany? What if being editor was too much for Dad and the drink was winning like it did with Aunty Merle and Uncle Ian? What if the government was right? Maybe Dad just needed to calm down a bit.

I fell into an exhausted sleep and dreamt of Dad running after a rhino, waving a donkey's jawbone.

4

NEXT MORNING, MOM HAD THE LOOK OF SOMEONE walking up a long hill without knowing where the top was. She mixed up the fillings on my sandwiches and forgot to put Kool-Aid in my bottle.

I was trying to read Dad's leaders every morning now while I ate breakfast. I hadn't been able to talk to Sol about the plot, so I looked for clues in what Dad wrote. Today, he'd placed his leader on the front page next to a story about the government starting to ban people they said were a threat to public safety. The story listed one hundred and two names, and in his leader Dad wrote that these people couldn't say or write anything in public and would be arrested if they talked to more than one person at a time. So if a banned man was walking along the street and bumped into his wife and child he couldn't talk to both of them.

That was just silly. Who could live like that? And who was watching them and counting the people they spoke to?

I continued reading. If, Dad asked, the country was at peace, like the government said, why couldn't everyone talk openly? Then he wrote something I didn't understand about the *spirit of Dr Goebbels living on in this rabble of petty gauleiters.* That was one for Sol. He would know about this Dr Goebbels, for sure.

As I read on, one sentence stuck out: *People disappear in the night.*

What people? The ones on the list? People who spoke out?

The leader was a blur now and I had to read the ending a couple of times before it sank in: *But why don't you make up your own mind about whether we live in a free society? Try this. Take this newspaper with you to a quiet place, sit a moment and read aloud the political debate we have printed below.* The rest of the page, all the way to the bottom, was blank.

I thought at first they'd stuffed up and Dad would give the subeditors hell. Then I read it again and got it. Harry Mac was looking for a fight. And if his name was put on that list, he wouldn't keep quiet. He would explode.

I looked again at the sentence, *People disappear in the night.* I wondered where they put them, and what would happen to us if Dad disappeared.

•

That day at school, Mr Frame, who could become violent after lunch because he had a metal plate in his head from the war and it heated up in the afternoon, was teaching us about Sir Isaac Newton. He said Newton had created laws in science, such as, *For every action, there is an equal and opposite reaction.* Mr Frame smirked. 'For example, if a newspaper editor pokes a mamba with a stick, it'll bite him.'

The other boys tittered. They didn't know what he was on about but they liked a dig.

My big mouth opened before I could think. 'You mean like if you make a bad refereeing decision they won't give you a big game.'

Mr Frame's face went red and the class was silent. We all knew he'd been passed over as a Currie Cup ref because he'd stuffed up in the Craven Week final. Luckily, the box of chalk he hurled at me hit Charles Marwick and cut his arm, so Mr Frame had to settle down. Anyway, he started it.

After school I was anxious to have another go at Sol, to get him talking and see if he let anything slip. I felt a bit like a secret agent. He wasn't home from work yet, so Millie and I played then I hung around until she became annoyed. 'You're dullsville, Tom-Tom. I'm going up the lane to watch the Incredible Hulk and see if he blows a foofy valve.' I knew Sol might be a while, so I went with Millie.

We followed the sound of Springbok Radio to Titch's garage, where we found him doing chin-ups, his face redder than Mr Frame's. Millie wrinkled her nose at the sweaty smell and settled down to watch. Millie said she liked to be there at the start of Titch's training to see the way his muscles puffed up and the veins stood out. Titch would grumble and tell us not to bother him, but you could see him watching us out of the corner of his eye when he made his biceps bulge.

I remembered something I wanted to ask him. 'Hey, Titch, how did your dad hurt his arm?'

He finished the set and dropped to the floor, panting and wiping his glistening chest with a towel. Millie's frog mouth was all rubbery. Titch had a body like in the magazines but his face was blank and he breathed through his mouth, even when he wasn't panting. He played rugby for Natal Schools and it was widely known he'd deliberately failed matric so he could make the SA Schools tour to Australia the next year. Unfortunately, the tour had been put off for a year because of protests over there. So Titch had to fail matric a second time, but now there was talk the school had had enough. Titch didn't really mind because something better had come along. He had taken up shot-put while waiting around to fail and found he was good at it. So good, he made it to the SA junior championships. Now he was focused on the Tokyo Olympics.

He looked at me now and spoke slowly, as if to an idiot. 'My dad was injured fighting for what he believes in—for the English-speakers.' Titch told us that Haas Cockroft had been with a group of activists who'd travelled to Ladysmith to sabotage a visit by a government minister. It was all very hush-hush. When the time came, they'd stood up in the middle of the minister's speech and sung 'God Save the Queen'. Haas and his comrades had then ducked out for a cigarette to celebrate their triumph. Unfortunately, some of the local farmers had been waiting for them.

'He should get a medal,' I said. Big mouth.

Titch turned on me, his small eyes disappearing. 'Well you'd never win a medal with that leg, *hoepelbeen.*'

Next to me I could see Millie's frog mouth working. She liked Titch's physique but that's as far as it went. Her voice was sweet. 'Tell me, Titch, is the school going to take you back next year?'

He turned away. 'Haven't heard yet.'

'Oh dear. So if the school won't take you back, I suppose you'll have to go to the army. You should ask the *Bosmoedertjie* what it's like . . .'

Titch's head jerked up and the frightened-animal look on his face made me feel almost sorry for him. I hadn't realised that might be the real reason he kept failing. He picked up his T-shirt and walked out of the garage.

Millie followed. The frog mouth hadn't finished with him. 'I suppose you could try to get into university and defer your service.' She always pushed the knife a little deeper.

Back up on the Liebermans' verandah, she celebrated with a bottle of ginger beer. 'Pompous thickie,' she said, pouring. 'I'm the only one who can call you a cripple.'

'Bringing up the *Bosmoedertjie* was cruel, Millie.'

She flashed straight back, 'Oh was it? While Titch builds his muscles and fails exams, people like your brother have to go to the border and get their legs blown off, like the *Bosmoedertjie*.'

'The *Bosmoedertjie* didn't have his legs blown off,' I corrected her. 'He was paralysed.'

She thumped down the bottle of ginger beer and rolled her eyes. 'Unreal!'

Mrs Lieberman had been giving me unfriendly looks from inside the house and kept calling Millie in to do her homework, so when Sol got home and sat down to talk to me, Mrs Lieberman slammed a book on the dining table. 'Oh, for God's sake, hasn't this child got a home to go to? What are you filling his head with?'

Sol glanced sideways at me, winked and waved me to a chair. He leant back and closed his eyes. The darkening lane smelt of freshly watered gardens, and a trickle of servants made their way up to the bus stop on the big road, their voices slow and tired. I thought I should leave Sol alone, but I had worked out a way to get him going again; I'd ask his opinion of Haas Cockroft's combat wounds from Ladysmith. But before I could say anything, Sol started up.

'Tomka, I've been thinking about all this,' he said into the evening quiet, eyes still shut. 'What's in the box in the garage?'

'I'm sorry?'

'The cardboard box in your garage; the one with the incubating light and the blanket.'

'Oh, the crocodile eggs.'

'Correct.' He opened his eyes and smiled like the *Pick a Box* man. 'What did Harry Mac want to do last year, before Liz put her foot down?'

'Uh, sell the house and travel around the country in an ox wagon.'

He was nodding. 'Do you want me to go on? Remember the motorcycle sidecar?'

'Dr Lieberman, I don't—'

He held up his hands. 'Tom, your father wants political justice, *ja*, but he has an equally powerful appetite for life. He takes big juicy bites.' He snapped his teeth and sat back, grinning.

I clasped my hands between my knees, miserable and confused. I looked around for Millie but she'd gone inside to do homework, waiting just long enough so it didn't seem like she was doing it because her mother had told her to. Why couldn't Sol talk simply? I wasn't doing a very good secret agent job on him.

Sol leant towards me. 'Sorry. Nothing in life is straightforward, least of all me. Listen. Your father lost five years of his youth to a war. Before that, he was a poor miner. Now he comes back and because he's clever the world opens like a flower: good job, beautiful wife, nice house. He doesn't have to sweat underground with a mile of rock waiting to fall on him. He can sit in an office with sunlight across his desk and write stories that thousands of people read and admire. He is still young. Anything is possible.'

He stopped and sipped his drink, holding up that warning finger.

'But there's a serpent in Harry Mac's garden. You see, he finds he has to fight the war all over again, just the details are different. And this time, the good guys are losing.'

Dad would hate that. Was he being drawn into Haas's plot to relieve the pressure inside himself?

Sol's accent had thickened the more worked up he became, but this time he wasn't putting it on. He stood and stretched, rolling his neck. He glanced back at the house and patted his pockets, pulling out a single bent cigarette and a box of matches. He motioned for me to walk to the end of the verandah, where he leant on the railing, lit up and sucked deeply. In the lounge behind us Mrs Lieberman's voice shrilled as it tried to cut across Millie's drawl. Maybe she'd changed her mind about doing homework. Sol blew out, shoulders relaxing, smiled at me and held a finger to his lips. The lane was dark now, and the smell of fried onions drifted up. Mom would be wondering where I was. I had thought Sol wanted to talk some more, but he just wanted to smoke. So we stood there leaning on the rail, watching the blue dusk coat Table Mountain.

I had to have one more go. 'What about you, Dr Lieberman?' It came out rude. The big mouth and the frog mouth. Quite a pair, me and Millie.

'What about me.' Sol said it like a statement, not a question. It sounded sad.

'I mean, don't you get angry? You know, all the Jewish stuff?'

'The Jewish stuff.' He laughed and coughed before flicking the cigarette into the night. 'Tomka, if we Jews got angry about everything that has happened to us over the last two thousand years, we would set the world ablaze.'

There you go. You think you're getting somewhere with Sol, and he throws that at you. I could imagine his eyes sliding in the dark.

'It's still not fair that Dad won't speak to us because he's angry with the Nats.'

He laughed again and turned to see Mrs Lieberman standing further down the verandah in the light from the lounge, hands on her hips. She looked anxious. Sol patted my shoulder. 'Go home, Tom.'

•

The silent routine at home was much the same. Mom not crying so much, just flat, and Essie muttering to herself in Zulu. Dad had told us a story once about a bad-tempered subeditor he'd worked under. The sub was rude to the native staff, who complained about him. But the native tea lady was always smiling even when the sub yelled at her. Dad had asked her why and she said that it was okay, she had got *muti* from a witchdoctor and was now putting it in the sub's tea to make him happy. I wondered if Essie was putting anything in

Dad's tea. If she did it wasn't working. I wanted so much to tell Dad about Mr Frame's dig—and my comeback—and to tell him about Millie frightening Titch with the army and the *Bosmoedertjie*. But he sat out on the dark verandah and didn't say hello or goodnight.

I lay in bed for ages thinking over what Sol had said about Dad. I kind of got what he meant, but it didn't make it any easier. Why would a man who wanted to take juicy bites out of life risk it by killing the prime minister? No, Dad must have it all under control. But as soon as I thought that, I knew I didn't believe it.

●

Something was scratching at my shoulder. I slapped at it and heard a giggle.

'Tom-Tom!'

I rolled over in bed and took in the silhouette framed in the window by the streetlight.

'What the hell are you doing, Millie?'

She rocked forward on the sill and tickled me again with the twig. My bed was right under the open window but I couldn't make out her face. 'C'mon, you can't chicken out now. We promised.'

I groaned and flopped back. 'That was a hang of a long time ago. We're too old for this, Millie. Anyway, I thought you were joking.'

'C'mon, let's agitate the gravel.'

I pulled myself onto the sill and Millie grabbed my arms, steadying me as I slipped down next to her. We were both in our shortie pyjamas and the night was warm, the grass cool under my feet.

'Do you need your caliper?'

I pushed her away. 'Go on. This is stupid. You could've been the Panga Man at my window.'

'He only attacks lovers. Half your luck. Get moving.'

We crept through the garden and out onto the lane, my feet feeling their way along the stones. We stopped at the corner of the big road and looked around. The street was empty, the houses dark.

Millie started ahead, 'Quick, it's nearly midnight.'

'This is so childish.'

Grumbling, I bumped into Millie's back. She had stopped at the Van Deventer gate and was looking at the *spookhuis*. I came up next to her. There were no curtains and the streetlight shone through a gap in the trees and into one of the front rooms.

I thought I would be scared, but I felt nothing. I looked at Millie and her face was blank, her mouth neutral.

'How will we get in?'

She shrugged. Neither of us had thought of that. We opened the gate with its bottle of coloured water and feathers, walked up the overgrown path and stepped onto the verandah. The cement was cold and leaves had started to collect against the front door.

'It's probably unlocked,' I said. 'Essie reckons the natives won't go near it.'

Millie leant forward and tried the handle, giving a start as the door opened. We peered down the dark corridor, cool air reaching out to touch our faces. 'Should've brought a torch,' I whispered.

'That's the point,' Millie said, trying to sound normal. She felt for my hand and pulled me into the house, the floorboards hollow under our bare feet.

We turned into the room that was lit from the street and looked around. It was just a room, an empty room. The house smelt of fresh paint and dust. As we stood there, I started to feel something. Not scared, just something about the house. We walked back into the corridor and through another door. This room was bigger and darker and as our eyes adjusted we could make out a fireplace.

'This was where it happened.' Millie's voice was over-loud and bounced around the walls.

'Sh! How do you know?'

'Just do.'

I looked around slowly. How did he do it? Were they all sitting around the fire eating tomato soup and toast and listening to a serial and Mr van Deventer walked in and just did it?

That feeling again. I took a deep breath and turned to Millie, who was still holding my hand. In the gloom, I could tell she was looking at the floor.

'Let's go, Tom.' Her voice was quiet.

'Are you scared?'

She shook her head, 'I just . . .' She shook her head again.

It was almost there, that other feeling, like something at the corner of my eye, but when I turned it slipped back into the shadows.

'Why do you think he did it?'

She didn't answer, but tugged at my hand and led me out of the house. We closed the door behind us and walked down the path, through the gate and out onto the pavement next to the big road. We turned and looked at the house, the blank windows reflecting back. Now I felt it was watching us. But I still wasn't scared.

Millie spoke in the same quiet voice she'd used inside. 'Tom?'

'Yes.'

'What's going on?'

'What do you mean?'

'You know.'

So that's why she'd called me out tonight. But I just couldn't talk about it.

We turned away and walked around the corner and back down the lane. We parted without speaking, me losing balance because we'd forgotten our fingers were still entwined.

5

IN THE END IT WASN'T TIME THAT BROKE THE SILENCE, but Essie.

Mom had driven Dad home from work a few days later and gone to sit in the kitchen, but Essie wasn't there. Mom waited and eventually went to the back door and called out. There was a light on in the *kaya*, so Mom and I went out and found Essie sitting on her bed, crying.

'Essie, what's the matter?'

The old woman shook her head. 'Windsor.'

Windsor was Essie's son, her only child, and both of them had been there from the start, from before I was born. When Mom and Dad bought the house from Haas Cockroft just after the war and moved in, they were surprised to find people living in the outside *kaya*. They'd asked Haas about it.

'Oh, that's Essence and Windsor,' Haas said. 'They come with the house.'

I never got to know Windsor because he lived most of the time with his gran at the family *kraal* in Kranskop. To me he was just a sullen teenager who sometimes stayed in the *kaya* during school holidays. He hardly ever spoke to Little Harry and me but seemed to get on with Dad, who paid him to work on garden projects, like pergolas that never got finished while they argued about the government. Windsor was clever and when he matriculated, Dad helped pay for him to go to Natal Medical School.

Now it seemed Windsor had disappeared.

Mom went and told Dad, who put his glass down and came straight out to the *kaya*. It turned out that not only was Windsor missing, but he hadn't been to lectures for months—in fact, hadn't been seen since he told a classmate that he was catching the train to join the Pan Africanist Congress protest at Sharpeville.

Essie could barely bring herself to say the word 'Sharpeville'. Her smooth brown face was twisted with crying and she held a hand over her eyes like she was ashamed to let us see her like this. 'I thought he was just busy and that's why he didn't come to see me for so long. A friend of his came today and told me and brought this.' She held out a worn booklet. 'The PAC said they must leave their passbook behind and go to the police station in Sharpeville and ask to be arrested.'

Dad didn't say anything. He took the passbook and went to bed early while Mom comforted Essie.

I stayed a while watching the two women and the way our shadows grew and shrank along the walls in the light of the paraffin lamp and I felt a sweet-sad rush of memory, of being wrapped in those plump brown arms. I hadn't hugged Essie in years. I looked around the *kaya*, with the small fireplace in the corner, the iron bed raised on bricks to keep away the *tokoloshe*. It had also been a long time since I'd stood under this blackened ceiling, with smoke tickling my nose, smoke that was the scent of Essie. She was a part of our lives every day, but we weren't a part of hers. And I remembered one

Sunday coming back from a picnic, and as we turned into the lane Mom said, 'Good heavens! Where did they all come from?' It was a sunny autumn afternoon and all the way down the lane, sitting on the little crescents of grass designed for cars to pass each other, were groups of servants, chatting, braiding each other's hair or polishing silver. Mom had rolled down her window, letting in the liquid sound of their voices. 'Hell, I never knew there were so many of them living in the *kayas*,' Mom had said.

•

The next day, Dad behaved as if the silence hadn't happened. In fact, he didn't shut up all evening. For someone who was so impatient about everything, he sure liked to tell a long story, and Mom and I sat there at the kitchen table, smiling at him. I don't think Mom heard a word.

He had contacted the police and found that Windsor wasn't on the casualty list from Sharpeville. Nor was he among those arrested.

Dad had then walked from the newspaper office around the block to the sandstone building that housed the security police—the Special Branch—and asked to speak to Kolonel Engelbrecht. Loftus Engelbrecht and Harry Mac knew each other well from their rugby days. Loftus was now known as the Kolonel, pronounced in the Afrikaans way, Kol-o-nel. It sounded foreign, more dangerous.

Dad was settling into his story now, hunched over a beer can at the table. Beer was fine, but something about his mood made me uneasy. His eyes were shining.

The Kolonel had kept Dad waiting on a bench outside his office while Special Branch men came and went along the corridor. 'People don't usually go into that building of their own free will, so I got plenty of narrowed eyes from the police who recognised me,' Dad said.

He would have been nicely steamed up by the time the Kolonel called him in, calm and polite and talking about the Springboks.

'Everything in that building is hushed,' Dad told us. 'Even the African office boy who brought tea and rusks walked on tiptoe.' The Kolonel had taken the passbook and sat leafing through it silently while Dad looked around, noticing a pile of newspaper clippings on the desk which he recognised as his own editorials.

Dad drained his can of beer and I hopped up to fetch another. He laughed and shook his head. 'A cop's a cop. Subtle as a sledgehammer.'

The Kolonel had finally looked up and said, 'Windsor Khulu Dlamini. Is he a troublemaker?'

That made Dad seethe. He told the Kolonel he just wanted to set a mother's mind at ease. He pointed out Windsor was only nineteen and a medical student.

The Kolonel had looked at him without expression and said, 'A clever kaffir, hey? Worst kind.'

Dad pushed away from the table and started pacing around the kitchen, going into a crouch, like the boxers do. Mom had stopped smiling. 'I hope you controlled yourself?' she said.

He spun around and shook a finger. 'You know, he used to do that on the rugby field if his team was losing; he'd just say something quiet in the scrum and before you could stop yourself you'd taken a swing at him and he'd be standing there with a blank look while you were being marched off the field. Jesus, he was good at that.'

Mom's face was stiff. 'What did you do, Harry Mac?'

He shrugged and sat down. 'I know he doesn't believe that rubbish, so I told him to fu—' At the look on Mom's face he broke off. 'I told him not to speak like a pig.'

The Kolonel had laughed and said he would make inquiries; no promises.

The story was over, but Dad stayed seated, slowly crushing the empty can in his hand and staring at the tabletop. Mom had started to get up, but stopped. She lowered herself back into her chair. 'Yes? And?'

Dad wouldn't look at her. 'I was nearly out the door when Loftus said my name, softly. I turned and he had this odd look, and he placed his hand on the pile of leader clippings and said, "*My vriend, it has been suggested you should get your house in order. Not from me, verstaan? Higher up.*"'

Mom was twisting her rings. 'Harry Mac?'

He lifted his head, and there . . . there was that shine in his eyes. 'I told him I would start worrying about "higher up" if I broke the law.'

•

Back in my room, all I could think about was that shine. From what Dad had told us, the Special Branch didn't make empty threats. I knew he wasn't scared of them, but I didn't think he would be excited. Was he about to take a swing at them? Through Haas's plot?

I switched off the light and in the darkness saw Mr Frame's red face under his boiling brain: *Equal and opposite reaction*. I wasn't so sure about the 'equal' part.

•

The end of the silence was like break-up day. Mom sang while making breakfast and Dad just leant back in his chair, grinning and teasing. That evening, Mom came home with her hair done and a flat cardboard box under her arm. For Harry Mac, this was better than the bioscope. He called it 'Liz's appro dance'. They would go into their bedroom and he would prop himself up on pillows on the bed with a glass of beer on his bare belly, one arm tucked behind his head, while Mom unpacked the swing skirts she'd taken out on appro. She'd turn the side mirrors on her dressing table and check the fit of a skirt, kick off her shoes and start spinning, the skirt floating up as her legs flashed and Dad chuckled, jiggling the glass of beer. Sometimes, they'd shut the bedroom door. The next day, Mom would return the skirts.

But it couldn't last.

While Mom and Dad got on fine now the silence was over, they weren't happy. The government was burning a hole inside Harry Mac, and there was something else. He complained to Mom that now he was editor he felt alone at work. The paper had a billiard room, and whenever I went into the office with Dad I used to watch him and the reporters talk about their stories over the clicking balls. But now it was hard for him to find a partner and a chunk of his day was taken up with staff problems. He'd come home from work and unload to Mom and you'd hear the same few names over and over— men he'd beaten to the top job. Every evening at the same time, the paper would call our home and Dad would discuss the news with the night editor, and you could hear how forced the jokes were.

It was during one of these calls, not long after the end of the silence, that Dad discovered our phone was being tapped by the Special Branch.

Our line had developed an echo and strange clicks, which only seemed to happen during the night call, and one evening when I answered the phone it was so bad I couldn't even hear the switchboard operator. I handed the receiver to Dad and told him the line was really crackly. He listened for a moment and then barked, 'If you're going to tap my bloody phone, at least make it professional so we can both hear.' There was a brief silence as the clicks stopped and then an Afrikaans-accented voice said, 'Sorry.'

Well, I hadn't heard Dad laugh like that for a long time. There were tears running down his cheeks.

But that was just one light moment.

Most of the time, the house felt like it was being squeezed in a vice. Little Harry returned from the coast, moody and not speaking to anyone, and started packing for the army. This in turn upset Mom, who was already worried about Dad and Essie. For her part, Essie did her work listlessly as the days dragged by with no word of Windsor. As well as not knowing what had happened to her son all those months ago, there was the problem that Windsor had left home without his passbook. The passbook now held by the Special Branch. Dad said Windsor would be thrown in jail if he was caught in a random police check. He could be sitting behind bars anywhere in the country, with no lawyer, no way of contacting anyone, and waiting indefinitely for a trial along with the hundreds of others caught in the swoops. Dad said he would automatically be found guilty and sent to prison. And no one would know.

I spent as much time as I could over at the Liebermans' to get away from our gloomy house, but Millie was annoyed with me because she knew I was hiding something from her. Even Sol seemed preoccupied, and when I tried my secret agent tricks on him, he just went 'hmm' and twiddled his toes inside his socks. The only one who hadn't changed was Mrs Lieberman, who snapped at Millie and sneered at Sol, once calling him 'a loony doctor' right in front of me.

To top it all off, the summer storms were late, and the heat triggered a Berg wind, blowing down from the mountains like the hot breath of a big dog.

6

EVER SINCE MILLIE AND I WERE SMALL, SOL WOULD READ to us. He loved the ancient world, and my favourites were the Greek myths and a big lump of a book, *The Great Civilizations*. Sometimes, he would read just a page and then talk. With the myths, he liked to explain what he called 'the context'. And sometimes he would read strange, unsettling books, like the one he had out now. He said it didn't matter if we couldn't follow it all, because something would seep in.

I'd walked up the front path and found Sol and Millie in aprons, bottling ginger beer on the verandah. Sol was filling the bottles and Millie capping them, so I helped for a while, stacking the full bottles in crates until we'd finished. Sol took the empty drum around the side to clean it, calling back to me, 'Don't go away, Tomka, I want to talk to you. Millie, get the boy a drink.'

'*Jawohl, Mein Führer!*' Millie saluted her father's back and marched inside. Sol's voice carried faintly from the garden, 'Don't joke about things like that.'

Sol emerged from the house a few minutes later, drying his hands on his trousers, a book tucked under his arm.

'This is for the boy with the questions. The boy who asked why I don't get angry, who asked about the "Jewish stuff". So I want you to remember this name: Primo Levi.' He ran his index finger down the gold lettering on the spine of the book. He didn't use the thick accent and he wasn't smiling.

He sat down, took a sip of his drink and started reading the story of the young Jewish-Italian partisan who was captured and sent to Auschwitz.

Sol only got past the first few lines when his voice stumbled and he lowered the book to his lap. The Berg wind gusted through the Liebermans' jacaranda, whipping off the late flowers and sending them spiralling around the garden like living things, glowing with light from the setting sun.

Millie sat next to me with her eyes closed; she hadn't made any smart comments since he began reading. Sol started to speak again, his gaze fixed somewhere in the restless canopy of the jacaranda, but this time he wasn't reading from the book. It lay closed on his lap and his voice was different, like he was talking down a phone line from far away.

'Tom, in 1935 I was in my last year of school when my father was thrown out of his job as a hospital pathologist in Hanover. Out on the streets and in the shops we weren't safe from the Brownshirts, so our extended family had a meeting and decided to get the young people out.'

He stopped and his face sagged. Millie's eyes opened, and fixed on him.

He continued, 'I ended up on a refugee ship, the *Stuttgart*, bound for Cape Town with about six hundred other young Jews. The deal was that once we were settled, the South African government would give our parents entry permits. We docked in Table Bay and I stood at the top of the gangplank, rain dripping off my hat, looking out at my new country. I heard a chanting below on the wharf and I looked down to see a bunch of men in grey shirts, their fists raised. One was waving a swastika.'

Sol turned to me and tried to smile, but it didn't work.

He got up and went to lean both hands on the verandah rail. Millie had closed her eyes again and as Sol passed, she trailed her fingers along his arm. He looked out over the garden then turned to us.

'This is not just one of "Sol's stories",' he said, nodding towards Millie. 'It has a point. We'd barely left the docks and the fists of the Greyshirts behind us, when a young university professor led a delegation to the government, describing us as a menace. Four days later, the government caved in to the pressure and clamped down on Jewish immigration. That young professor's name was Hendrik Verwoerd and he is now our prime minister.'

Sol laughed but, like his smile, it cracked. 'He's moved on from Jews since then.'

'So what are you going to do about Verwoerd?' Big mouth, big mouth. Why did I say that?

Sol jerked and looked at me wide-eyed. 'What do you mean, Tomka?'

'I'm sorry, Dr Lieberman, I didn't mean to be rude. But I still don't understand how you can be so calm about it all.'

'Because—and you listen to this, too, young lady.' He leant forward and tapped hard on the arm of Millie's chair. 'Because we have to bear witness. Someone has to bear witness.'

Millie spoke without opening her eyes. 'Like a linesman waving a flag from the sidelines.'

Shit a brick. Harry Mac would have backhanded me without thinking. But Sol looked like he might cry. He hung his head, then straightened. 'Okay, *freche Kinder*. In the car.'

Something in his voice made us both get up without asking why and climb into the old Austin. We didn't even look back to see if it was all right with Mrs Lieberman. Sol kept the motor running outside our gate while I went in and told Mom I'd be late for dinner, then we turned onto the big road and drove down the hill, through the quiet tree-lined streets, across the Duzi bridge, all the way into town and up another long hill to the railway station. Sol parked and led us into the red-brick and wrought-iron building where people bustled about, gathering their bags for the arrival of the overnight train from Durban to Joburg.

Millie had got her voice back and asked Sol if we were meeting someone.

'Sort of,' he grunted.

He eased his way through the crowd, looking around as if trying to find someone or something. We passed the two glass cases holding the scale model engines and Millie demanded two pennies. Sol looked like he was about to argue but relented and gave us a coin each. We fed the machines and the trains lit up and the wheels turned. When it was over, Sol called us away, impatient. He stopped on the platform and held his arms out, turning a slow circle, grinning. Oh my God, he's going to dance, I thought. But Millie grabbed my hand and led me to a bench outside the nearby waiting room. 'Lecture time. C'mon, Dad, hurry up, I'm hungry.'

'Okay, but only because you called me Dad.' He cleared his throat. 'I am standing on one of the most significant places in modern history.'

'Yeah, right,' muttered Millie. 'Dullsville Central.'

'Millie shut up. It is a cold midwinter night, 1893. The Durban to Johannesburg train steams in through the mist from over there, and in a cloud of smoke and grinding metal . . .'

'Sol!'

'Okay, okay. The train stops, people get off, people get on, but the train just sits there hissing steam, and after a while a policeman arrives, boards the train and shoves a small man out of a carriage and onto the platform. The man's luggage follows. The policeman leaves the station and with a piercing whistle and a belch of black smoke, the train resumes its journey. All is quiet. The station is deserted. The little man picks up his suitcase and walks into the waiting room—that one behind you—and sits down. He sits there all night, huddled in his coat, thinking. At first he plots revenge, but as the freezing night wears on, he decides he should get out of the country and return to his homeland. But then as dawn nears, his mind clears. Now he knows what he must do.'

With that, and Millie and I just getting into the story, Sol turned and walked out of the station.

Millie was furious. When we caught up with him at the car, she demanded to know what happened to the little man.

Sol had a smug look as he opened the door. He liked having something Millie wanted to know. He started the car, shrugged and said, 'Oh, he just went on to defy the greatest empire in the world and lead his country to freedom. And he didn't have to point a gun at anyone. He just sort of—how did you put it, Millie?—waved from the sidelines.'

He stopped the car in the middle of the road and turned to us. 'His name was Mahatma Gandhi. He was thrown off the train because a white passenger objected to his presence. He said later that the seeds of his non-violent resistance, *satyagraha*, were sown that night. He stayed in South Africa another twenty years, fighting racism, and then went back to India to inspire the independence movement. He of course did a lot more than wave from the sidelines, but you get my point.'

We drove on in silence until I asked, 'What happened to the little man after independence?'

'They shot him.'

'Sol, can we have a Moolk?' We were passing the petrol station that had installed a new vending machine, and there was a cluster of cars around it.

'*Ja, ja.*' There was disappointment in Sol's voice as he turned back.

We bought our cartons of flavoured milk and leant against the car, slurping, watching other kids doing the same.

I was wrapped up in Sol's story, working it out. He had been jumpy when I asked him what he was going to do about Verwoerd, but now I thought he was saying violence was not the way. If Sol's way was what he called 'bearing witness' then maybe I could trust him. I had to speak to someone soon, though, about Dad.

I watched him come out of the shop carrying half a loaf of bread wrapped in tissue paper. He jammed it between the front seats and we drove off, his left hand reaching down to gouge out lumps of bread and stuff them into his mouth.

'Mom will kill you,' Millie chirped.

'Momf nof here.'

I sat in the back and watched his jaw muscles make his ears jump. 'Dr Lieberman, did your parents get their entry permits?'

He chewed and swallowed hard, nodding. He glanced at me in the rear-view mirror. 'They did, Tomka. But those Greyshirts, and others like them, forced the government to withdraw the permits.'

'So did they ever get out of Germany?'

He nodded slowly. 'Yes. To Poland. To Auschwitz.'

We drove back to the lane in silence. As I climbed out of the car at our gate, Sol put a hand on my arm. 'You know, our faith has it that we are God's chosen people. But there's an old Jewish joke which says, "Why doesn't God choose somebody else for a change?" What it means in reality, Tomka, is that we are outsiders. Here, the black people are struggling against their Afrikaner oppressors, the Afrikaners feel cheated by the English, and everyone hates the Jews.

Which gives us kind of a free hand, really, because we've nothing more to lose. But I choose to live a non-violent life down an obscure lane in an absurd town, whose inhabitants' greatest desire is to find an English aristocrat among their ancestors.'

He laughed and the old waffly Sol was back. 'You know, I chose this town because I saw on the map there was a place nearby called New Hanover and I thought it might help with the homesickness.'

'Do you miss Germany?'

He thought about it. 'I'm sorry I never got to see Jesse Owens run at the 1936 Olympics. Ah! To watch him fly, and to see the look on Hitler's face would have been priceless.'

'Sol, that's enough! Let him out of the car, I'm bloody starving.'

'Foul-mouthed girl.'

1

A FEW DAYS LATER, DAD TURNED HIS EDITORIAL ANGER on the English-speakers.

Who are we? What do we stand for? We've been here one hundred and fifty years, but where are our songs, our heroic stories, our roots? We don't even sing the national anthem in our own language. Our children are taught the Afrikaner legends at school: the Wolraad Woltemades, Rachel de Beers and Dirkie Uyses. The black people have their Shakas, Moshoeshoes and Bambathas. Who do we have? Imperialists and warmongers like Cecil Rhodes. Men who incited wars for diamonds and gold.

The Afrikaners and the Africans are engaged in a titanic struggle for domination and survival—and have been since 1652. Where do we fit in? Napoleon is supposed to have scorned the English as a nation of shopkeepers, so what does that make us, the disregarded colonial offspring of Britain? Peanut-sellers. Snack merchants on the sidelines of this great contest.

African liberationists may loathe the Afrikaners, but they see them clearly for who they are and what they want. Sadly, many English-speakers in this province feel a kind of shame about being South African. They still run to the 'Mother Country' to help them secede from the Afrikaner and return to the comforting embrace of the British lion, moth-eaten as it is.

Peanut-sellers? Another one for Sol. Was Dad going mad? He was lashing about in all directions. Sol had said Harry Mac was like Samson, going at everything with the jawbone of an ass. I'd asked Mom about Samson but all she could remember from Sunday school was that he killed himself when he pulled down the pillars of the temple. I hoped this wasn't where Dad was heading, but the pressure was building and I didn't know who would burst first, him or me. *Peanut-sellers?*

•

I'd been half expecting it for a few nights now, so when I felt my shoulder roughly shaken I woke up and without speaking climbed out the window, took Millie's hand and we walked up to the *spookhuis.* The Berg wind had spent itself, and as usually happened, soft grey clouds had swept a cool change up the coast.

We walked into the lounge where we had now decided Mr van Deventer had done it, and stood for a while in the dark. The air was warm and stuffy, left behind by the Berg wind.

'I never told you,' I said, not looking at Millie, 'but whenever I came past the house before, I was scared to look in case they hadn't gone away.'

She seemed to think about it. 'And now?'

'I don't know. I feel like they could still be around but I'm not scared. Well, maybe a bit.'

Millie crossed the room and stood at the window that looked down the lane and over the valley. She was being stand-offish and it made me jabber.

'Hey, Millie? Why d'you think he did it? I reckon he was a secret agent and was found out and so he had to erase all traces . . .' My words dribbled away as she remained staring out the window, her back to me.

She turned the latch, letting in a stream of cool, damp air. I sniffed at the new air because Mom could smell rain, but the rest of us never could. I was about to say something about it, but caught myself. Millie perched on the sill and swung her legs out. She sat there facing away from me. 'You're a shit.'

'I'm sorry, Millie.'

'We said no secrets.'

'Sorry.'

I climbed up and sat next to her, our heels against the wall of the house. The weather change had triggered storms over the coast and the distant skyline pulsed with white light, silhouetting the slab of Table Mountain.

Something way down the valley caught my eye; two sets of headlights flickering through the gum plantation at the sewerage farm. They were heading up the back way towards Hesketh, where the fence was slack and you could hold it down, lay planks of wood over the barbs and drive through. Little Harry had told me how you did it. Once on the track, you took off down the straight, changing into fourth through Henry's Knee and then flat out until you had to brake, sooner than you realised, at Quarrys Corner. Quarrys was so tight you were automatically careful, no matter how drunk you were. After Quarrys, it was full-bore down the back straight, sweeping into Beacon Bend, where it just kept tightening and tightening like a screw. And that's where the cars rolled.

'And?'

'Huh?'

'What you're keeping from me.'

So I told her. Just like that.

Then neither of us said anything for a long time. Even though the night was still, with the window open you could feel air moving in and out of the house like it was breathing. I felt lighter, but not sure if I'd done the right thing.

Up at Hesketh, lights flashed down the main straight. More lights waited at Beacon.

A white hand crept along the windowsill and squeezed mine. 'Thank you.'

She tried to rest her head on my shoulder but it didn't work because of her neck. Instead, she turned her body and rested her forehead against the side of my head. It felt like warm water flooding through me. I hadn't felt so happy for ages.

Silence again, but she was working up to something.

'I've got one.'

I couldn't see her mouth and so I waited. Across the valley it was dark. The cars up at Hesketh had gone. Below us, the lane was quiet except for the murmur of Titch's radio and the chink of barbells on concrete. He was training late tonight.

We heard the black car before we saw its lights. Its wheels were already crunching gravel at the bottom of the lane and it would be able to see us in a few seconds. It moved slowly, like its wheels were seeking out each stone to crush. We scrambled back inside and I reached up and pulled the latch shut. We crouched below the window and the black car stopped, as it always did, idling for a minute or so, then continued its slow grind up the lane, staying in first gear so the strain of listening to it was like hearing someone speak with phlegm in their throat and you wanted to cough for them.

'Sol has secrets, too.'

'What?'

We were still crouched below the window and I barely heard her whisper. Our foreheads were touching, so I leant back to try to see her face. It was too dark. I held her shoulders and strained my eyes. 'Millie? Is Sol involved with Harry Mac? Millie? You have to tell me.'

A slight move of the head. 'They're his secrets, not for me to tell.'

I wanted to shake her. It wasn't fair. I'd told her mine. But shaking wouldn't get anything more out of Millie, and if I tried to argue she'd just tangle me up with words. I relaxed my grip and we heard the black car turn out of the lane and accelerate down the big road.

Millie pulled away and helped me up. My leg had stiffened and I rubbed it before checking the window was closed. When I turned around she was gone.

I stood there listening to the fading sound of the black car. It was the only car that ever came out of the bush below the lane, and they must have had a key for the padlocked gate that blocked the faint track coming out of the trees. Wherever it came from, the black car would have to go to a lot of trouble. It would have to skirt the entire town, drive through the sewerage farm and then a long way through the plantations, up the valley, over the *spruit* causeway and along the bush track before it got to the gate at the bottom of our lane. We never knew when it would arrive or why, but it always did the same thing. If I was awake, sometimes I'd hear it brush against the hedge outside my bedroom window and I'd roll away from the wall. We just thought of it as a lane thing. If you asked an adult about the black car, they'd wave you away and make a sound like you'd said something rude at the table. Little Harry had been face to face with the black car one night after he'd sneaked out of the house to have a cigarette in the lane. It kept coming straight at him at the same slow speed and he had to jump into the hedge. He said he'd looked into the car as it glided past and there was no one inside. Millie and I reckoned he was lying, because the black car had darkened windows.

I looked over the room again, feeling its stillness. It was the first time I'd been alone in the *spookhuis*.

'Shame.' The walls slapped the word back in my face. It was as if someone else had spoken through my mouth. But that's what the feeling in the house was. Shame.

I walked home, chewing over what Millie had told me. Just as I was getting closer to talking to Sol, he slipped away again. Sol had a secret. I didn't know what it was but it obviously upset Millie. And now she knew mine.

8

AFTER DAD CAME HOME FROM WORK NEXT DAY, I WENT looking for him. I had this lump like a big belch of words sitting in my chest and I needed to talk to him before it exploded.

I found Mom in the kitchen mixing *frikkadels*, while from the lounge came the awful warbling of Jeanette MacDonald and Nelson Eddy singing 'Will You Remember', one of Mom's favourites since she was a girl. Mom said that when he was younger, Dad had looked a bit like Nelson Eddy, which I thought was rubbish because Nelson Eddy had a girly face, and if he'd made eyes at Mom, Dad would have knocked his block off. I watched Mom from the doorway, singing quietly to herself (thank God) and she looked up and saw me. She did a little whirl across the kitchen and squeezed me to her, holding her hands clear so the mincemeat didn't get all over my shirt. I think I fell in love with Mom every day.

'Where's Dad?'

'Don't know, poopie-boy. Might be out checking those damned crocodile eggs. Nice to have you home in the afternoon. How's Millie?'

'All right.'

'I think we all need to get away, you know. Maybe go down to the caravan for a weekend.'

I shrugged and resumed looking for Dad. As I was passing through the house I heard the murmur of men's voices. I stopped and listened. It was coming from Little Harry's room. I walked over to the door. Dad and Little Harry were sitting side by side on the bed. They didn't see me and I hung back. The first thing that struck me was how alike they were. Little Harry had been called that since he was a baby but he was nearly as tall as Dad now, although not as scary. I'd never seen the two of them like this. For a start, Dad wasn't lecturing, pointing, accusing, and Little Harry wasn't glaring, defending, swearing. He was no longer the big brother who left me down at the front of the bioscope while he smoked up the back with his friends; who stood in front of the mirror and flopped his hair and practised his Ricky Nelson smile; who hit me when I asked if Ricky Nelson also had pimples.

Here were two men talking together about men things. About the army. And I was just a boy.

I backed away and went to my room.

I waited until I heard the slow thud of Dad's feet walk down the hall to the kitchen, heard the fridge door open and close, the clink of glass, and then Mom and Dad's voices join in with Jeanette MacDonald and Nelson Eddy in 'Indian Love Call'. Jesus wept!

Then Dad's heavy footsteps moved to the verandah. I waited for a few minutes and then joined him. Dad was drinking a glass of beer, the bottle on the floor next to him, his gaze fixed on the garden, but you could tell he wasn't looking at anything in particular. He turned to me without smiling. 'Boykie.'

I touched the big round shoulders and pulled a chair close to him and told him about the student teacher's pamphlet with the drawing of the man protecting himself from the atom bomb by holding a bucket over his head. I sat back and watched how his whole body shook when he laughed, and I felt so much better.

But after a while he went still and quiet again, so I said, 'Mom's going to miss Little Harry.'

He sighed. 'They've all got to do it. You're lucky.'

It was the first time anyone had said I was lucky to have the bad leg. He smiled, showing those big yellow teeth, swatted my head and sang '*Jannie met die hoepelbeen . . .*'

'Dad?'

'Mmm?'

'Is it dangerous?'

'What?'

'Where he's going.'

Another sigh. Why did adults sigh so much? 'Look, Tom. For the first couple of months he'll do nothing but run off his baby fat on the *highveld* and get shouted at by corporals. After that, who knows? He could end up driving trucks, become a medic, work in the stores, anything.'

'Or be sent to the border.'

'We don't know if there's anything happening on the border. The government says we're not involved.'

'But the *Bosmoedertjie . . .*'

He swung towards me and grabbed my arm. It hurt.

'Now listen to me. None of that, d'you hear? You want your mother to go to pieces?'

I sat back, stung, feeling my arm where his fingers had dug in. But the belch of words wouldn't stay down.

'Do you agree with him going?'

'It doesn't matter, he's got no choice. And it'll probably do him good. Knock some bloody sense into him.'

'Dad, what's "azania"?'

'Where did you hear that?'

'What is it?'

'Azania is the name some people will call South Africa when—if—they overthrow our government.'

'The people Little Harry will be fighting?'

'Jesus Christ, Tom!'

And then it boiled and blubbered and babbled out. If Little Harry was going to protect us, didn't it mean the government was right? What if we ended up like the Congo, where they raped nuns; where Uncle Ian ran for his life when the rebels attacked the mine? Wasn't it true our country was peaceful? Look, Millie and I can walk home from school bioscope night on our own. And weren't the natives happy, the way they smiled and lifted their hats? Look at Essie.

He got up, squatted in front of me and held my arms until I settled down. I was sobbing, and I hadn't even had the guts to tell him the really big thing: what I'd overheard in the dark lounge.

'Boykie, boykie. Come on now, come on now. You take everything too seriously. This is not the only country in the world with problems. Listen, I'm not going to treat you like an idiot, but please, Tom, there are things you don't know about, things you may still be too young to fully understand. It's helluva complicated. What you see on the streets and what you hear on the radio is not the whole story; it may not even be the true story, okay? Come on now. It's going to be all right. And Little Harry will be fine. We have to be strong for your mother.'

•

That evening we had an early dinner and did something we hadn't done for years. The sun had just set behind Swartkop but the sky was full of light. Mom laid out our tartan picnic rug on the back lawn and I grabbed the cushions. Dad fetched the drinks—wine for Mom, ginger beer for me, and beer for him and Little Harry. We sipped our drinks for a while then lay on our backs, Little Harry and Dad on the outside, Mom, me and Laika in the middle. Above us, the sky was a bluey-purple dome and huge V formations of egrets started to pass over on their way back to the bird sanctuary on the other side of town. They came in silent hundreds from the *bushveld* near the Valley of a Thousand Hills, where they'd spent the day darting at ticks and grubs. In between the formations were solitary herons, which you could tell by the bulge under their heads where they curled their necks, and occasionally a big bird with slow unfurling wings that Dad said was a crane. As the sky darkened the formations thinned out, and by the time we'd wished on the first star, they'd all passed through. We lay there in silence, our sides touching each other. Eventually, Dad let out a breath and said, 'Ah, well.' He grunted to his feet and went inside, followed by Little Harry.

•

Within a week, Little Harry was gone. The day he left, Mom kept packing things in his duffel bag and Little Harry kept taking most of it out when she left the room. Socks, tins of rusks, handkerchiefs, extra underpants, even little chocolates stuffed down the side pockets for him to discover on the train. He didn't throw those out. Dad had bought him a pocket-sized transistor radio, and he took out the batteries to show me the size I should send him.

When we arrived at the station, it was packed with families; mothers fussing and pushing things into their sons' pockets, fathers proud and know-all, and the boys just embarrassed and desperate to get away. When she was worried about us, Mom had this annoying habit of spitting on her hankie and wiping imaginary dirt off our faces, so Little Harry watched her carefully. He was actually excited and went off and hung around with his friends who were on the same call-up. When the train came in it gave an extra hoot and the

Durban boys were all hanging out the windows shouting insults as though they had already been in the army for months. Little Harry and his friends yelled back and you could see there would be trouble all the way to Joburg.

After Mom and Dad had said their goodbyes, Little Harry punched me on the arm and said, 'Batteries, okay? I'll send you my address as soon as I'm posted. Don't forget. Batteries.'

Mom wouldn't leave until the train had gone so we stayed until it chuffed off, arms waving from the windows. While Mom walked slowly down the platform, watching the red light disappear into the night, I told Dad about the little man, Gandhi, and the overnight Joburg train.

He nodded. '*Ja*, but you know even Gandhi put on a uniform. He was a stretcher-bearer in the Boer War.'

•

In the days after Little Harry left, Mom seemed to drift and I'd come across her standing somewhere in the house with a distracted look on her face, as if she'd misplaced something. But when Little Harry's first letter arrived with his rank, number and a camp address on the back, she seemed to feel he was solid again. He was settled.

To be honest, I didn't really miss Little Harry. I now moved up a bit in the house and at school it was something to have a brother in the army.

9

ONE DAY, MILLIE AND I DECIDED TO SEE IF WE COULD get closer to the *Bosmoedertjie* and find out what Little Harry might be in for with the army. I thought it might also help me to understand why Dad criticised the government but then thought it okay for Little Harry to do his national service.

Like a lot of things in the lane, the *Bosmoedertjie* was just there, part of it and largely ignored; he was a noise, a confusion of screeches, threats and giggling that you got used to on the days when Mr de Wet wheeled him out onto the verandah.

We liked little Mr de Wet, even though he was the secretary of the local National Party branch and a *diaken* in the Dutch Reformed Church who tut-tutted when anyone worked in their gardens on a Sunday. He always said '*goeie môre*' in his soft voice and he would lift his hat, smiling with crinkly pale blue eyes. We felt sorry for him because Mrs de Wet had died of a heart attack when the army said the *Bosmoedertjie* had been killed on manoeuvres. And then the broken son had been found alive and returned and Mr de Wet had to look after him all on his own.

The boy's real name was Arno, but everyone in the lane called him the *Bosmoedertjie* because on weekends he would sit on the verandah in his Davy Crockett hat and listen to Esmé Euvrard on *Springbok Rendezvous* reading out requests and playing records for the army boys. Out in the remote camps the troops called her the *Bosmoedertjie*, the Little Bush Mother, who comforted them when they were far from home. In the lane, our own *Bosmoedertjie* would shriek, '*Sy het my lewe gered!*' She saved my life.

When he had been in the camps, he had written home to his own mother telling her what a comfort Esmé Euvrard was to him, so Mrs de Wet had planted an Esmé Euvrard rose in the garden in honour of his return. It was still there, its pale pink blossoms tended by Mr de Wet.

None of us were game enough to ask what had happened out there in the *bushveld*. We stayed out of the De Wets' garden because if we came too close, the *Bosmoedertjie* would aim his walking stick at us, going, '*Tok-tok-tok! Tok-tok-tok!*' When he first came home and Mr de Wet thought his son was only injured in the body, he gave the *Bosmoedertjie* a pellet gun to shoot toppies that flew into the fruit trees. But one day a native delivery man in a khaki uniform had walked up the path and the *Bosmoedertjie* had screamed, '*Terroriste aanval! Terroriste aanval!*' and started firing at the man. So now he had the walking stick instead, and he would present arms whenever *Springbok Rendezvous* played his favourite songs, 'The Longest Day', 'Soldier Boy' and 'For Your Precious Love'.

But what Millie and I really wanted to know was what was in the small red cardboard box he clutched on his lap and which he would sometimes wave in the air while shrieking, '*Vyftien persent af!*' But fifteen percent off what? Most of us thought the box held a piece of shrapnel they had pulled out of his spine, but Little Harry said it was his testicles.

So one Saturday morning when Mr de Wet was digging in his garden and the *Bosmoedertjie* was safely out of sight, Millie and I said hello and hung around the gate.

Mr de Wet straightened his back and looked at us. He wiped his face with a handkerchief and leant on the garden fork, his blue eyes studying us from under the brim of his hat. 'So your brother has gone to do his duty, hey?'

His voice was thickly accented, like someone who never used English.

I nodded. 'Yes, *Oom*.'

'What is his base?'

'Middelburg.'

'*Ja*, a lot of them start there.'

He nodded, put his foot on the fork and thrust it into the soil, then realised we were still watching him. 'Do *julle* want a cool drink?'

We followed his muscular bandy legs onto the verandah. He told us to sit and said, 'It's okay, he's sleeping, hey?'

Mr de Wet went inside and came out with Kool-Aid and ginger nut biscuits and asked how our families were and about school. Millie chatted away as though they were old friends and I could see he really liked her, so when she asked about the *Bosmoedertjie*, he told us the story like he'd been dying to speak to someone for a long time.

But first he ran his hand over the stubble of his crew cut and fixed us with those eyes. 'Arno believed in what he was doing, *nè*? He joined a special unit, so what I'm telling you did not officially happen, *verstaan*? No questions, just listen.'

Arno had been out in a forward observation post to watch movement across a river—Mr de Wet didn't say where. The soldiers had been there for days and were bored sitting in the hot, dusty bush where nothing moved but the flies. They couldn't swim in the river because of crocodiles and the danger of ambush. Their only relief was drinking brandy, and using the camp radio to listen to Esmé Euvrard—which was also forbidden. One night the post came under mortar attack, but they couldn't radio for support because they'd flattened the batteries.

Mr de Wet leant forward, rested his elbows on his knees and looked down at the verandah floor, rubbing the red line where his hat brim had pressed into his forehead.

'Arno was still in his sleeping bag when the first mortar landed and he said it felt like someone had thrust a hot knife into him. *Net so!*' Mr de Wet sat up and pressed his thumb into his lower back. 'He passed out and when he came around it was daylight. His sleeping bag was sticky with blood but he felt no pain. All around him were the bodies of his comrades, and the *terroriste* were looting the camp. They connected their own battery to the stronger army radio and were trying to tune into the base camp to check patrol movements. What they got was Esmé Euvrard, *ja*. They squatted and listened to her messages and music, passing around the bottle of *brandewyn* they'd pulled out of a dead soldier's rucksack. All the time, over here right next to them is Arno, playing dead—well, he *sommer* is nearly dead, *jy weet*? His *dors*—what you say: thirst?—is driving him mad, but lying there with the flies crawling up his nose, not daring to move, he hears that voice on the radio saying there are *min dae* and to *vasbyt*.'

Mr de Wet looked away, absently rubbing the spot on his back where he'd pushed his thumb in. His voice was so soft I could barely hear him. 'My son believes Esmé Euvrard was talking to him, telling him there were only a few days to go, and to hold fast. But I know it was the Lord's work.'

He stood up and took a couple of steps towards the garden then stopped and spoke with his back to us. 'Another patrol chased the *terroriste* back across the river and radioed in that Arno's unit had been wiped out. By the time we heard he was alive, it was too late; Marie—Mrs de Wet—was gone. Too late, *ja wat*.'

He fell silent and dropped his head, and I wondered if he believed it was also the Lord's work that killed Mrs de Wet and sent home a shattered son. But even thinking it seemed smart-arse.

The thought seemed to hang in the air and he turned and squinted back at us, nodding. '*Ja, die Here beweeg in vreemde maniere.*'

Millie and I thanked him for the Kool-Aid and left him standing on the garden path thinking about the strange ways of the Lord.

He'd been so nice to us we hadn't asked about the little cardboard box on the *Bosmoedertjie*'s lap. When I mentioned it to Millie later, the frog mouth twisted and I couldn't tell if she was going to cry or hit me.

•

Hearing the *Bosmoedertjie*'s story just confused me even more. Who was right—Dad or the Government? I was now more afraid for Little Harry and I promised myself I would send him batteries in Mom's next parcel. Mr de Wet had told me he would pray for my brother, but I wasn't sure about that. I couldn't talk about it to Millie because she had gone stand-offish again since visiting Mr de Wet, and that made it worse.

And then an old fear returned to my dreams. A few years ago, I'd been to the Saturday morning bioscope with Little Harry, and as usual he'd left me alone down the front. There was a Flash Gordon serial, and the episode ended with Flash and Dale trapped in a prison with the walls closing in from all sides. I'd felt sick about it all the next week and pleaded with Little Harry to take me back the next Saturday to see how it turned out, but he didn't and I was stuck with that picture in my mind. That's what I saw now in my dreams: the walls edging closer.

A few nights after our talk with Mr de Wet, I tapped on Millie's window. She must have been awake because she got straight out of bed and climbed over the sill without saying anything. She didn't look at me once while we walked back up the lane, and instead of going to the *spookhuis*, I led her by the hand to the grassy bank near the bottom of our garden. There was no moon and the Milky Way was a thick mist of stars just above our heads. We lay down and stared up, waiting for Sputnik to cross over, pretending Laika was still on board—not my Laika but the first one, the Russian one. We weren't stupid, but this was our game, although Little Harry once overheard me telling Mom how the original Laika had landed safely and was living in a special home, and he'd laughed and said, 'You know what really happened to Laika—fzzzt!' I had mentioned it to Millie and she did a frog mouth and then a few days later told one of the girls who fancied Little Harry that he put a sock inside the front of his swimming costume.

Tonight there was no Sputnik and Millie felt a thousand miles away. But I could still feel her thoughts scratching inside my head. I sat up and showed her the packet of cigarettes and matches I'd found under Little Harry's bed. We took one each and lit them, then turned up the inside of our wrists. Together, eyes locked, still not speaking, we lowered our cigarettes onto the other's wrist then lay down, holding hands. With our free hands we clutched the warm kikuyu grass and screamed, our fingernails clawing at the soil to prevent us spinning off into the Milky Way. We only stopped when Titch Cockroft threw down his weights and walked to the fence and yelled he would *bliksem* us if we messed up his training and he didn't get to the Olympics.

•

The next weekend, our parents bundled us off to the beach. After the first questions and head-shaking, and our silence, our parents hadn't mentioned the burns again. I wasn't even scared of what Dad might do. I felt safe inside my silence, looking out. Maybe that's how he felt during his silences.

Mom, Dad and I stayed at the caravan park but Mrs Lieberman refused to camp, so they went to the hotel. The kids at the park looked at our waterproof dressings and wanted to know why Millie and I had the same wound so we told them it was a tattoo for a secret society and we couldn't talk about it.

I don't think the weekend at the beach helped much, although Mom seemed glad to get away from the lane and she wore a new bikini which nearly gave Dad a fit. Other than glaring at any man who looked at Mom on the beach, he was quiet and I would catch him watching me. He couldn't hold my eye and would get up and walk away.

The park had for years been a favourite holiday spot for the newspaper staff and their families, and the adults sat around in their camp chairs in the early evening, drinking and joking. This time, though, the men were more serious than usual, discussing the election, the republic and the new censorship laws which were making their jobs more difficult by the day. They all kept turning to Harry Mac, and although I was proud of him and sorry for them because they couldn't have him in their families, I wondered what they would think of him if they knew about the plot.

These were the men who had been his friends and, although they had always looked up to him as a sort of leader, they were now edgy around him: Mr Albrightsen, talking fast as though he was afraid to stop, and with his ginger testicle that always bulged out of his shorts like a startled eye; Mr O'Neill with his rat face and the way his nose seemed to bend towards whoever was winning the argument; Mr Farrar who never wore a shirt and was always touching his SAAF moustache and sucking in his stomach when the women brought fresh drinks, his eyes flicking around the group after he'd made a joke. Millie and I didn't like Mr Farrar. He told rude jokes to the women and stared when they bent over. He did this thing when he stood up of flexing his left arm like Charles Atlas, and then he'd run his hand slowly across the bicep and the angled muscle of his chest, and then his hand would hesitate and stop when it got to his pot belly, and flick away like it was irritated. Now, as the adults gathered on the first evening of the weekend, Mr Farrar caught me and Millie watching him stroke his body. He glared and I did my blank face and just wasn't there. He was about to say something when I sensed Millie start her frog smile, wider and wider, her eyes never leaving his, until he shuddered and turned away. 'Jesus, you two give me the creeps.'

I brought my face back but Millie kept staring after Mr Farrar and I swear the skin on his back twitched. She always took it one step too far.

'Is it the way he looks at your mother that bothers you?' I asked.

She answered without taking her eyes off Mr Farrar's twitching back, 'I don't like the way *she* looks at *him*.'

'Why don't you get on with your mom?'

She pointed at her victim. 'That's one reason. But it's the way she treats Sol. She wants him to go into private practice and make more money, then we won't have to drive an old Austin and she can act the lady at her tennis club.'

'Well why doesn't he?'

She looked across at Sol, who was hunched forward arguing with one of the newsmen, and her mouth went wide and beautiful. 'Because he says the people at Town Hill Hospital need him more.' By now, Millie and I had closed the gap between us and at that moment I almost felt I could ask her what his secret was, but I knew it would spoil things.

Dad was standing to one side listening to one of his reporters, Ken Brady. Ken was excited and Dad was nodding and looking thoughtful. He beckoned to Sol, and got Ken to tell his story again.

Later, back at the van, Dad said to me, 'When we get home, I'm going to show you something.' He wouldn't say any more than that.

I pestered him for days once we returned home but he'd clammed up, and the gloomy atmosphere soon settled back over us, overshadowing the glow of the beach weekend.

•

A few nights after we got back, I was woken by shouts, screams and doors banging. There were headlights in the lane, motors running and boots crunching. Mom and Dad were coming out of their bedroom and we went out onto the verandah from where we could see two vans blocking the lane and men shouting instructions in Afrikaans and Zulu.

'Bloody police,' Dad said and went out the back to check on Essie. She was already up and wrapped in a dressing gown, so he brought her onto the verandah and we sat and waited for the raid to finish.

'Where's Henry?' Mom whispered to Essie.

'Not tonight,' she said with relief in her voice.

A policeman with sergeant's stripes walked into our yard like he owned the place and shone his torch over us on the verandah, lingering on Essie before he turned to Dad. '*Naand, Meneer.* I'm going to check your *kaya*.' He jerked his head at a native constable and they walked around the back.

They soon returned and left the yard without even saying goodbye. Further down the lane we heard a woman sobbing and a man's voice, angry, arguing. Metal doors clanged shut and the vans drove out of the lane.

Essie sagged in her chair and Mom brought her a cup of tea. If Essie's new husband, Henry, had been staying the night with her, as he sometimes did, he would be in the back of the van now.

No visitors were allowed overnight in the *kayas*, not even family members.

The next day Essie brought the lane news back. A husband and a teenage son had been caught in two *kaya*s further down. And that was the net result of the raid.

10

ABOUT A WEEK AFTER THE RAID, I WAS SITTING ON THE verandah watching a storm building when Mom and Dad came home from work. I could see they were having words as they got out of the car. I half got up but realised it couldn't be too serious because Mom was doing most of the talking. Still, I hurried over to make sure it didn't get worse.

They both stopped and turned towards me. Mom said, 'Look at him, just a boy and with the leg and everything. It's not right, man.'

But Dad had made up his mind. 'He's the one who's been snooping, pushing and asking questions, so maybe he'll learn something useful. Okay, fine, *Wagter*, go and get dressed. Put on your blazer.'

Mom knew she'd lost so she fussed and stuffed a handkerchief in my pocket. She made me wear my caliper and tightened the leather straps until they pinched. Then she wanted me to take a raincoat but Dad scoffed, saying we would be indoors.

Mom turned on him next. 'You are not wearing that old thing.'

He looked down in surprise and fingered the brown tweed jacket. 'Why ever not? It's my favourite.' But Mom knew that Dad only wore it to places where a good jacket might get spoilt.

She went into the kitchen, shaking a finger back at him. 'You behave yourself, Harold MacGregor. No nonsense. You've got Tom to think of.'

'Where're we going, Dad?' I said as we ate a quick meal. I didn't care. I just wanted to be with him.

'Your first political gathering. Get a move on.'

We kissed Mom goodbye and went out to the car, where I was surprised to find Sol waiting. I looked for Millie, but Sol said, 'Men's night out.' Millie would hate him saying that.

It had all happened so fast I hadn't had time to wonder if this was the Verwoerd meeting Haas had talked about to Harry Mac. I wasn't ready for this.

The two men were silent as we drove towards town. My thoughts were still swimming when, instead of going to the city hall, we turned onto a side road and headed out past the industrial area towards Edendale township. So it wasn't the Verwoerd meeting. Now I really didn't have a clue, so I loosened my caliper and leant on the windowsill. Storm clouds were rolling in from behind the Edendale hills and a lightning flash lit up the sawtooth roof of the Bata shoe factory.

'The venue's been changed,' Dad said to Sol. 'They found police bugs so it's now at the Indian hall in Plessislaer.'

'Is he still coming?' There was an edge to Sol's voice.

'Ken Brady says he is.'

The rain had started, fat drops warm against the window, and it was dark when we arrived at the hall where a huge crowd of mostly Africans and a few Indians had gathered. A row of Black Marias was parked off to one side and huddled next to them was a group of policemen in greatcoats with the collars turned up. Ken Brady stepped off the hall porch and hurried over. 'I can make room for you inside with the reporters.'

But Dad shook his head. 'No, we'll find a spot.' He looked over at the row of vans. 'Big turnout. The police informers have been busy.'

I retightened my caliper and we went around the side of the hall and stood by an open window looking onto the front table, where a number of men in suits were seated. A man with a priest's collar was at the microphone, talking to the crowd in Zulu. As the rain came down, we pressed in under the eaves and were hit with a thick fug from hundreds of damp bodies crowding the hall. It was hard to see over the heads of the men who filled every available space, even jamming behind the official table. I felt a tap on my shoulder and a native man placed a wooden crate next to me and hoisted me up by the elbow. I had a better view now, next to Sol and Dad leaning on the windowsill.

'Okay,' Dad said to me, turning his back to the hall. 'You wanted to know what's going on in this country—well, here it is.' He jerked his thumb over his shoulder. 'This is what people do when their political parties and their leaders are banned. Look around. Go on.' He had his angry baboon face on, the way they shot their foreheads back and thrust out their jaws. It made me feel like I'd done something wrong.

I leant in and looked around. It was as if, for the first time, I was seeing a crowd of Africans as individual people. They were tight-faced and hard-eyed, and they smelt of earth. They were not like the blurred faces I passed on the pavement from school; faces that smiled and stepped aside.

'These men have walked here, many without food. They have slept out in the veld. This is what people do when you take nearly everything away from them.'

He swung back towards the hall, where people were shouting

encouragement at the speaker, echoing his words back to him. Some of the men spoke in English, but I couldn't really follow any of it and after a while my leg started to hurt. I didn't want to complain so I sat down on the crate and leant against the wall, wishing I was home in bed and far away from Dad's anger.

Then I was being shaken and dragged to my feet. It was later in the evening and an expectant hum came from the hall. Outside in the rain, the crowd had grown and there seemed to be even more police. Dad nudged Sol and pointed to the shadows, where a tall man stood behind the police line on the edge of the light. Sol nodded. 'Ah, the infamous Kolonel Engelbrecht. So this is not a simple law-and-order turnout—it's a Special Branch show.'

The sight of the Kolonel shook the sleep out of me. This was the man who'd warned Dad that 'higher up' was telling him to get his house in order. It was too dark for a good look at the Kolonel, but I had the impression of something hard with sharp angles, like the long wooden T-square Mr Frame threatened us with.

Above me, the noise in the hall swelled and I grabbed the windowsill and pulled myself back onto the crate. A big man built like Harry Mac and about the same age had stepped up to the microphone. He wore an expensive-looking suit and had a neatly trimmed beard. He placed his overcoat on the table, picked up a handful of papers and started to speak in English.

I can't remember what he said; he had an odd voice, as though speaking with a mouthful of porridge, but like everyone else in the hall and outside, I was fascinated. Something poured out of him and filled us all up. He didn't talk for long, and then suddenly he and the coat were gone, with the crowd roaring, '*Amandla! Ngawethu!*' Power! To us!

Ken Brady had turned from his seat among the reporters in front of the main table and was grinning at us through the waving arms and fists. I looked at Dad and Sol and their faces were alive.

Dad grabbed my arm. 'That's it, *Wagter*, let's go.' The anger was gone and there was a lightness in his voice I hadn't heard for a while.

It had stopped raining and as we came around the side of the hall, a cordon of policemen was blocking the doorway, checking everyone who came out. The next speaker had started and some of the police had moved inside the hall to scan the crowd. The Kolonel stepped out of the shadows and walked stiffly up and down his line of men. He saw Dad and stopped, his face twisting as if trying to find the right expression, and he spoke without moving his lips. 'Why am I not surprised to see you here?' His glance at me was the touch of a cold knife, before he turned and looked Sol up and down.

Dad shrugged, leaning forward onto his toes. His voice was still light, but there was that look on his face that always made Mom reach out and dig her fingers into his arm. 'It's a free country—or so you and your "higher-ups" keep telling us. Who are you looking for?'

'None of your business.' The Kolonel walked away, eyes raking the crowd.

'I think he's given them the slip,' Sol murmured.

As we walked to our car, a uniformed sergeant made his way through the crowd near us, stopping men and lifting their hats. As he drew nearer, I saw it was the policeman who'd been in our yard the week before. Dad recognised him too and smiled. I thought of digging my fingers into his arm.

'Well, well, *sersant*, so you're a Special Branch man, hey? Now tell me, what was a Special Branch officer doing on a simple *kaya* raid at my house?'

The sergeant looked straight through Dad and reached out to push him aside with the back of his hand, saying, 'Move on, move on.'

Now that's two things you don't do to Harry Mac: manhandle him and tell him to move on.

The policeman's hand had barely made contact with Dad's arm when he found himself stumbling back, his peaked cap rolling in the mud. As the sergeant reached towards his holster, the Kolonel stepped between them and held up a hand. At the same time, Sol, with surprising strength, grabbed Dad and started hustling him away. In the spill of light from the open hall doors, a circle of African conference delegates watched in silence, their faces stone. And then I saw a face I knew at the back of the group.

It was Windsor Dlamini.

He caught my eye and stepped back then his face disappeared into the surrounding dark.

'Get him out of here,' the Kolonel barked at Sol, which was exactly what he was doing. Dad seethed and surged in Sol's grip but allowed himself to be moved away. I grabbed the back of Dad's tweed jacket for balance and did my best to keep up.

We got back to the car and fell in. Terrified, I looked back to see if the police were following us, but Dad started to roar with laughter and thump the steering wheel, and even Sol couldn't keep a straight face.

Dad reached across and pulled a half-jack of whisky out of the cubby-hole. His shoulders shook as he tipped the bottle to his lips then passed it to Sol with a splutter.

Sol stopped laughing first and prodded Dad on the shoulder. 'You! The great strategist.'

Dad waved him away and reached for the bottle. From where we were parked we could see the police still checking people coming out of the hall, while other officers worked their way through the crowd outside, shining torches in faces. Around the grounds, black constables checked behind trees, along ditches and aimed their torches into parked cars.

'He's gone. They've missed him.' There was satisfaction in Dad's voice.

'Are you talking about the man who spoke? Who was he, Dad?' My leg was aching but I didn't want him to know. I loosened the straps of the caliper, pushed my fingers inside the frame and rubbed my calf.

They swung around in their seats as if they'd forgotten I was there.

'That man . . . that man is—'

'He is our hope,' Sol interrupted.

Dad waggled his head slowly from side to side. 'That's a bit grandiose, Sol. No, I wasn't going to say anything like that, but he's certainly someone they should be listening to.' He started the car and looked at me in the rear-view mirror. 'His name's Nelson Mandela. He's a lawyer from Johannesburg, and the police just made a big mistake.'

'Why?'

'Mandela's banning orders expired yesterday and the police forgot to renew them. So, legally, he was free to talk here tonight. That's his first public appearance in years, and it was supposed to be a secret, but Ken Brady heard about it—and so, it seems, did the Special Branch. They were there to arrest him, but they didn't have the guts to do it in front of the crowd so they were going to grab him afterwards.'

He started the car and we headed back towards town. Dad was silent and I could tell he was stewing over something. He looked at Sol and slapped the steering wheel. 'You know, I still don't understand why a Special Branch sergeant would take part in an ordinary bloody *kaya* raid in the lane.'

Sol took the bottle of whisky off Dad's lap and put it back in the cubby-hole, 'You won't find out by assaulting him, you *moegoe*. When are you going to learn that up there is for thinking, not here?' He leant across and poked Dad on the side of the head and then slapped him across the knuckles.

Dad grinned. You could see he liked Sol doing things that no other man would dare.

'Did they do your place, too?'

Sol blew out through puffed cheeks. '*Ja*, they did our place. Raided most of the *kayas* in the damn lane. Edgar's place, obviously.'

'Obviously.'

'Edgar Lambert? Mr Lambert?' I piped up from the back seat.

They both turned again and I felt like an eavesdropper in a bus.

'Yes, he's banned.' Dad said it offhand, like the way you might say someone was a member of a sports club.

He glanced at Sol with a little smile. 'Our hope, hey?'

Sol shrugged. 'Mandela's the new generation. He's also smart and he knows how to play white people. He's one to watch.'

'If he stays alive long enough. Tell me, Sol, you really believe we can have change without fighting for it? *Wagter* here told me about your Gandhi performance.'

'Depends what you mean by fighting. We Jews take the long view.'

'Don't give me that crap. The Jews fought back in the ghettoes, Warsaw, the death camps.'

'And most of them died. I just believe there are other ways.'

'And when the other ways don't work?'

Sol sat staring through the windscreen and finally put an arm across Dad's shoulders and said, 'What you don't do, Samson, is pull the temple walls down around you.' He gave Dad a brief squeeze and pulled his arm away.

11

THE NEXT MORNING AT BREAKFAST, WHEN ESSIE CAME
out of the kitchen carrying her mug of tea, I remembered.

'Essie! I saw Windsor.'

She staggered and hot tea slopped across the lino. '*Hau! Nkosane*,
not a nice joke.'

Mom and Dad turned on me, but I insisted. 'I did. I promise. It
was when Dad pushed the poli—' I caught myself. 'I mean, when the
police were checking the crowd. He was there. He saw me looking at
him and he ducked out of sight. I promise, true as Bob.'

Dad didn't believe me. 'Tom, it was dark, there were hundreds of
Africans, and . . . there was all sorts of nonsense going on with the
police. You shouldn't say things like that. You'll just upset Essie and
give her false hope.'

Mom took Essie back into the kitchen, settled her on a stool and
went to fetch the mop. While she was out of the room, Dad leant
across the table, doing his scary eyebrow thing. 'You keep your big
mouth shut about last night, hey!'

It was later in the day, much later, that he came to see me. I was lying on the bed because my leg had been cramping on and off since the night before, and he walked in and sat down, picked up my leg, his hand closing around it as he worked his thumb along the tight calf muscle. I wished he would do it more often. He put the leg down and rubbed his face with both hands. 'Tell me again, Tom.'

I told him what I'd seen and he nodded. 'Okay, I'll check with the police.'

•

The cramps bit at me all that night, only easing towards dawn, leaving me weak and exhausted. This caused a problem because it was Mom's day at Malnutrition Relief and she couldn't stay home to look after me.

'It's okay, he can come into the office,' Dad said. There were always kids coming and going at the paper, but I thought Dad had been a bit quick to offer. Maybe he felt guilty about taking me to the All-In Africa Conference and seeing me end up with leg pains. Good.

So a short while later, carrying my lunchbox and a satchel full of schoolbooks, I followed him down the corridor to where his secretary, Miss Hammond, fidgeted outside his office. She was bursting to talk to him and seemed annoyed I was there. She half pushed me into the adjoining boardroom and swung the door closed behind me. But it was the easiest thing to turn and put my foot in the gap. She didn't notice in her rush to tell Dad her news: the Kolonel had called and wanted him to come around to police HQ 'immediately you arrive'. She took a deep breath. '*Immediately*, Mr MacGregor.'

I couldn't see Dad's face but his voice was normal. 'Tell the news editor and the chief day sub I'm ready for morning conference.'

Miss Hammond squeaked and hurried out.

I left the boardroom and went to roll balls around on the billiard table for a while, then wandered down to the telex room, where I sat and watched the news chattering out of the bank of machines in long curling sheets. Bobby Naidoo was on duty and I helped him tear the stories and stack them into their separate piles. I had a cup of tea and a samoosa with the operators then went back to the boardroom, opened my schoolbooks and read a comic. I made sure the connecting door into Dad's room was open just a crack.

Late in the morning, Miss Hammond poked her head into Dad's office. Her voice was miserable. The police wanted to know when he was coming.

'Tell them if the Kolonel wants to talk to me he can come here.'

'This is the *police*, Mr MacGregor!' she said. She saw me watching through the gap in the door and mouthed to him, 'Special Branch.'

'And they are our servants. Tell them eleven thirty would be fine.'

I checked my watch. Plenty of time. I pulled the blinds, switched off the light and went through to Dad, who was hunched over his typewriter. I yawned and stretched and told him I might have a lie-down. He grunted and continued with his leader. I looked back into the boardroom and it was completely dark but for the narrow shaft of light from Dad's office across the carpet. I took a pad of newsprint with me and wedged the door open just enough so I could see the chair facing Dad's desk. He would have his back to me but that was okay.

By the time I heard Miss Hammond's voice go squeaky again when she welcomed the Kolonel, I was ready, sitting on my chair in the dark just to one side of the shaft of light coming from Dad's office, as still as a bird. It's movement that gives you away, they told us at Cubs.

The Kolonel didn't like being there, but Dad got up and greeted him with a handshake and used his first name. He called out to Miss Hammond to bring tea and biscuits, and when he turned back to his desk, he had this stupid grin on his face. Uh-oh.

The Kolonel put his cap on the corner of Dad's desk, ran his palms along the side of his hair, lifted his trousers a fraction by the crease and sat. No part of his body moved until Miss Hammond, bobbing and tiptoeing, had clicked the door shut behind her.

Then he sighed and crossed his legs, gesturing around the office. 'We don't have to play games, Harry Mac.'

'Games, Loftus? That thug who tried to push me around at the conference; since when does one of your Special Branch officers waste his time breaking down *kaya* doors and pulling the blankets off sleeping couples?'

The Kolonel waved the question away and got up. I could still see him as he walked to the window and looked out at the provincial gardens across the road, staring straight at the statue of Queen Victoria. 'This *verdomde* town,' he muttered, and turned away.

He sat down again. 'Look, Harry Mac, here it is—and I will ask you to do me the courtesy of not interrupting until I have finished; I am sure you will have plenty to say then. *Stem jy saam*?'

Dad agreed to nothing, crunched a biscuit, and waited. I could hear him chewing and the look on the Kolonel's face showed how little he enjoyed watching those big teeth at work and the crumbs that would now be tumbling down Dad's tie.

The Kolonel looked towards the window, gathering his thoughts, then shook his head like a horse bothered by a fly. 'I've never understood why that damned woman's statue is outside Parliament House.'

'Because she was our queen, just as Elizabeth is now, and when Lizzie dies they may put her statue next to old Vic.'

'Not bloody likely, as you English are fond of saying.' He reached for a chocolate biscuit, seemed to think better of it and settled back in his chair. 'Okay, that's as good a point to start as any. This country will be a republic in two months. No more running to the old flag. No more statues of dead queens. We're on our own. All of us. Now, I'm going to let you in on something that is for your own good.'

He leant forward and touched the edge of the desk with a long finger. 'As we sit here, the pen-pushers in Pretoria are tidying up a new law effective almost immediately we become a republic.'

I could hear Dad sucking chocolate off his fingers, but still he said nothing.

The Kolonel's eyes were fixed on Dad and his voice was so soft I had to lean forward, nearly into the light, to hear him.

'This law will indemnify anyone working under government authority from any action they take to maintain good order. That's the simple version, but, my friend, I ask you to consider the key phrases—*any* government agent taking *any* action to maintain order is indemnified. What's more, the law will be backdated for a year.'

Indemnified? I didn't know what it meant but it sounded serious.

The Kolonel leant forward again and that long finger tapped on the desk. 'So if, for example, a few days ago a police officer— let's call him Sergeant Viljoen—had been assaulted by a member of the public and the officer had then shot that man, there would be no action taken against the officer. Do you understand? No action taken.'

He left the finger there a while then slowly drew it back, watching Dad. 'You smile, but this is not a rugby scrum, Harry Mac, because I'll tell you what's next. My government—your government—will soon introduce the death penalty for sabotage. We haven't worked out everything that actually constitutes sabotage, but here's a hint: you wouldn't want to damage so much as a fire extinguisher in a public building, *verstaan*?' He paused. 'Or incite public disorder— say, through an inflammatory newspaper article.'

He picked up his tea, drained it, and carefully put the cup down. He took a handkerchief from the top pocket of his uniform, dabbed the corners of his mouth and sat back, his eyes never leaving Dad.

'Harry Mac, last time we met, you said you would only start worrying when you broke the law. Well the law is not waiting for you, *my vriend*.'

I was now so tense my leg was cramping but I didn't dare to stretch it out. I couldn't follow everything the Kolonel was saying, but the threat was plain. I didn't need to look up indemnify anymore. Now I started to worry about what Dad might do and I wished I could see his face. He had been quiet for far too long.

But instead of knocking the Kolonel's block off, Dad reached over and tore off a sheet from a news pad. He cleaned his fingers and tossed the crumpled paper over his shoulder, where it hit the edge of the wire basket and bounced onto the carpet, landing next to the other balls of paper. He was nodding. 'Very impressive. Tell me, Loftus, there's something I'm keen to know.'

The Kolonel leant forward a fraction. '*Ja?*'

'Do you love animals?'

'*Wat sê . . .?*'

'Simple question. Do you love animals? You see, I know you don't smoke and you're careful about what you eat. So I was just wondering if, like that other vegetarian teetotaller—Hitler—you also love animals?'

The Kolonel's face reddened and he uncrossed his legs. For the first time, he looked like an ordinary man. I would rather Dad had smashed his face, but this was good.

Dad continued, as casually as if he was chatting about rugby. 'Oh go on, you do. Don't be shy. I bet it's an Alsatian with a name like Wodan and your wife is jealous.'

The Kolonel was working on his breathing, and he laughed, a little squeaky like Miss Hammond. '*Ag, man.* Harry Mac, I like you! You've got guts. Pity you're on the wrong team. It'll be a shame if we have to hang you one day—that's a joke, by the way; we haven't got a rope thick enough. Actually, you missed your target with the Hitler insult.'

He crossed his legs again. He was enjoying this now and a few feet away in the dark I was gasping with pain as my leg spasmed under me.

'You see, I'm not one of those *verligte* modern Afrikaners who reinvent themselves. I was interned during the war for my support of the Nazis and I'm proud of it. What have I and my people got to thank the British for, hey? As for Hitler . . .' He shrugged. 'He was just a necessary catalyst to get things moving. Yes, he went a bit far, but after the final victory we would have replaced him with moderates.' The Kolonel smiled easily. 'Yes, I did say "we". But don't get excited. There's no secret organisation, just a broad international movement with common beliefs. I would happily have been there, by the way, among the Greyshirts on the day your Jewish friend stepped off the *Stuttgart* in Cape Town.'

Here we go. Harry Mac's shoulders hunched and rhino started to leak into the boardroom. My leg was rigid and I couldn't have moved if I'd tried. I was on the point of shouting something, anything, when the Kolonel laughed and held up a hand. '*Ag*, come on, Harry Mac, you'd expect me to know he was on that ship. Hell, it's my job to know everything about anyone of significance. How is your brother Ian, by the way? Recovered after his escape from the Congo? Hm?'

If this was a rugby scrum, the Kolonel would be flat on his back and the whistle would be shrilling. But Dad somehow calmed himself. 'I'm a newspaper editor, Loftus, I expect you to check on me and my family—but a psychiatrist in a state mental hospital? Hardly significant.'

'He's a Jew, isn't he? Ah! Now who's upset, *nè*?'

I couldn't stop myself. I jerked in the chair and fell over backwards, rolling on the carpet. But Dad's rising bulk blocked the doorway and they couldn't see me. Oh shit, shit, I thought, as I scrambled back into the dark, pulling the chair with me. Then I heard the Kolonel laugh.

'*Ag*, sit, man. Let's leave the Jewish thing alone. I'm sorry, I shouldn't have let you get under my skin. But you were the one who brought up Hitler, and do you really think a *Pax Germanica* would have been worse than what your Allied victory produced, hey? Every day wondering whether the Americans or the Russians will be the first to press the button? Do you think the Good Lord's judgment will find much difference in the balance between Hitler, Churchill, Roosevelt and Stalin?'

'Or Verwoerd.'

The Kolonel stood, picked up his cap and brushed imaginary fluff off his trousers. The two men stood eye to eye.

The Kolonel spoke first. 'I didn't come here to threaten you, Harry Mac, but I do want to warn you—there is a difference. I like you, but that won't stop me doing my duty. One more thing, and don't take it the wrong way. We are not interested in you and your jottings; we have much bigger fish to catch. Just don't get tangled in the net. Oh, and by the way, the dog's name is Siegfried and he sleeps on the bed.'

Dad saw him to the door. 'Loftus, I feel sorry for you. For all your new laws, your night raids, your God-given right, it amounts to nothing against what I saw and felt the other night.'

The Kolonel bowed slightly to Dad. As he turned to leave he looked straight at the crack in the door behind where I crouched, and touched the brim of his cap.

The jet of piss was hot inside my underpants and I knelt there, unable to move as the piss ran down my thighs and into the carpet.

Dad closed the door behind the Kolonel and I prayed he wouldn't come into the boardroom, but instead he went over to the window and stood staring out. I managed to push myself off the floor and make it out of the other door, checking the corridor was clear before hobbling to the toilet. As I sneaked away I heard a smack like a fist hitting a wall.

My underpants were soaked and I bundled them up and flushed them down the toilet. It took three goes and the back of the brush. But I still had a stain on my shorts, so when I got back to the boardroom I grabbed my drink bottle and splashed orange juice on my fly and on the carpet, and that's when Dad pushed open the door and switched on the light.

'What in hell's name is going on here?'

I mumbled about trying to get a drink in the dark and spilling it. But you can just tell when your parents don't believe you, and that's the long hard look he gave me now.

I had to stay like that for the rest of the day, sticky, tired and stiff, and wondering if anything could be done to stop Dad disappearing one night.

Just before it was time to go home, Miss Hammond entered Dad's office and handed him a pale brown envelope. 'A police messenger dropped this off,' she said and hovered near the door. There was a funny look on her face, like she was almost glad the police were visiting Dad. 'Mr MacGregor, are you in trouble?'

'We're all in trouble,' he said, slitting open the envelope. He would have enjoyed saying that. The previous editor had been an English professor, and Miss Hammond felt she'd come down in the world when Harry Mac took over.

He shook something onto his desk and sat staring down at it.

'*Wagter!*'

I scurried in and looked over his shoulder. It was a copy of a photograph showing several African men. It was grainy and poor quality and the date written in a corner was from two nights ago. About four of the men's heads were circled and a number was written next to each. The photographer had snapped them from the side as they all craned towards the lit entrance of the Plessislaer hall. There was no mistaking the circled head of Windsor Dlamini.

12

ESSIE WHOOPED AND DANCED AROUND THE KITCHEN AT the proof her son was alive. She couldn't stop staring at the photo, touching Windsor's face. 'Master, what is this long number next to his head?'

Dad had been dreading this and had told me to say nothing. He put a hand over hers. 'Essie, it means the police have a file on him.'

'*Hau!* Master, but Windsor is a good boy. He's not a *tsotsi* or a *skabenga*.'

'Yes, we know and they know. But he may be mixed up in politics.'

For Essie, that was almost as bad as hearing he was dead. She didn't like the word. It was something you left to the local chief. The stuffing went out of her and Mom made her take the rest of the day off.

That morning, I read Ken Brady's report on the All-In Africa Conference. It was very long and parts of it were quite boring, but it said that the fourteen hundred delegates had come from all over the

Union to attend the conference, and that it was the biggest political gathering of Africans ever held in the country. By the end of the conference on Sunday, the delegates had voted for a non-racial, democratic constitution and called for a national convention of people of all races.

I asked Dad what they wanted and he said for everyone in the country to have the vote.

'Even the people in huts in the *bundu*?'

'Even them.' He picked up the paper, glanced at the report and shook his head. 'Poor buggers. Not a hope in hell.'

The story also said that the main speaker, Nelson Mandela, had slipped away from the meeting, evading the police.

I thought the reporter left out the best stuff—how the men were different to the ones we usually met, with their hard eyes, hungry faces and that smell of earth. And of course Dad's scuffle with the policeman, particularly because he won it. But maybe it was better to leave that out.

•

That afternoon I was over at Millie's when Sol came home early from the hospital, so I told them about Dad's visit from the Kolonel, including the bit about him knowing Sol had been on that ship.

'Doesn't that scare you, Dr Lieberman?'

He shrugged, lips turning down at the edges. 'Why should it? The Greyshirts and the other Nats have been anti-Jewish from the word go, so I would expect them to keep tabs on us, particularly such a symbolic event as the arrival of the *Stuttgart*. But the Nats aren't stupid, you know; they realise how much the Jews contribute to the economy. These days, they leave us alone as long as they know where we are and that we're being good boys and girls. Believe me, it's a relief after what I went through in Germany.'

I liked Sol but the way he seemed to accept all the bad things was starting to annoy me. 'But you told me before how much the people running the country hate the Jews and the English-speakers and the natives.'

'*Ja*, but you asked me if I was frightened because they know so much about me, and I answered you. I think the Nats have things other than Jews on their minds at the moment.'

Sol was too slick for me, and even though what he said made sense, it seemed selfish. For all I knew, Dad was planning to risk his life for the country, and Sol was talking about keeping his head down. I didn't want to be a secret agent around Sol anymore.

'Anyway,' I grumbled, 'the Kolonel's a pig and I hate him.' I didn't add that he had made me piss myself.

'Ay ay, Tomka! Hate doesn't fix things. There's a saying: you need to walk a mile in another man's shoes before understanding how he feels and why he acts the way he does.'

'I don't need to walk a yard in the Kolonel's boots to tell what he's like.'

'Is that so? Okay, time for another drive.'

Millie had had a fight with her mother, a boring one about music lessons, and so was happy to get out of the house. Mrs Lieberman had been a concert violinist when she was young and wanted Millie to learn to play. Of course with her neck, a violin was out of the question, but Mrs Lieberman was pushing Millie towards the piano.

In the car, Millie complained about it to Sol, who just smiled and said all barbarians could do with a little culture, and who knew? One day she might play jazz like her American uncle. That shut her up and we enjoyed the mild early autumn day, the best time of year in our town, and drove towards the sun, soaking up its warmth.

'*Ag*, no, Sol, not the blooming railway station again,' Millie said as we swung up the long hill. He ignored her and soon we were heading out of town under a canopy of jacarandas. It was greener here and the gardens were bigger. Sol slowed the Austin and we turned through a tall gate flanked by trees and banks of shrubs.

'This is more like it,' said Millie when Sol parked and we climbed out. She raced away down an avenue of plane trees, kicking her way through the fallen leaves. But Sol leant against the car, pulled a wrinkled cigarette out of his jacket, lit up and puffed away, waiting for Millie to realise we weren't following her.

'Nice? You like the botanic gardens, hey?' he said when she returned with an armful of leaves and flung them over the car and us.

I knew Sol wasn't here to admire the gardens, so I waited.

'Very nice,' Sol said, nodding. 'Not sure how I feel about it, though. Did you know we're standing on the site of a concentration camp?'

'He-e-ere we go!' said Millie, pulling herself up on the car bonnet and drumming her heels against the tyres. 'Better be a good one, Sol; Tom's eyes are already heading towards glaze-ville.'

'Cursed child. Actually, it was just over there.' He pointed across the road and his voice took on its lecture tone. 'The year was 1900 and the British had started to recapture the land lost to the Boers. The Tommies were rounding up the Natal Afrikaner farmers who had joined the Boer commandos, and because Natal was a British colony, these farmers were regarded as traitors. They were jailed, their properties confiscated and their wives and children sent to concentration camps.

'One of the first camps was right here. Of course it wasn't all nice lush gardens and trees in those days, just hundreds of tents out on the bare veld. One family, a woman named Maria Labuschagne and her seven children, were forced off their farm near Ladysmith and placed here with thousands of other Boer women and children ripped from their homes and husbands. The British didn't set out to ill-treat them, even though they regarded the Boer families as barely human.'

'Sol, you're rambling. Get back to the point—if there is one. I'm getting cold.'

Sol blew a last long blue plume into the crisp air then stubbed out his cigarette. '*Ja, ja*. The point. Well, they tried to win the prisoners over with the bribe of better food if they became sympathetic to the British—what the Boers called a *hensopper*, a hands-upper. But Maria, like her jailed husband, was a *bittereinder*, a bitter-ender. She toughed it out, refusing to accept the British bribe. A year after the camp was set up, measles ripped through the detainees, followed by pneumonia. Among the scores who died was Maria Labuschagne, along with six of her children. Bitter to the end. The only survivor was four-year-old Hettie Labuschagne, who emerged from the camp after the war to find herself an orphan, her Boer father having died in exile in Ceylon. Even the family farm was gone, the homestead burnt down, the animals and the land confiscated.'

Sol turned and looked at us. 'Hettie Labuschagne was the Kolonel's mother.'

That shut Millie up, and me too. I couldn't think of anything to say, but after a minute, Millie's eyes narrowed. 'Okay, Dr Know-all. How come you know so much about the Kolonel? You sound like the Special Branch yourself.'

Sol laughed. '*Ag*, that's easy. It's a small town. The Kolonel's sister is deputy matron at Town Hill and she'll tell the story to anyone, whether they want to hear it or not. I've been hearing it for years. Angry woman. Bitter, bitter. Come on, let's go, I want to pick up some bread on the way home.'

'Can we have a Moolk?'

'No.'

'Then you can't have bread.'

I sat in the back seat while they argued, and I thought about the Kolonel. There was an image in my mind that clouded out everything else: four-year-old Hettie Labuschagne standing at the gates of the concentration camp at the end of the war. She had a cloth bag slung across her shoulders and she was wearing one of those little Dutch bonnets. She wanted to ask one of the big men in khaki, smelling of tobacco and sweat and carrying a gun, what she should do, where she should go. But she couldn't speak their language. And so she stood in the mud at the gate as the wagons creaked past and the soldiers swore at the mules.

I remembered one dark night my family were downtown, driving home from visiting my grandparents, and I boasted from the back seat that I could find my way home from where we were. Harry Mac hit the brakes, leant back and opened the car door. 'Off you go then.' I hopped out, smiling at him until he pulled the door closed and drove away. I watched the tail-lights turn the corner, then burst into tears. He drove around the block and picked me up again. But did anyone come back for Hettie Labuschagne?

I sniffled and turned away from Millie to wipe my nose on my sleeve. Then I saw the Kolonel look at me and touch his cap brim, and I felt again the hot piss in my pants, and I knew the walls were closing in on all sides.

13

IF THE KOLONEL THOUGHT HIS VISIT WOULD INTIMIDATE Harry Mac, he was wrong.

Dad wrote a leader like the earlier one about the lamps going out over Europe before the First World War. But this time he said it was our government putting out the lights. And he said they were doing it deliberately because people were afraid of the dark and would crowd into the government's *laager*. He wrote that the government hated the English-language press for telling the truth.

The leader ended with something I didn't understand but which worried me: *We have been warned it is our duty to uphold law and order; to be patriotic. Well, you know what they say about patriotism. As for law and order, what is a citizen's duty when those very laws are a threat to society's order?*

Dad was often quite pleased with his leaders, but he didn't say anything about this one. In fact, the day the leader came out he plunged into a silence.

He didn't turn to gin, but poured a beer and went to the garage to sit with the crocodile eggs. Mom and I ate in the kitchen and talked about whether the Special Branch had threatened him over the leader. But of course we couldn't ask. Mom waved away my questions about patriotism and citizens' duties, 'Tom, I've got enough to worry about at home let alone the bally country.'

After a couple of Drosteins, Mom began to think it was her fault again because they had just done the monthly accounts and Dad had grumped at the size of the grocery bills. I told her not to be silly because he did that every month. But that just made her feel worse.

The silence only lasted a day and the next evening he snapped back like one of those people you read about in the magazines who come out of a coma after years and start talking like they were in the middle of a sentence.

He told us what had happened the morning his leader came out. He was summoned into the office of the newspaper's owner, a piggy-eyed Scotsman named John Dewar. The Old Man, as everyone called him, had the year before appointed Dad as editor, although the board of directors didn't like him: he was too coarse, they said, never seen at a club, and only made it to corporal in a Transvaal regiment. To keep the board quiet, the Old Man said he would control everything Harry Mac did. Mom loved to tell what happened next, speaking in her naughty voice: how Dad told the Old Man to 'shove the job and the newspaper up your arse'. There hadn't been a problem since, and the Old Man smiled every month as sales went up.

But he knew what the government was planning and was worried by the latest leader's suggestion that it might be time to break the law. 'Keep going like this, laddie, and we may have no paper, no sales. Stick it to the buggers, by all means, but remember you cannae score tries if you put your foot into touch.'

Dad's Scottish accent was terrible but we laughed anyway, and I couldn't imagine anyone actually calling Harry Mac 'laddie'.

Mom told me later that Dad had been upset because he knew the owner was right from a business point of view. What led to the silence, she reckoned, was Dad knowing the Old Man was right about the political strategy, too. He was playing into the Kolonel's hands and giving the government an excuse to close the paper down when the backdated laws kicked in.

I thought Dad was getting angry because the Kolonel was doing the rugby trick on him.

●

Meanwhile, Haas Cockroft had been in combat again. He stopped Dad at the fence one afternoon when we got out of the car and told him about The Group's latest revolutionary act. They had disrupted a National Party meeting in Ixopo by switching off the hall lights and turning on the fire hose.

'You should have heard them howl!' Haas giggled, pink cheeks quivering.

'Lucky they didn't catch you like last time,' said Dad.

'Well, we're getting better at it, hey? Good training. Of course, I couldn't actually go into the hall.' Haas held up his arm. The plaster had been on for some time now and was cracked and dirty, and I'd seen him use the arm in the garden. 'Someone had to wait in the car with the motor running. Just in case, you know. They're real thugs.'

●

It was about this time, just as the weather was getting cooler, that something happened in my leg. I was used to cramps and twitches, but this came on hard in the night, just before dawn. The contraction shot up my leg, bending my foot backwards and making me gasp. I lay there waiting to see what would happen. The last thing I wanted to do was call out. Mom was barely holding things together as it was, keeping an eye on Dad and watching the post for letters from Little Harry, quickly turning over the envelope to check the address on the back even before she opened it to make sure he was still at a safe camp.

As I lay there in the dark, the spasms eased and I smiled, remembering a visit to the doctor a few years before. My ankle had been giving way and the specialist had told my parents that he was going to break the bones and fuse them so the ankle wouldn't collapse. 'Of course, it won't bend either, and he won't be able to walk properly.'

I don't recall what Dad said exactly, but I remember a roaring and him throwing me over his shoulder and carrying me out, even though I could actually walk. There were other parents in the waiting room with their children, staring, and I smiled down at them as we swept out, trailing a smell of rhino.

But these days, Dad was so angry who knew what he would do if I told him the pain was back?

The pain didn't return that day, so I didn't say anything to anyone other than Millie. She listened quietly, pulled a frog mouth, and then nearly let me win the pushover game on the lawn.

Behind the hedge, somebody walked up the lane, one shoe scraping. 'Hey, Millie,' I whispered, nodding towards the sound. 'Did you know he was banned?'

'Mr Lambert? Of course.' But you couldn't tell if she really had known.

Mr Lambert was one of the sounds of the lane that we hardly noticed anymore. Little Harry did the best impression of his scraping shoe and nodding head.

When Sol got home Millie and I asked him why a sick old man was a threat to the government.

After changing out of his work clothes, Sol had set himself up on the verandah with a cloth and a bottle of alcohol, and was wiping down a large animal skull. 'Isn't it a beauty?' he said. He had found the eland skull while hiking in the Berg, but Mrs Lieberman wouldn't have it in the house, so Sol kept it in the garden rondavel he used for private consultations. He called the skull his *memento mori*, and said it was to remind him that nothing lasts.

He stepped back from the skull and pointed down the lane. 'They're not worried about what Edgar Lambert might do physically,' Sol said. 'But there's a helluva mind inside that frail body. He's under house arrest, too, but because of his medical condition, they allow him to walk to the shop to get the paper.'

It turned out Mr Lambert had been the leader of a political party until it was banned. By placing him under house arrest they could keep a close watch on him.

It struck me. 'The black car!'

Sol shrugged, his eyes sliding back to the skull. 'Who knows?'

I told Sol about Haas Cockroft's latest adventure with The Group at Ixopo, and how Dad had teased him. Sol made a noise of disgust and flicked the cleaning cloth at the verandah rail. 'Those people. The Group. Albrightsen, O'Neill, Farrar. Men with weak pasts hoping for rescue from a mediocre present and an empty future.' I guessed from the distaste in his voice that Sol probably wasn't mixed up in Haas's plot. That was good. I got my best secret agent results when I didn't try too hard. But what, then, was the secret Millie had mentioned?

It was also the first time I'd heard that some of the newspapermen were in The Group. That meant Dad must know who was in Haas's plot, even though their names were supposed to be secret. Did they know whether Harry Mac was in or out? My brain hurt.

Sol took the skull back to his rondavel and told us to wait because he felt like reading to us. I thought about how much Dad enjoyed reading and then telling stories, usually from some thick African history book with a gloomy cover. The last one had been about a

German missionary doctor with a big moustache. Maybe that was why Dad and Sol got on so well. They both loved telling stories. I hadn't seen Dad read one of those books for a while. These days you'd find half-finished Westerns by Louis L'Amour lying around face down. I wanted my old dad back. But more than that I didn't want anyone to take him away, angry or not.

Millie and I were settled down with our ginger beers when Sol came out of the house, talking. 'You know, Tomka, what you were telling me about the Kolonel and the Greyshirts; those guys were serious, hey? The Nazis and Afrikaner politicians exchanged visits and talked about how Africa would be carved up after the war. The Germans of course wanted South West Africa back, but said South Africa could run everything else south of the Sahara.'

Sol read more of *If This Is a Man* to us and talked about the author Primo Levi's struggle to survive in Auschwitz and to understand human impulses. Sol was trying to make a point, comparing South Africa with the camp, where the 'moral code became warped, affecting both the jailers and the jailed.'

Sol had lost me, and Millie's face was closed. There was a long silence and when Sol started speaking again, his voice was dreamy.

'For me, there is more.' With Sol, there was always more. 'My father was sent to the same sub-camp and he was there about the same time as Levi was put to work in the Buna synthetic rubber factory. That's where any record of my father ends.'

Sol looked down at the book on his lap. 'My father was a pathologist and would have had similar skills to Levi, who was a chemist. I know there were ten thousand people in his camp, but I fantasise that my father also worked in the rubber factory, maybe alongside Levi. I read this book over and over to get a sense of my father's life in the concentration camp, and maybe on some reading I will come across a reference to him. Fantasy, hey? But what else do I have?'

'What about your mother?'

'When the train arrived, they separated the women on the platform, and walked them straight into the gas chamber.'

The dreaminess died when he said that. I felt like I'd trodden on something I shouldn't have. I didn't know what to make of Sol now. I was sickened by what had happened to his family, but it also made me feel more strongly that he should act, do something; bugger trying to understand 'human impulses'.

Millie had sat through the story in silence, her mouth unreadable. She would have heard this before—these were her grandparents—and yet she never spoke of them. Had Sol taught her the best way to survive was to keep your mouth shut and your head down?

14

A LETTER IN THE FOLLOWING WEEK LIT UP MOM'S FACE and we had to endure Nelson Eddy and Jeanette MacDonald for days on end.

The letter was from Little Harry, saying he was being posted to the Natal Carbineers HQ in town for a few weeks, because the government was doing manoeuvres. He would try to get a leave pass but thought it unlikely. He would, however, have to do guard duty and we could come and see him at the sentry box outside the drill hall, as long as we didn't talk to him.

One day, with 'Indian Love Call' threatening to shatter every window in the lane, and Dad outside checking his eggs for the third time that day—'These things are taking forever'—Mom said she would let me in on a little secret.

It turned out that every night when she was closing up the house, Mom would sneak out to the garage and switch off the incubator light. Next morning she would be up early to put it back on. 'If you think I'm having those bally things slithering around my house, think again,' she told me.

I wasn't comfortable sharing this secret with Mom; I had been looking forward to the baby crocs ever since Dad brought the eggs back from one of his Umfolozi trips to write game conservation stories.

•

A couple of weeks later Little Harry rang from the phone box inside the drill hall to tell us his unit had arrived. Mom hogged the phone but Little Harry wouldn't tell her anything about his posting or when he would be on guard duty. Mom wanted to know why all the secrecy, but he just said, 'Ask Dad.'

'*Ag*, it's bloody Nat paranoia,' Dad told us. 'That man we heard at the conference, Mandela; even though he's on the run, they've made him secretary of something called the All-In National Action Council and they've called a three-day stay-at-home strike around the time we become a republic.'

The republic hadn't been a big issue in our house. Dad said it was stupid on one level because it isolated us further from the rest of the world, but he liked the idea of the country standing on its own two feet and showing some gumption. Despite what the Kolonel had said to goad him, Dad and many people like him felt no connection with Britain and resented being called English.

He said that the three-day strike would give the government an opportunity to frighten people, to tighten their grip and declare another state of emergency, like the one a few months ago. All police leave had been cancelled this time and the army was going to guard the native townships. Dad guessed that was what Little Harry would be doing.

Mom wanted to know if Little Harry would be in danger, but Dad laughed. 'I'd be more worried for the safety of the poor people in Sobantu Village, being watched by jumpy eighteen-year-olds with guns.'

And then, casually, like it was of no interest, he said, 'Of course, the uncertainty means they've postponed Verwoerd's visit. Not even sure if he'll come at all, now.'

Something rushed out of me and I slumped back in the lounge chair, gripping the arms in case I squealed around the room like a runaway balloon. How could he just say it like that? What about the plot? Was it all over?

I watched him closely for days after that but he didn't behave any differently, although once I saw him talking at the fence with Haas Cockroft, who had taken off his cast since hearing that Verwoerd wasn't coming.

And it seemed like the good news wasn't over. The Panga Man had attacked another couple parked down at the fish hatchery, but the man in the car had fought back and managed to wrestle the panga off his attacker. The Panga Man had fled but his victim got a good look at him and said he had been well-spoken with a quiet voice. Police were now confident they would get their man.

•

As the republic and the native strike drew closer we started to hear the throb of helicopters every day crisscrossing the town and hovering over Sobantu Village and out towards Edendale. One landed in the field opposite our school and we were taken out in groups to look at it and sit inside next to the soldiers.

One morning the window frames in the classroom started to vibrate. We rushed over and saw a column of Saracens rumble by. One pulled into the school and at little lunch we clustered around the khaki armoured car but weren't allowed to climb inside. One of the boys said they were worried we'd find the red button that worked the gun. Best of all was the shriek of three Sabre jets tearing through the sky. The next day's paper had a story about a woman living on Blackridge who said her windows had cracked. No one else reported any damage. I told Mom the pilot had probably been singing 'Indian Love Call' as he passed over the woman's house.

The radio news at night was cheerful, full of stories about the republic celebrations, the 'new era dawning', and how everything in the country was normal. B.J. Vorster came on at the end and warned that anyone threatening to disrupt the internal order would 'feel the full force of the law'. He said a peaceful transition to the republic would be ensured by the full military call-up.

Everything seemed to be going so well. Little Harry was safe, the country was under control, and Haas's plot must surely be off. The only one who didn't seem to be feeling the good cheer was Dad.

•

It was late afternoon when Little Harry rang. I answered the phone and he said in a gruff voice, 'Seven o'clock. Bring me some batteries,' and put the phone down. I told Mom and she scolded me for not calling her to the phone and then went into a tizz because she hadn't baked anything. She rushed about opening and closing the fridge, stepped on Laika and didn't say sorry, and you couldn't get any sense out of her. She told Dad we would have to get our own dinner and then shouted at us when we started eating the Viennas she had been saving for Little Harry. Eventually, Dad and I took a tin of bully beef, a bottle of tomato sauce, a block of butter and a loaf of bread out onto the verandah and ate sandwiches while Mom baked. It felt like we were camping out there, just him and me, and Laika cleaning up the scraps.

Well before seven we drove into town, crossed the Duzi bridge and turned into a narrow side road, slowing down as we approached the streetlight next to the gates of the drill hall. A skinny figure in khaki with a long rifle stood in the sentry box next to the gates, and Dad had to pull over he was laughing so much. I didn't mind that, but Mom slapped his arm until he stopped and we drove on and parked opposite the gates. Mom gasped when she saw how much weight Little Harry had lost. He seemed to have grown a couple of inches, too. We sat in the car and waited, while Little Harry stood with the rifle at his side, staring straight past us.

'What do we do?' whispered Mom.

Dad, shoulders starting to shake again, said in a strangled voice, 'Give Tom the parcel and he can go and find out what's what.'

So I crossed over and stood in front of my brother holding out the big cardboard box. He didn't move. I opened the box and the smell of Mom's butter biscuits wafted under his nose. He muttered without moving his head.

'What?'

'Put the fucking thing down behind me,' he hissed.

I went back to the car and told them he had used the F word but had accepted the box.

'Bugger this,' said Mom, climbing out and crossing the road. She marched straight up and hugged him, causing the rifle to clatter to the pavement. After a few seconds he hugged her back. Dad went over, picked up the rifle, hefted it and shook Little Harry's hand, while I was told to keep an eye out for the corporal who was always looking to make his life miserable. He briefly grabbed my hand and asked if there were batteries in the box.

●

The national stay-at-home strike started three days before the republic. Essie told us that men had come to the lane, ordering servants to stay away from work, and she didn't know what to do.

She was worried about angering the activists but didn't want to lose wages. Mom thought it easier all round to give Essie a few days off and send her home to the *kraal* at Kranskop.

On the first day of the strike, riding to school, the streets were quiet and almost empty. I'd never realised that most of the people who walked the pavements were natives. No one was working in the gardens, either, and I missed the bubbling voices.

On the second day, I was woken just before sunrise by two men arguing, trying to keep their voices down. The voices were familiar and coming from outside, below the verandah. I got up and walked out into the cold grey light, following the sounds.

'You could at least have made contact with your mother, you know. It's bloody selfish.' That was Dad.

'Who are you to say what's selfish? You lie here in your warm bed, protected by Saracens, while my people are shot down like dogs or disappear.' That was Windsor.

Windsor!

The voices stopped and I realised I'd said his name aloud. Two heads peered around the hibiscus bush they'd been crouching behind.

'Tom, go inside!'

'Hello, Windsor.'

He looked embarrassed and started to smile, then thought better of it, turning his head away. 'I must go, Mr MacGregor.'

'See your mother first. And you just think about what I said.'

'And you think about what *I* said.'

Dad came up the steps, his breath steaming. He put an arm around my shoulders and led me inside and back to bed. He pulled the blankets up to my chin and sat heavily next to me, elbows on his knees, saying nothing. He took one of Laika's ears and flipped it back and forth, which she hated. I watched him, dying to ask what was going on, but knowing he would only tell me if he felt like it, and after a while he shook his head and sort of laughed.

'Everything is so *deurmekaar*. It would be nice to say Windsor is like another son to me, but that's foolish sentimentalism. Or maybe just guilt. It's almost like we're an incomplete version of each other: I've got the public life, he the secret inner life. I know which has more value. Mine is the idiot's tale, *full of sound and fury, signifying nothing*.

I reached over and pulled Laika away. 'Dad, what did Windsor want?'

He jerked and I knew he had been talking to himself. 'Want? What did he want? Nothing. And everything. *Wagter*, you can't tell anyone you saw Windsor, okay? Not even Millie.'

Sure, Dad.

'So what did he want?'

'Windsor has chosen a path which means trouble for him. Lots and lots of trouble. God, I admire him. He's such a stubborn bugger, won't listen to sense. *There comes a time when it lies within a man's grasp to shape the clay of his life.*'

'Dad, *you're* not making sense.'

'Jesus, now I'm quoting Louis L'Amour. Nothing makes sense, boykie. Windsor is doing things that are completely logical—in fact it would be odd if he wasn't doing them, because you see there's a direct line between who he is and the action he's taking. It's the same with the Kolonel: a direct line, clear, strong. For people like me, like us, the line is all twisted, with loose threads hanging off. Our line gets tangled with Windsor's and the Kolonel's. We think it makes all the lines stronger, but it just causes knots. And so you end up with a son standing guard over a rotten cause, and you crouch in the bushes counselling a young man whose courage and ideals you support, but who may kill your own son in the pursuit of them.'

'Dad, please.'

He ignored me, his big head grim, hulking between his shoulders.

'And the reason we find ourselves in these situations is because life is simple and complicated at the same time. It's one thing to see right and wrong with crystal vision; it's quite another thing to live your life, where the everyday stuff—food, family, ingrown toenails, toothache, a grumpy boss—overwhelms and clouds that beautiful vision.'

I gave up trying to understand him. But I didn't care what nonsense he spouted as long as he stayed on the bed and I could feel him warm against my legs.

He sighed, stood and rolled his head on his neck. He looked down and was back with me again. 'Little Harry says his unit is being posted soon; he doesn't know where but the rumour is somewhere in the bush. Don't say anything to your mother. Let her enjoy having him nearby for a while.'

●

That night I tried to explain this conversation to Millie. She kept stopping me and asking me to repeat things. It was hard trying to remember everything, but it seemed to make sense to her. We were sitting in the window of the *spookhuis* huddled under a blanket, and with her hair across her face I couldn't see what she was thinking, but she would nod every now and then.

We were regular visitors to the *spookhuis* now and even talked about camping there one night, maybe when the weather warmed up. But the place still had an in-between feeling, like you get in some people's houses when you're not sure whether you're welcome or not. So we would stop at the front door and ask Mr and Mrs van Deventer if it was okay to come in. We reckoned as long as someone didn't say 'no' it would be. We'd checked out every room and even worked out which was Gillian and her brother's bedroom, but we didn't spend time there.

'So what do you think?'

Millie shrugged. 'Obviously the plot has been dropped because Verwoerd isn't coming anymore, but it seems to have made it worse for your dad. From what you've told me, he envies Windsor because he knows what to do. Don't you remember what Sol said on the verandah the other day?'

I shook my head. Sol had said lots of things.

'He said that your dad is frustrated because the English-speakers are trapped between Afrikaner nationalism and the African liberation struggle. They're in the way.'

How the hell did she remember that?

'Have you noticed any change in Sol now that Verwoerd's not coming?'

She jerked her body around, her face inches from mine and her mouth a funny shape. 'What do you mean?'

'Y-you know, his secrets . . .'

'I never told you his secrets.'

She turned away again and let her hair fall back. It was a cold, clear night and our breath misted around us. She seemed to move away from me a little under the blanket. It was a long time before she spoke again.

'I think Mr van Deventer had secrets. I don't know what they were, but Sol says something funny was going on—he overheard the servants talking about the Van Deventers but they clammed up when he asked them about it.'

I'd messed things up by asking about Sol and I hated seeing Millie upset, so I said, 'Hey, do you think he could have been a secret agent?'

'Get real. No, I think it was about romance. Mrs van Deventer was having an affair so he shot her.'

'That's not romantic.'

We were both quiet then. It was so cold Titch had put his weights away early and there were no insect sounds. All the houses were dark and the lane lay there like a shivering creature waiting for something to warm it up.

When Millie spoke her voice was clear and sharp. 'One day, Tom-Tom, you and I are going to remember all this quite differently.'

15

THE STAY-AT-HOME STRIKE HAD PASSED AND, AS THE SABC
said, everything was normal. Men in overalls and gumboots came
back to work on the roads, spraying the tufts of grass around street
signs, causing thorns to grow in their place, and the ice-cream boys
rang their bells and parked their three-wheelers on the corners, and
the servants sat on the crescents of grass in the lane and plaited their
hair and polished our silver. I rode my bike to school past the native
bus queues, and the voices from the gardens like water running over
rocks, and if I was walking on the pavement and stumbled, the first
hands to help me up were black. As far as we knew there had been
almost no trouble, although Essie told us that she had been travelling
on a bus that had been fired at near Kranskop. She thought it was
because there were men on board who were going to work during
the strike. But it might also have been a clan feud, a 'faction fight' as
the police called them. She and her friends were more concerned with
the new rands and cents which had replaced pounds, shillings and
pennies, and they were certain the new money wouldn't buy as much.

The police issued statements saying the strike had been a failure, even though there were reports of factories closed throughout the country and we had seen how quiet the streets had been. Anyway, it all got lost in the republic celebrations, and at school we were given medals and taken to see the tanks and helicopters and watch the bands and soldiers march at Jan Smuts Stadium.

Mom and Dad came down to the stadium to see Little Harry march past, eyes-right towards the provincial administrator in a top hat on a podium while three Sabre jets streaked overhead trailing orange, white and blue smoke. I looked for Little Harry, but couldn't see him among the glittering bayonets.

The best news for Mom was that Little Harry's unit was given ten days' leave now the strike and the republic were safely behind us. He came home and spent the first couple of days eating and sleeping, then put on his old jeans, which hung loose from his hips, and went looking for girls.

I hadn't seen Mom so happy for a while. She spun through the house in some new long pants she'd bought and when she was like this not even Dad could bring down a silence. He called it sashaying, and I thought the pants were too short, but she said that Princess Grace had worn them to the Isle of Capri and that was good enough for her. Dad wasn't sure about the Capri pants, saying he preferred the swing skirts, but he seemed to change his mind the more he watched her twirl through the rooms. Haas Cockroft didn't mind them either and when Mom came home from shopping one day and bent to get the bags out of the car, Haas sprayed the garden hose all over his shoes.

Even Dad perked up and for the first time since he became editor we felt like a family again; in fact it was better than before because he and Little Harry didn't fight at all. Mom's music filled the house and she couldn't make up her mind which was her current favourite— 'Moon River' or 'Itsy Bitsy Teenie Weenie Yellow Polka Dot Bikini'.

Dad grumbled about the bikini song, but I thought anything was better than 'Indian Love Call'.

Actually, I couldn't remember a better time. I started to wonder if the whole plot business had just been my imagination. Even Dad's leaders had calmed down. He started talking about other things, arguing with Mom over which horses to back in the July Handicap and laughing at her choice. 'Kerason? Sounds like something you burn in a lamp. Kerason? It's fifty to one. Let's find a picture. I bet it's got long ears and goes "hee-haw".'

I had no more dreams about walls closing in, and the pains and cramping in my leg had gone.

Little Harry was more relaxed around the house and had grown serious since being in the army. He and Dad started sitting on the verandah in the late afternoons, drinking beer, and they didn't mind me being there. But their voices changed when I left and went inside.

One morning I saw Little Harry across the lane sitting on Mr de Wet's verandah, talking and drinking Kool-Aid like they'd known each other all their lives—which of course they had, but I'd never seen Little Harry so much as greet Mr de Wet.

I was a bit irritated with Little Harry to be honest, coming home like a new adult in the house, making Mom giggle and being able to sit and drink beer with Dad. And now here he was chatting away on the *Bosmoedertjie*'s verandah.

When he came back across the lane I was waiting on the top step and told him that Millie and I had been over there and we already knew the *Bosmoedertjie* story. Everything, I said. We knew everything, even the secret stuff. He squinted up at me, smiled and brushed past. 'Everything? Oh well, I don't need to tell you, then.'

The shit. I followed him to his room, demanding to know what they'd talked about and hating the whine in my voice.

Little Harry stretched out on his bed with a smirk, but he soon lost interest in teasing and let out a long breath. Now he was even sighing like an adult. 'I was passing and said hello, and Mr de Wet came to the fence and asked me how my army service was going. Behind us Titch was grunting and blowing air like a whale in his garage and Mr de Wet said he'd heard the school had taken Titch back but the rugby tour was cancelled, so now it was the Olympics or nothing. So I told him it would probably be nothing because we would be banned unless we included blacks in the team for Tokyo.'

I wasn't interested in Titch's Olympics. 'Did Mr de Wet say any more about the *Bosmoedertjie*?'

Little Harry rolled over to face me. 'Did you know South Africa had natives in its Olympic team before the rest of the world even allowed women to run?'

I narrowed my eyes at him but kept my mouth shut. I'd been caught too many times before. After a while I said, 'How do you know?'

'Mr de Wet told me. We had two natives in the marathon at St Louis in 1904. They were over there with a Boer War pageant and decided to have a run. One did really well and might have won a medal if he hadn't been chased off the course by a mad dog. Mr de Wet says the Olympics has never been fair, so who are they to point the finger at us.'

I kept my eyes narrow and watched his face but nothing showed. I would look this one up in the school library. A mad dog. Please.

'How come Mr de Wet knows so much about the Olympics?'

'Because he nearly got there himself in 1928. He invited me in and showed me a picture of himself at the trials. Flyweight boxer. Knocked out by the man who went on to fight for the bronze.'

I pictured the muscular legs and wiry body. Little Mr de Wet with the soft voice and crinkly eyes.

'So did you learn anything else about the *Bosmoedertjie*?'

You would have thought I was talking to the wall.

'I don't think the poor old bugger has talked to anyone for ages.

I had to sit there and listen to him go on about how life itself wasn't fair, about how he joined the National Party because the British had been unfair to the Afrikaners. How did he put it? "The British always do things to suit themselves and then make the morals fit."'

Little Harry lay back with his arms behind his head. 'Actually, it was quite interesting. He said the Boers were the only ones to sign a treaty with the natives, settling on land emptied by the Zulu invasions.'

I knew this one. We got it often enough at school. How in 1838 the Voortrekker leader Piet Retief and his men signed a treaty for the empty land with the Zulu king Dingaan at the royal *kraal*. Afterwards, the king held a big feast, with dancing, and then stood up and shouted to his warriors, '*Bulala umthakathi!*' Kill the wizards. And they did, and an *impi* went straight out and slaughtered hundreds of men, women and children waiting way back at the wagons.

'Yes,' I said with a wave of the hand. 'Piet Retief and all that.'

But he carried on as though I hadn't spoken. 'Mr de Wet said his ancestors were among the survivors and took part in the big revenge battle, Blood River. Dingaan was crushed and the Zulus left them alone after that and the Voortrekkers settled in the lands they'd negotiated, and set up their own republic.'

I'd had enough of a history lesson from Little Harry, who'd mucked up so much at school that he didn't even remember we'd learnt this stuff. And he'd obviously not found out anything new about the *Bosmoedertjie*. I got up, stretched my leg and started walking out of the room. His voice stopped me.

'I thought he was just rambling but he was building up to a point.' Little Harry smiled at me, propped himself up and did quite a good imitation of Mr de Wet's soft, high-pitched voice. '"Don't forget it was the *rooinekke*, the British, who took over our Voortrekker republic and then invaded Zululand, *nè*? So now that we've finally got rid of the British, who is to tell us that we must hand back all this country, hey? Does anyone tell the Zulus they must give back the land they conquered in the great scattering, the *Mfecane*? If you start down that road, you'd be *verspreing* land all the way to the Congo, and then probably have to keep going."'

Little Harry flopped back on the bed, pleased with himself. He obviously understood Mr de Wet's argument, so I nodded. I would go away and think it over. I nodded again more slowly, like a grown-up, and left.

'Hey, *Wagter*!'

I poked my head back in.

He was grinning. 'Don't you want to know what he said about the *Bosmoedertjie*?'

Swine.

After Mr de Wet's little talk they'd sat on the verandah with a cold drink, laughing at Titch huffing and groaning across the lane. Little Harry had asked Mr de Wet if it upset him that his own son was badly injured while someone like Titch did everything he could to avoid call-up.

The old man had frowned then shook his head. 'At one time, *ja*. Arno believed in what he was doing. I did too. Now, I don't know, man. While I agree with Verwoerd's policy of separate development, we are becoming *boewe*, thugs, in the way we do it. Your kaffir has always stood up to us. You can't sit on him forever. The time for fighting is over. There must be another way.'

Little Harry said Mr de Wet had picked up a biscuit and was about to take a bite when he stopped and pointed it towards Titch and then tapped the side of his head. 'He is a *dikkop*, that boy, but if he keeps himself from harm, who can blame him? As for my son, that is the Lord's work and my cross to bear.'

I waited but Little Harry seemed to be finished. 'Did you find out what was in the *Bosmoedertjie*'s little red box?' I asked.

He stared at me. 'You make me sick,' he said, and turned away.

Which wasn't fair, because he was the one who'd said it contained the *Bosmoedertjie*'s balls.

•

But even though Little Harry had become more serious and could drink beer with Dad, he still did things with the family. Like one Saturday during his leave when Dad announced we would all go down to the racecourse to watch the starts. 'There's a life lesson I want you to observe,' he told us.

It also turned out Dad wanted to see some horses that he fancied for the July Handicap in a few weeks. He hadn't been able to talk Mom out of Kerason and wanted her to see some 'real horses'.

There was a gap in the fence near one of the main starts, so the local families would climb through and crowd the rails at that spot.

'Now watch number three,' Dad said after we'd wormed our way to the front. Down the rails a bit I saw Haas Cockroft and he was watching Dad. Something cold passed over me but it was only for a moment. Verwoerd wasn't coming. That was over. Finished. Everything was normal again. But the sight of him nearly spoilt the outing for me.

Dad was talking again so I put Haas out of my mind. The start barrier was a piece of rope stretched across the course with a bit of netting hanging off it. The jockeys would have to time it so that their horse was settled at the exact moment the starter released the lever and the rope sprang up.

Dad told us that the jockey on number three was the famous Tiger Wright, who had won the July four times and was about to leave to race in England.

'Watch him, watch the colours,' Dad said.

There was such a confusion of rearing and circling horses, flying froth, bit-jingling and jockey-swearing that it was hard to pick anyone out. But suddenly the light flashed, the rope jerked and they were away, Tiger Wright's colours leading the field.

Behind them they left a horse squealing and kicking as it struggled to get up, and next to it on the grass lay its jockey, still.

'Okay, that's enough,' said Mom, grabbing my hand and pulling me back through the gap in the fence to the car while the race caller's excited voice echoed through the loudspeakers from the grandstand across the course. Dad and Little Harry, meanwhile, had ducked under the rail and run to the jockey, along with half the town it seemed. I struggled against Mom's grip, but she wouldn't let me join them.

After a while, they came back to the car, grinning and teasing each other. Dad handed the keys to Little Harry and climbed in the front next to him.

'Who won?' I asked.

'Who do you think?' said Little Harry, starting the car and glancing at Dad, and I felt a lurch, realising they had shared something private.

I sulked on the way home and refused to ask what the life lesson was, while Mom kept asking about the fallen horse and jockey.

'They'll be fine,' said Little Harry like he was a doctor or something.

It was only on Monday morning at breakfast when I read the paper that I found out what it was all about. On the front page there was a picture of the jockey in his hospital bed with rope burns on his face. He was an apprentice and it was his first race, and the other jockeys had told him that Tiger Wright had an arrangement with the starter that when his horse was set, he would nod and the starter would release the lever.

'So I watched Tiger and when I saw him nod, I gave my horse heels and whip. That's the last I remember.'

The apprentice's horse sprang straight into the rope and the net wrapped around the jockey's face, whipping him and the horse backwards.

The story didn't say whether he'd misread the nod or whether such a nod existed. Tiger Wright won the race by half a length.

It was a good story but I couldn't see the lesson Dad wanted us to learn.

'Well, the start is supposed to be fair to everyone,' he said, chewing, smiling, talking and pulling a piece of bacon rind from his mouth at the same time. 'I wanted you to see Tiger nod to the starter, to make you realise that things might not be what they seem. Life is not always fair. Take nothing for granted, and be your own man.'

He chuckled and tapped bacon grease on the photo of the injured apprentice. 'I think that reinforces my point.'

I wondered what he was trying to tell us, but you know, sometimes I think Dad just liked good stories and then built something around them afterwards.

But a few days later the stories turned bad.

16

THE ROUTINE IN OUR HOUSE FOR COLLECTING THE MAIL was that Mom would go to the letterbox after she'd fetched Dad from work. This day, I'd ridden my bike in through the gate and seen something sticking out the box. I'd been expecting a Captain Condor figurine I'd written away for and I didn't want Little Harry to know I still read *Lion* comic, so I grabbed the envelope and took it into my bedroom. Mom was in the kitchen and Little Harry was lying on his bed listening to music.

I closed my door and tore open the envelope, but it contained only a sort of smallish newspaper folded up. It was in a foreign language and had a red star on the top. Also in the envelope was a sheet of paper with Dad's name on it and, written in English, *Your annual subscription is due for renewal*, with details of where to send a cheque. I looked on the outside of the envelope and saw it was addressed to Harold MacGregor. I put everything back in the envelope, changed out of my school uniform and went down to Millie's, taking the paper with me to ask Sol if he could understand the language. Maybe it was something from Dad's POW days.

Sol wasn't home so I left it on their verandah and went to play with Millie. About half an hour later, a man we didn't recognise, wearing a safari suit and smoking, walked down the lane. He turned without looking at us and walked back up towards the big road. A while later we heard a van turn into the lane and stop. It seemed only moments later Essie came huffing down the lane, eyes wide.

'*Nkosane*, come quick. Police! Little Harry has a gun!'

Millie grabbed my hand and we raced up the lane, past the police van blocking our driveway and into the house, from where we could hear angry voices.

Two men stood in our lounge. One was the smoker in the lane and the other was the sergeant who had been on the *kaya* raid, Viljoen. Mom was sitting in a chair crying, holding a handkerchief to her face. Between her and the police was Little Harry holding his army .303 across his chest.

The police turned when we ran in, then ignored us and carried on glaring at Little Harry. Millie and I went straight to Mom and sat on the arms of the chair.

'We are giving you one last warning,' said the sergeant, who was trying to control the situation, but his voice was uncertain. 'Put the gun down now. Do you have any idea of the consequences of what you're doing?'

'Well you won't be around to see them, will you?' said Little Harry. The safari suit man moved to one side and Little Harry slid the bolt of his rifle and raised his eyebrows at him. The man went pale and stepped back.

I gaped at Little Harry. His expression was terrifying, his eyes never leaving the two policemen. He looked just like Harry Mac but a helluva lot scarier. 'Tom, phone Dad.' His voice was quiet. 'Tell him the police are harassing Mom.'

I edged over to the phone and dialled the newspaper, my fingers shaking. The policemen flinched when they heard Dad's roar down the line.

I turned to them. 'My dad says if you don't get out of our house right now he'll . . .' My face felt hot and I glanced at Mom. 'He'll rip your fucking heads off and shove them up your hairy arses.'

The police looked at each other then back at Little Harry. 'Put down the gun and we will continue this outside. We are within our legal rights to question you over the possession of banned or seditious publications.' Viljoen said it all like he was reciting it.

'Fine,' said Little Harry. 'Do your sneaky little job. But what gives you the right to walk into our house and start threatening my mother? Is that the way you operate, you cowards? Wait until the husband is away then intimidate his wife? You see, I am a member of the armed forces. This gun is legal and loaded. You—' he pointed at safari suit '—are an intruder, maybe a terrorist. You've got no uniform. "Kapow!" Bullet through the heart. Only afterwards do we find out you are a policeman, when this other piece of shit comes around the corner in his pretty blue uniform. *Ag*, shame! And guess what? We have three—no, four—witnesses to back up my story.'

It was completely mad and I was sure Little Harry had been reading too many detective stories in the army—he'd even said 'kapow!'—but the policemen didn't know how mad he might have gone out in the *bundu*.

'Now get on with your police work. And you might want to be quick. It takes my father not even ten minutes to get home—less if he's in a hurry. And he's not as nice as me.'

Sergeant Viljoen spoke again to Mom in that rehearsed voice, but speeded up. 'We have reason to suspect your husband is in regular receipt of banned publications. We have observed your mailbox and believe it may contain such material. Have you collected your mail today?'

Mom shook her head.

Sergeant Viljoen had now recovered and was starting to enjoy himself. He looked at safari suit man. 'We will record that as a "no". We now ask you to accompany us to the mailbox.' He sneered at Little Harry. 'You're welcome to witness this, or are you going to try to stop us in the execution of our duty?'

Little Harry looked like he'd run out of ideas and seemed unsure what to do next. I was standing to one side, trying to catch his attention without the policemen seeing me. Little Harry noticed and I nodded and smiled and indicated with my head outside. He turned back to the police with a shrug.

Little Harry put down his rifle and we all walked outside. When we arrived at the letterbox, the sergeant made a show of standing next to it like a magician, opening the lid and pulling out letters one at a time. Most were bills, including one from the shop where Mom had bought her Capri pants.

They got to the end and looked inside, then spoke hurriedly in Afrikaans to each other. They ripped open each letter and shook the contents on the ground. They searched the area around the letterbox and the sergeant became angry and accusing towards safari suit, who defended himself, pointing at the letterbox.

'If there's nothing else, gentlemen, I'm going back to listen to my radio,' Little Harry said.

Red-faced, Sergeant Viljoen flipped open his holster and put his hand on the pistol. 'You do realise, don't you, that I am indemnified if I shoot you right here for obstructing me in the course of my duty?'

Little Harry was unworried. 'Even if you weren't just boasting, I'm sure not even you are stupid enough to shoot an unarmed man in front of so many witnesses.'

'What, this lot of cripples and freaks?' Viljoen laughed, looking at Millie and me.

'No,' said Little Harry, his gaze passing over the sergeant's shoulder. 'This neighbourhood.'

The sergeant turned and saw half-a-dozen servants watching from the lane. Behind us Mrs Cockroft and Titch leant on the fence and across the lane Mr de Wet sat on his verandah.

'One day . . .' the sergeant said through gritted teeth, looking at Little Harry.

They got back in their van and drove off, showering gravel. As they passed, safari suit stared at Little Harry and cocked his finger against the side of his head.

I wonder what would have happened if Harry Mac had skidded into the lane at that moment.

●

Of course, that wasn't the end of it. The next day Dad kicked in the Kolonel's door and demanded to be arrested.

Once again we were around the kitchen table listening to him. There were crushed beer cans everywhere, including one Dad had crumpled while it still had beer in it, but he ignored the mess. And this time Little Harry was with us, riding back in his chair and chewing a toothpick like Wild Bill Hickok. He saw me watching him and grinned. I couldn't help smiling back. I wondered if this was a story I could tell at school.

But Dad was different. When we'd sat at this table after he'd visited the Kolonel to get information on Windsor, his eyes had had that dangerous shine, like someone squaring up for a fight. Now he looked like he wasn't sure where the next blow would come from. I think he was worried for the rest of us. Well, good. But from what he told us, the Kolonel was becoming more dangerous.

Dad told us that he'd marched into the Special Branch headquarters and demanded to see the Kolonel. When the secretary tried to fob him off he walked straight past her and kicked the door open.

'Oh, Harry Mac,' said Mom.

Little Harry stopped riding his chair and we both leant forward.

'That same office boy who tiptoes around like a creeping Jesus was serving the Kolonel tea, but he scuttled out quick-smart,' said Dad. I bet the room stank of rhino.

Dad had slapped the newspaper with the red star onto the Kolonel's desk and said, 'Is this the best you can do?'

Apparently the Kolonel didn't stop stirring his tea while he glanced at the paper and then back up at Dad.

'How would you feel if I just kicked my way into your office?' the Kolonel had said.

'How would you feel if I just pushed my way into your house and terrified your wife?'

Mom was nodding now. She poured a glass of wine. 'Good, yes. Did you tell him about that Viljoen?'

'Hang on,' Dad said. 'I'll get to him.'

Dad had then demanded to be charged for 'being in possession of seditious literature'. He wanted it to go to court, to prove they planted it. Mom stopped nodding.

Dad took a mouthful of beer and sat rubbing the condensation on the can.

'Well?' Little Harry wanted to hear some more action. But Dad got up and walked to the fridge, opened and closed the door, and came and sat down again.

'He didn't know anything about it,' Dad said, rubbing his face.

'Oh, bullshit.' Little Harry pushed himself away from the table and looked like he might also go and open and close the fridge.

Dad held up his hand. 'No, no. I know him.' He chuckled. 'He was actually a bit hurt that I would accuse him of such a clumsy plan. Told me we weren't in a Wild West film.'

'Viljoen,' Mom said.

Dad nodded. 'He all but admitted it could be Viljoen's work. The Kolonel apologises to you, by the way.'

I thought Mom was going to spit in her wine. 'Well that's all very nice, but what's he going to do about it?'

'Nothing. He does nothing to stop the Viljoens.'

Little Harry had been tapping an empty beer can on the table. 'So what did you say? Sounds like you were almost holding hands by this stage.'

Harry Mac's heavy head swivelled slowly towards Little Harry, who this time did get up and walk to the fridge. Dad's voice followed him. 'And what would you have done—put a bullet through him?' Little Harry's ears were red and he kept his back to us.

Mom stepped in. 'Did you discuss anything else?'

'He gave me a lecture about the past dragging us down. He even mentioned Hitler again, saying there were people in his department who believed Hitler was still alive, living somewhere in Africa with ex-Afrika Korps men and planning some sort of comeback.'

'Viljoen,' Mom said.

'But he said Hitler was the past. If we combined our energies under the government, together we could step into a bright future— Afrikaner, English and Bantu. He really believes it.'

The Kolonel had offered tea, but Dad had refused. He told us he felt like a mouse in front of a swaying cobra.

And then, when Dad got up to go, the Kolonel had said, 'I'm not asking you to change your beliefs, but you must understand that this government—your and my government—is serious about taking all necessary steps to ensure a secure future for this country. Deadly serious.'

Dad finished his beer. 'And then he told me there was an arrest warrant out for Windsor because he didn't have his passbook.'

Dad had stared at him and said, 'You mean the passbook I gave you.' And the Kolonel had just shrugged.

Dad had then cursed the pass system, but the Kolonel had the last word on that, too, pointing out it had been introduced by the British a hundred and fifty years ago.

Little Harry had been listening with his forehead against the fridge. He brought up his fist and bunched it against the door. 'Jesus, Dad, didn't you even get one good shot in?'

'I told him that if Viljoen ever sets foot on my property again it will be the last time.'

'Thank fuck for that.'

And you know what? No one even noticed he'd sworn.

●

After the communist newspaper affair the feeling in the family changed again. We'd been relaxed for the last couple of weeks but now we clutched at each other like something was slipping through our fingers. Little Harry's leave was ending and Mom was the only one who didn't know he was being sent to the bush. I don't think she could have handled it on top of everything.

On his last weekend Little Harry took me with him to Hesketh to watch Mike Hailwood. We'd missed the Easter bike races that year, but Mike Hailwood was special, and at this meeting he was going to ride in three different classes on one day.

There was a huge crowd on the hill, a warm day with the sun flashing off hundreds of windscreens, and the smell of hot oil and rubber. We hung around the pits, the riders strutting in their black leathers peeled to the waist and the knees all scuffed, while the mechanics revved the bikes so loud you couldn't speak. We wandered up to the wooden stand at Angel's, where we could watch the riders come through the Sweep, throw their bikes over and then accelerate as they entered the straight.

I'd been feeling strange for most of the day and Little Harry was being extra nice, like he didn't want to go back with bad memories. And as I watched him, bare-chested, drinking beer and cheering Mike Hailwood to victory in the 250cc race, my stomach started to knot. I had the sensation of looking down at myself sitting next to Little Harry. I went to put my arm around his shoulders and heard a boy screaming and someone spilled his Coke over the person in front of them.

And the boy was me and I was on my back in the grass at the bottom of the stand with the sun in my eyes and bikes roaring past and Little Harry shaking me and shouting. And the pain in my leg was like nothing I'd ever felt before.

17

WHEN I CAME AROUND THE FIRST THING I SAW WAS
Little Harry's face and I started apologising for making him miss
the races, but he did a Harry Mac eyebrow thing and told me to
shut up. Mom was holding my hand and her eyes were red. In the
background I could hear Dad talking with another man. I tried to
focus and sit up but a hand pushed me back. I still had the sensation
of not being completely in my body. I fell asleep again realising there
was no pain in my leg. No pain anywhere.

It was dark when I awoke and Mom was sleeping in a chair next
to the bed, her hand still holding mine. I lay still until everything
cleared then lifted my head. There were four other beds in the room,
with glowing red lights on the wall and the smell I knew so well,
clean and scary. The smell of a hospital.

My movement stirred Mom and she sat up, confused, and then
leant over me. 'Tom, are you okay, boykie?'

I nodded, tried to speak, but just croaked. Mom helped me up
and gave me a sip of water. I was woozy and a dull ache throbbed

through my leg each time the muscles spasmed.

'Why am I so dizzy, Mom?'

'They gave you something to help you sleep.'

'What's going on?'

'Wait for the doctor.'

A nurse, drenched in hospital smell, entered the ward. 'How are you feeling, Tom?' she asked as she fussed with my pillows.

I nodded.

'Doctor will be here soon.' She checked the other beds and walked out, the smell lingering behind. Imagine living with a nurse. You'd wake up every morning thinking you were in hospital.

'Where's Dad and Little Harry?'

'Dad's coming. He had to drop Little Harry off on the road.'

I was sorry not to have seen Little Harry before he left, but I knew soldiers had to get on the road early or they had no hope of hitching a ride back to camp in time.

When Dad arrived I thought I detected rhino underneath the hospital smell. And then I knew he was worried because he started going at Mom about the number of blankets I had and whether I could reach the glass of water.

The doctor came, prodded, stretched, squeezed and bent my leg, shone bright lights in my eyes and then stood at the end of the bed and spoke to Dad as if Mom and I didn't count. I wished Millie had been there and I smiled, imagining her saying, 'Excuse me! Are we just Scotch mist over here?'

'Is he exhibiting any unusual behaviour?' the doctor said. 'Trouble at school, emotional problems? Is he anxious about anything?'

Dad muttered something I couldn't hear, but the doctor was already leafing through the pages on his clipboard and looking towards the next patient. He nodded to Dad and walked on.

Dad sat down and tugged at the sheet. 'He said it's a post-polio relapse.'

I had no idea what that meant. 'When will I be better?'

Dad flicked a glance at Mom and I knew that what came next would be a lie. 'The doctor said everything's fine. They'll keep you here a few days and then it's home again, because someone has to keep an eye on your mother and me, hey, *Wagter*?'

I hated that hollow talk. I turned my head away and wouldn't look at him.

He touched my shoulder. 'Sorry, Tom. Look, I don't think these buggers have a clue what to do. They don't know how to treat it, okay? But they say it will help if you rest and try to relax.'

'Can you bring Millie?'

'After school.'

He stood and looked at me and then bent down and kissed me on the forehead. It burnt long after the smell of clean and scary had wiped out all trace of rhino.

•

Dad had left the newspaper for me to read, and later, when Mom had gone home to bathe, I went through it.

He hadn't taken the attempt to plant a communist newspaper on him lying down. In his leader he said twenty thousand people had been arrested since the state of emergency and the government was now going for people who simply argued against the new laws. People like him. Bullets were fired into homes, cars sabotaged and threatening phone calls made. He said there was evidence the government was even hunting down activists in neighbouring countries. About the newspaper plant, he wrote: *We could say this is simply the clumsy handiwork of those Special Branch officers with IQs lower than their jackboot size. But the frightening implication is that these thugs have the freedom to operate in this way within the unlimited powers the government is according itself.*

Lying in bed, I chuckled at the bit about the IQs and wished Dad was there to laugh with me. I hoped Sergeant Viljoen read it. If he could. But then I thought what good would it do? It would just make the Special Branch meaner.

The really interesting story was in the sports pages, where there was a long interview with Mike Hailwood. He had won all three of his classes at Hesketh and said how much he enjoyed racing there. I was sorry Little Harry missed it.

Mike Hailwood also joked with the reporter that he felt safe racing motorbikes these days since visiting a fortune-teller who told him he was safe on the track but would be killed by a truck when he was forty.

I didn't think that was a good thing to joke about, but I knew Little Harry would like the story so I kept the paper to send to him.

•

After the warm, sunny weekend, the temperature dropped sharply and it was freezing in the hospital ward. Two other beds were occupied. In one was a skinny old man with tubes coming out of him; he lay on his back with his eyes closed, breathing and choking. In the other was a younger man with a dressing on his stomach. He listened to his radio all day and got up every now and then to cough and smoke on the verandah, leaving the door open so the fumes and icy air blew in.

Because the doctors and nurses didn't know how to treat me they sort of left me alone, which was fine because I didn't feel like talking or seeing anyone. Actually, that's not quite true. From the moment I woke up I watched the sun on the tin roof outside the window, and when the shadow of the chimney reached a certain point I knew Mom would arrive soon. I didn't really want her to speak either; I just wanted her to hold my hand and be there.

It was awkward when Millie came because I wanted her there nearly as much as I wanted Mom, but I didn't have anything to say to her, so she sat there and watched me with watery eyes and a thin frog mouth.

And then one grey afternoon it rained. And when it cleared, a pale sun the colour of a lemon touched the wet wall outside and with it came the memory of a terrible sadness.

The first time I got sick I was about five years old. I don't have many memories before that other than running around a lot with Millie, and jumping off rocks into a beach pool with Little Harry. All that ended with the first shooting pains and a long time in hospital, and after that I couldn't run or jump so well and was supposed to wear a caliper all the time. I hated it and, luckily for me, so did Dad. He never minded if I went to school without it and only wore it if I was tired and wobbly.

But what I most remember from that first stay in hospital, maybe in this same ward, was a day when it rained, and after it cleared, the pale sun slanted on the wet wall and a feeling settled on me that was like losing a toy you know you'll never find again.

I got better and, apart from not being able to run properly or jump, it wasn't too bad, but every now and then I'd see that same wet light and sink like a lilo with a slow leak.

Now I was back in hospital and the pale sun had found me.

To make it worse, the chimney shadow passed over the rooftop and Mom still hadn't arrived. By the time she did, flustered and apologetic, I had turned my back and wouldn't look at her. Millie would have slapped my arm and said, 'Stop sulking,' but I wasn't feeling sorry for myself. True as Bob. I honestly just didn't care. I stayed that way when Dad arrived. He grabbed me and turned me over, but I flopped in his arms and stared at the ceiling. I wanted to tell them not to worry, it was just the pale sun. But I couldn't.

Mom had to leave the room when she started crying and I

heard Dad's voice booming down the corridor demanding to see the doctor.

Eventually, the doctor came and did the usual prod and twist and paper-shuffle. Then he and Dad stood at the foot of my bed and talked like I wasn't there.

Dad had the eyebrows and forehead furrow working, and now something extra—the big yellow teeth were showing. This was his scariest face, like the baboon at Ben's Den that would throw itself at the bars of its cage, peeling its lips back off its teeth. The doctor looked frightened, like he was worried Harry Mac might bite him, and I thought he might, too.

The doctor was umming and erring and when he started leafing through his notes, Dad snatched the clipboard out of his hand and flicked it into the corridor.

'If you don't bloody know what to do with him then just say so. Stop pretending you're God Almighty.'

'Look, Mr MacGregor, we are starting to see patients with this sort of relapse, but there's no treatment that we—'

'Is he going to get better?'

'Well, a prognosis is always—'

'Is he going to get worse?'

The doctor's shoulders slumped and he glanced at me. 'Possibly. Probably. We just don't know. The night nurse says she came into the ward and saw him getting back into bed and she thinks he walked down to the toilet on his own. It seems there's something else going on here. What happened to his wrist?'

I was wondering when that would come up.

Now it was Dad's turn to sag and stumble with words. This made the doctor feel a whole lot better and he took charge again in a hoity-toity drawly voice. 'As far as we can tell there has been no, or little, physical deterioration. But I am going to keep him here another week to monitor any changes.' He took Dad's arm and led him across the ward, but I could still hear him. 'And we're also going to do a psychological assessment.'

Dad went quite still, and if the doctor had known him better he would have shut up then and there because he would have realised he was talking to thin air. In fact, when the doctor continued drawling and tapping his clipboard—which the nurse had fetched from the corridor—Dad was already on his way back to my bed.

'Want to go home, boykie?'

I turned my head and looked at him but didn't say anything. He bent down and I thought he was going to kiss me again, but instead he rolled me into a cocoon with the blankets and threw me over his shoulder.

'Harry Mac! Harold!' Mom was panicking and looking back at the doctor and nurse, who stood with mouths open as Dad walked unhurriedly towards the door.

I burrowed my face into his neck and breathed him in. No rhino. Just earth, heavy breath and big warm animal. Harry Mac had rescued me again. I breathed deep, closed my eyes to the pale sun and knew that nothing could touch me now.

18

THE PROBLEM WITH BEING RESCUED BY HARRY MAC
is that it's never the end of the story. He refused to talk with the
doctors or anyone from the hospital and of course Mom had to pick
up the pieces, returning the blankets and fetching my stuff from the
ward under the glare of the nurses and having to sign a form saying
the hospital was no longer responsible for my wellbeing.

I preferred being at home, away from clean and scary, but wasn't
interested in reading or listening to the radio. Laika didn't mind.
She spent the day at the foot of my bed, scooting and scratching and
pouncing on my toes when I wiggled them. Millie took a dim view
of it all and declared she would no longer visit me, but she started
coming to the window, leaning on her elbows and giving me such
a frog mouth stare that eventually I got out of bed just to get away
from her.

Little Harry wrote me two letters, the first telling how he stood
on the side of the road for ages before he got a lift. As a result, he
didn't get back to camp in time and the corporal who hated him put

him on report. Little Harry told the duty officer that the reason he was late was because his little brother was dying and he had to stay by his bedside. They let him off with a warning, which pissed off the corporal, who said he would check to see if the story was true. *So you'd better make sure that's the story if the army contacts home*, Little Harry wrote. He ended the letter, *P.S. Hope you're not really dying, or maybe just enough to convince the army. P.P.S. Send batteries.*

I wrote back saying the doctor had given me six months to live so he probably wouldn't see me again. I said it was my dying wish that he give me his Elvis record collection. I included batteries and the clipping of the story about Mike Hailwood.

His second letter was all about how boring the army was and ended with a request for a lot of batteries. *P.S. Touch my Elvis records and I'll come back and finish you off myself. P.P.S. Don't write again after you send the batteries. I won't be at this address by then.*

I knew what that last bit meant, and I didn't say anything to Mom. I showed it to Dad, who said, yes, Little Harry had written to him at work.

As for my leg, it was true what the night nurse had said. I could walk, almost as well as before, although it hurt. Mom and Dad said I should just rest and move when I felt like it. What I most felt like doing was walking down the lane to the Liebermans' and waiting for Millie and then Sol to get home. So I did, and Sol was happy to have what he called 'a captive audience' and over a couple of weeks read the whole of *If This Is a Man*. Although the story of Primo Levi in Auschwitz was terribly sad and I couldn't follow quite a lot of it, I could see how much it meant to Sol and some of that moved into me.

Seeing me getting around lifted Dad's spirits for a while, as always happened when he solved a problem by knocking its bloody block off. But that soon wore off and he became not sad and not grumpy but something like that. I discussed it with Millie and she came up with the word 'morose'.

One evening, I was on my way to the toilet when I heard him talking in the lounge to Mom. It wasn't an argument, even though she was disagreeing with him. I stopped in the dark to listen.

Dad was saying, 'Yes, but if I wasn't involved with the bloody paper none of this would have happened. He'd be normal.'

'He is normal.'

'Of course he's bloody normal. I just mean the cigarette burns, shutting everyone out, even the relapse.'

'That's no one's fault.'

'Oh no?'

Back in bed I thought about what I'd heard. Dad blamed himself for what was happening to me. I hadn't thought of it like that, but maybe he was right. If that was so, he would want to do something about it and that worried me even more, because like I said, he solved problems by charging at them.

But what was there to charge at? Polio? Mom? The Kolonel? Verwoerd?

•

The first thing he did was dig up the back lawn. All of it. I sat on the verandah and watched the excavator rip off the kikuyu and smash through the layers of shale, lifting it out in slabs of red, yellow and blue. Sol had told us about this shale which was under everyone's gardens, how it was sediment formed when the ice sheets melted two hundred and fifty million years ago. I went and fetched Millie and we watched together.

I said, 'In one week we're undoing what took millions of years to form.'

She looked at me with a semi-frog mouth and smiled. 'That's good, Tom-Tom, you're starting to talk crazy again. You must be getting better.'

Dad had reckoned that swimming would be the best exercise for me, so he'd decided to put in a pool, and of course you could see Haas Cockroft grind his teeth as he watched over the fence. It wasn't only that we were getting the first pool in the lane, but the fact that Haas had just put in a new *braai* and laid expensive crazy paving over half his backyard. And here the same stuff was being dug out of the ground a few yards away by a madman who was giving the shale slabs away. Before the week was out, Haas cut down the last tree on our boundary.

Dad was excited about all the noise and construction work going on, but his mind was already leaping ahead to another idea.

This time, he had a harder job convincing Mom.

'Uh-uh. Not on your nelly. I thought you wanted him to get better, not be killed by a bally charging rhino. No, no. Not a chance, Harold MacGregor. *Ag*, shame, look at him, poor little thing, it's all he can do to drag himself around the house. Just look at him.'

And that was her mistake.

Because they both did look at me, and instead of the sullen, non-talking child of the past few weeks they saw a boy smiling and nodding at Dad's plan, pink-cheeked and standing without leaning on anything.

Mom went cold on Dad and backed away, but he grabbed and held her to him so she couldn't speak. He grinned at me over the top of her sobbing head and we both knew she was crying as much over me smiling again as over Dad's plan.

Actually, I don't know if that was true, but it's what flashed between Dad and me.

•

I said at the start of this story that I'd tell you later how I knew what a rhino smelt like. It was because the game reserves in Zululand were a second home to Harry Mac, and if we weren't on holiday at the beach, we were game-spotting in Hluhluwe, Umfolozi or Mkuze. And in between, Dad would grab every chance he could to go up to the reserves on his own on 'newspaper business'.

He came back with stories and pictures of crocs, hippos, elephants and mambas, and we would have movie nights that often featured a close-up of his nostrils because he had to adjust the lenses by turning the camera towards himself.

So we packed our khaki shirts and shorts and our *veldskoen*s, and Dad and I went into town to buy sheath knives, and hats with fake leopard-skin bands.

Despite Mom's tears, she seemed secretly happy to see us go. I wondered if it had something to do with Dad buying her the LP of *West Side Story* and the fact she'd have the house and record player to herself for days.

Now, while we joked a lot about Mom's singing, the truth was Dad was the only one who had actually broken glass with his voice. We'd been driving on a dirt road in the Free State a few years before, and at the exact moment Dad had started on the big drawn-out '*O-o-on the road to Manda-lay-ay*', the windscreen shattered. A truck had been passing and stones were flying, but we knew it was Dad and so the song was banned.

That didn't matter because I knew most of his other songs and when he got to the end of the first verse of 'Uh-oh, I'm Falling in Love Again', he would hold his hand out to me like I was his partner on stage and I'd sing the chorus in my deepest voice. I wondered if he thought about Mom when he sang it and whether he still felt that way about her.

We crested Fields Hill and dropped through the slow roller-coaster sweep to the coast, then stuck our heads out the window to feel the Durban air that clung to your skin like a warm facecloth. We skirted the city, singing all the way, and headed north through rolling hills of sugar cane and clusters of Indian houses nestling in the bush with their fluttering red triangles on bamboo poles. Mom used to say the flags told whether there was an available girl in the house and she would threaten to marry us off into an Indian family if we didn't behave.

The further we drove, the lighter the mood in the car became. Just leaving the lane had felt like climbing out of a hole and gulping sweet air. I glanced at Dad, who was singing an army song, and his forehead was smooth and his eyes had lost the muddy look that had been stealing their sparkle.

He broke off and started telling me a war story. That was a sure sign he'd let go of the paper, the Kolonel and Verwoerd.

Harry Mac had grown fond of Italians during the time he fought them. He said they'd never had their heart in the war and many were happy to be captured. Mostly, he remembered their singing, and that's what led to the story he was now telling. But it was a new story and different from the jokey ones.

His unit had been guarding a group of Italian POWs in Abyssinia, 'but our job wasn't to keep the Eyeties in, it was to keep the Abyssinians out.' The natives hated their colonial masters and would sneak into the POW camp at night.

'It was a makeshift bush camp with no wire and the prisoners sat in a group on the bare ground. But no matter how carefully our guards watched, every morning we'd find a POW with his throat cut.'

And so Harry Mac had walked the perimeter with his rifle at the ready while the Italians clutched each other in the dark and sang to keep their spirits up.

Dad said that's when the war turned for him and why he never wore his medals or marched in parades or drank with Haas and his crew down at the Shellhole.

He went quiet after that story and I felt sad, but grateful he had told me something so important. Funny stories weren't the only ones swirling around inside that dark head. Maybe he kept telling the funny ones to keep the sad tales away. And maybe that was why he was so angry with Verwoerd for bringing it all back. Sol had said something like that. The Nats were telling us to huddle in the dark and keep singing while they protected us from the natives who wanted to sneak in like the Panga Man and slash us.

He stayed quiet for miles and I sang through our favourites, searching for our light mood again. He was watching me out of the corner of his eye, and it was only when I faltered in the 'Hot Diggity' song that he came to my rescue and we were okay, singing our way over the Tugela, the river boiling brown from distant rains and marking the magic entrance to Zululand.

As he always did when we passed here, Dad pointed out a wild fig on the riverbank—the Ultimatum Tree—where, at the end of 1878, the British high commissioner to South Africa gave the Zulu king thirty days to meet his demands. 'They were impossible terms, which included handing over men for trial, a huge cattle fine and disbanding the entire Zulu army,' Dad said. 'It was meant to fail, and the British army was already lined up in four huge columns. When the thirty days were up, they invaded. The high commissioner hadn't even told the British government he was going to war with an independent nation.'

Harry Mac was back in full stride, leaping from one story to another, waving his arms and thumping the dashboard, and I sat back, half listening and half enjoying the show. But I was beginning to understand something Sol had once said.

I'd been complaining to Sol about Dad's anger and frustration when he tapped on the verandah rail. 'Look, Tomka. Harry Mac has seen something of the outside world and he wants to be part of it. He wants to write about the bush, argue about books, marvel at the Hindu gods and snorkel the Great Barrier Reef. See? He doesn't want the rest of his life to be defined by one issue.'

The cane farms slipped behind us, replaced by tall gum plantations bending in the north-easter that blew in from the Indian Ocean. And now the cultivation ended and we parted another magic curtain into hills covered in *bushveld* and the mysterious glowing fever trees. We started passing families in donkey carts, and bare-breasted women swaying along the side of the road under bundles of firewood they carried on their heads. And we seemed to drift into a spell, with settlements floating by like Zulu chants—Gingindlovu, Empangeni, Kwambonambi, Mtubatuba, Dukuduku, Shikishela.

Dad was out of stories for now and sat behind the wheel, a certain smile on his face. Somehow I knew what was coming. I leant forward and pressed my hands to the windscreen like they said to do to stop it from shattering, just as he launched into the first verse: '*O-o-o-n the road to Mandalay.*' I was laughing so hard with my face up against the glass that the windscreen misted over and we couldn't see the road ahead, but neither of us cared.

•

Dad had recently written a leading article about the English-speakers having shallow roots in this country, about not really belonging. But I thought he was wrong. Watching his eyes drinking up the *bushveld*, nostrils flaring, cheeks flushed, it was obvious he loved this place as much as anyone, and he cared about it as much as anyone. So why shouldn't he belong? Why couldn't he just keep visiting Zululand, write about rhinos and mambas and tell stories of Abyssinia and the Zulu War?

The urge to let on that I'd heard him and Haas Cockroft talking in the dark house was strong, the words forming in my mouth like a bubble that needed popping. But he was so happy next to me in the car that I couldn't break his spell.

In a Zululand winter, the late sun dusts the hills blue and gold and it was in this light we drove through the gates of Hluhluwe and turned south into the Umfolozi reserve. We pulled up at the camp's thatched white-walled rondavels, with the setting sun silhouetting the thorn trees and all around us dust and bustle: teams of barefoot native handlers, game rangers with guns and horses, Land Rovers, and trucks with solid cages on the back. I'd almost forgotten why we were here: for a rhino capture.

A man of about Dad's age and wearing a ranger's uniform limped over to the car, grinning and holding his hand out. 'Hullo, you horrible old bugger. Better keep out of the way or they may dart that big arse by mistake.' He saw me in the car and leant in. 'Howzit, boykie? Come to keep your dad out of trouble, hey? Go and see Mr Watts over there behind the horses, he's got something to show you.' He slapped the windowsill. 'Okay, see you two later at the *braai*. Gotta get this mob into shape for tomorrow. Early start, hey.'

Brian Locke was in charge here and he walked off, shouting instructions in Zulu, showing off a little, and Dad and I took our bags into one of the rondavels.

When we'd unpacked, I went looking for Tony Watts and found him squatting under a thorn tree with a grey bundle in one hand and a bottle with a teat in the other. Tony was a young ranger I'd met on our previous visit. He looked up and smiled, holding out a baby baboon, which wriggled and tried to bite his finger when he took the teat away. The baboon had a dog collar around its waist and a leash clipped to Tony's belt.

'Meet Mephisto. His mother was killed by a leopard.'

I tried to play with the baboon, but he got irritated and snatched at the bottle.

'Are you coming tomorrow? Good, you can look after Mephisto in the Land Rover because I'll be on horseback.'

That evening we sat around the fire and the men drank beer and talked about rugby, poachers, the election and the next day's hunt, while around us the night hooted and chittered, bushes rustled and dainty impala hung at the camp edge, their eyes reflecting the firelight.

Brian Locke stood to one side of the group, talking for a while with Enoch, the senior native ranger, who pointed into the dark and shaped his hands like he was showing the position of something.

We finished our *boerewors* and steak, and then a man I didn't know brought out a rifle and passed it to Brian. It turned out the man was a vet and he said they were trialling a new tranquilliser because too many rhino were dying under the old drug.

Brian showed the rifle to Dad and allowed me to hold it, explaining how the gas fired a dart into the rhino. I looked up at Dad with the gun in my hands. This was better than drinking beer with him on the verandah like Little Harry did.

Brian took the gun and gave it to Tony with a smile. 'Nice thing about this rifle is that you have to get really close to your rhino. Enoch says the big cow is down near the calving thickets between the rivers, so it'll be tight.'

Tony grimaced and shrugged. '*Ag*, it'll be okay.'

'He also said there was a herd of buffalo in the area, so we're going to have to be careful she doesn't get among them. If she does, there'll be a real bloody hullabaloo and we could have a buffalo charge on our hands.' His eyes flicked to me and then to Enoch. 'Keep this boy in the Land Rover when we ride in.'

Dad had been listening closely to all this, working an empty beer can in his fist. 'What about me?' he butted in. 'You said I could ride in with you.'

This was the first I'd heard of it, and Dad obviously hadn't told me in case my big mouth blabbed in front of Mom, and then the hullabaloo would be nothing compared with a buffalo charge.

Brian lifted an eyebrow at Dad. 'And so thou shalt, oh great white hunter. You can ride in with Tony and then hold his horse when he goes in on foot. But you're not going anywhere in that bloody hat, Buffalo Bill.'

He leant forward and grabbed Dad's hat, holding up his other hand. 'Don't worry, you'll get it back in the morning and it won't look like a prop from a safari film. Tom?'

I handed him my hat and he passed them to Enoch squatting next to him and spoke quickly in Zulu. Then he straightened his back and rubbed his knee. 'Okay, early to bed and we leave at five thirty.'

•

It was freezing as we lurched through the grey bush. The sun wasn't up yet and I sat wrapped in a blanket in the open Land Rover next to Enoch, who drove half standing, watching out for warthog burrows. Under the blanket and clipped to my belt was Mephisto, asleep with the bottle teat in his mouth. I picked up my hat and stroked the new grey fur band, which Brian said was kudu but which Enoch told me was from the mother baboon killed by the leopard. I wondered what Mephisto would make of that.

Lurching behind us was the truck with the vet, the handlers and the cage. The others had gone ahead earlier on horseback, Dad a sight in old grey work pants, his trouble-making tweed jacket and his hat, complete with baboon fur and a vulture feather.

Just as the sun was tipping the hills, we caught up with the riders looking down into a shallow valley where the two wide, sandy rivers converged. I loved the names, White Umfolozi and Black Umfolozi, as though the rivers had different natures, good and bad, like the white and black rhinos.

I couldn't see Dad among the horsemen and then he came riding down a hillside to be met with a lot of head-shaking by the rangers.

'What?' he said. 'You were the ones going on about black rhinos around here, so I thought I'd see how this chap goes uphill if we're charged.'

The others were still laughing when one of the native rangers scanning the thornbush and grassland of the river valley said, '*Laphaya!*' and pointed. Everyone hushed and strained their eyes until a tail flicker gave her away. The white rhino cow was just inside the trees lining the river.

Now the rangers turned to the surrounds, looking for the buffalo herd but also checking the dongas and sandbanks for wallows where *daga* boys—single male buffaloes—kept cool. They were the angriest animals in the bush and would charge without hesitation.

It was time to move. While Brian rode to high ground to keep lookout, Tony and Dad worked their way downwind of the rhino, then Tony handed over his reins and crept through the long grass towards the flicking tail. Enoch had joined Brian so I slipped out of the Land Rover when Dad came back grumbling about being a bloody animal handler. He held the harness tight to stop it from jingling and I patted the horses, which looked like something from *Prince Valiant* in their leather armour to protect them from the thornbush.

Tony was now swallowed by the trees and it wasn't long before we heard the gun's report, followed by the sound of branches cracking as something big crashed through the thickets. The noises moved deeper into the bush and died away.

We turned and looked up at Brian, who shook his head and called out, 'She's headed towards the river but she won't get through, there's a steep bank. She'll turn and keep running so we'll have to wait and see where she breaks out.'

He was still talking when Enoch shouted and pointed to where Tony came flying out of the thicket and scrambled up a thorn tree. Not too far behind, the rhino burst through, charging blindly but heading in our direction.

'Let go the horses!' Brian shouted down to Dad. 'Let go the fucking horses!'

Dad released the reins and bellowed, slapping at the horses' rumps with his hat and yelling at me to get back in the Land Rover. The native rangers scattered into the surrounding trees, while Dad jumped in after me and we watched the rhino thunder closer. You could feel rather than hear its feet pounding the earth. Dad hoiked me and Mephisto onto his lap and sat in the middle of the seat, away from the sides.

One horse bolted back up the hill but the other hesitated and came back. In an instant the rhino had caught the horse in the girth and hoisted it clean off the ground like it was a bag of *mielies*. The horse squealed and landed on its side, legs thrashing.

The rhino hardly broke its charge and kept going up the hill, past Brian and out of sight.

Everyone ran to the stricken horse, which had now got to its feet, legs splayed, quivering, snorting, its eyes rolling white. Tony dropped from his tree and moved in slowly, murmuring, taking the reins and calming the animal down. He checked its side and turned to us.

'Jesus, he's lucky. She caught him with the base of the horn, hardly scratched the leather. There was four thousand pounds of rhino behind that, so he'll be bruised to buggery, but I think he's okay.'

The other horse had circled around and trotted back to the vehicles, where the handlers caught it and brought it to Tony. He gave the gun to Enoch, clipped on a walkie-talkie, mounted and galloped up the hill after Brian and the rhino.

Dad was talking to the bruised horse, stroking its neck and scratching its ears while the vet checked it over. I got out of the Land Rover and stood next to Dad, my hand on the trembling animal's neck. We looked at each other and smiled. I'd never seen him so alive.

This was ours. You could keep the racehorses and jockeys.

•

The walkie-talkie crackled and Enoch signalled to us. '*Ubhejane* is tired now.'

We drove about a mile through *bushveld* before we caught up with Brian and Tony. They were bent over, examining the collapsed rhino.

'She's an absolute beauty and may even be pregnant,' Brian said as Dad opened his camera case. Brian looked over at me. 'Come on, Tom, she's out for the count. But leave that bloody baboon in the car.'

I clipped Mephisto to the steering wheel and walked over to the heaving mound, and the rhino smell hit me: big, unhappy, wild creature.

I knew Operation Rhino was saving the animals from extinction but I felt sorry for her—shot, charging in blind panic through the bush as the drugs wore her down, and now struggling to get to her feet again as the antidote worked its way through her. I looked at Dad, who was filming the rhino being hauled into the cage for her trip to Kruger National Park. He put the camera in his coat pocket and walked over to grip the iron bars. I joined him and he turned and smiled at me. But it wasn't the same smile we'd shared after the charge.

•

We rested that afternoon, had another *braai* in the evening, fell into bed and slept without moving, and the next day Dad and I went for an early game drive. We had a bird-spotting contest and watched the rising sun flare on the feathers of the lilac-breasted rollers. We saw giraffe heads glide above the treetops and lone male wildebeest guard their territory until we got too close then, with a toss of the head, rock away from the car. We stopped and laughed at a family of warthog rooting in the mud and then fleeing with tails erect when a hyena slunk out of the trees. We returned to the camp in the heat of the day, ate cold kudu and chutney sandwiches and then went out again for another drive when it cooled off.

It was the first time Dad and I had been away on our own, and now, after two days in the bush, he was different. He'd taken Sol's big juicy bites and was swallowing them whole. He didn't sing and bang the dashboard or hunch his shoulders and lecture me while doing the eyebrow thing. He spoke to me like I was more of a grown-up, pointing out new birds and the habits of animals. It was nearing the end of the dry season and herds of pregnant impala waited in the shade. Dad told me they were holding on to their babies until the rains came. We spent time at a hide where nyala and kudu tiptoed to the waterhole, watched by a pod of hippos with only their nostrils, eyes and teddy-bear ears showing. A herd of zebra came down, sniffing and snorting and frightening each other until one squealed and they galloped off, kicking and farting. And later in the day, a lone black rhino trotted out of a thicket of tambotie bush and lifted its blunt head towards us in challenge.

•

Dad must also have noticed a change in me. I was interested in things again and, when I thought about it, the hospital and the pale sun had been a long time coming.

Our time in the game reserve was nearly up and Brian and Tony wanted to treat us to a taste of the Wilderness Area. Dad often talked about the Wilderness, and he had come here the year before when the huge stretch of bushland and river valleys was first set aside as a reminder of what he called Old Africa.

You could only enter the Wilderness on foot, horseback or canoe, so we set out along rhino paths, the men walking and me on one of the pack donkeys. My leg ached a bit but after a while I forgot about it as a new feeling took over. We weren't sightseers any more, we were part of the bush, and there was no door you could close to keep it out. This was what it was like to be an impala or reedbuck, nose twitching, ears flicking, watching the thickets from where death could burst out at you or freezing still at night to avoid the silent snatch of a leopard. Now I felt bad for laughing at the snorting, farting zebra. As Dad said, 'Out here, seeing the sun rise is a triumph of survival.'

We moved along a mostly dry riverbed, Enoch out front with a gun, skirting the pools linked by narrow channels, and keeping to the sandbanks scored with the tail-swish of crocodiles and, once, a cluster of hyena tracks from a gang out on the prowl. We rounded a bend and Enoch held up his hand and pointed. A few hundred yards upriver a young elephant was leaning headfirst against a thorn tree growing out of the bank. He leant and rocked, leant and rocked until we heard the tree snap. The elephant tucked into the new growth and then slowly swung his way across the river and into the trees.

We followed the riverbed until we came to a stand of spreading sycamore figs and climbed the bank to make our camp. Some of the trees were fruiting and we disturbed a troop of feeding baboons, who barked and shook branches before moving to a new stand.

After setting up camp in the fading light, the men went down to a shallow pool below the bank. The water was clear and we hadn't seen crocodile tracks for some time, but Enoch stood guard while the others undressed and waded in. Out here in the Wilderness the men were quieter and Enoch moved among them like an equal. It was as if they had all stopped pretending. The world seemed to slow down and I watched the figures move silently into the pool and cup water in their hands to pour over their bodies. Dad straightened, turned and beckoned to me. The others lifted their heads too. I looked at these pale animals with water dripping through the dark hair matted from chest to groin, and it was like a prehistoric drawing from a book come to life. I stepped closer to Enoch. I wasn't ready to be one of them.

Sitting around on logs watching our strips of kudu sizzle on skewers, water boiling in a dixie, the men slipped into storytelling, their voices dreamlike.

Tony talked of how a century ago this area was a Zulu royal hunting ground and the whole tribe would turn out, beating drums and driving herds of animals into a funnel trap. Brian told of how rhinos were nearly wiped out in the great game slaughter of the early 1900s because cattle farmers blamed wildlife for hosting the tsetse fly, carrier of *nagana*, the deadly sleeping sickness.

Dad hardly spoke. He scribbled away, his notebook turned towards the firelight, working up a story about the park and the growing threat of poachers.

We chewed our scorched kudu, and the men drank beer cooled in the pool. We went to bed early and the fire was stoked to last through the night, Brian warning us not to leave any meat scraps lying around because it would attract hyenas. 'But don't worry, the dogs and the donkeys will let us know if the buggers sneak around.'

I'd been dozing through the stories, leaning against Dad. But something was building inside me, something I couldn't control.

We unrolled sleeping bags on the sandy ground and I tucked mine in close to Dad. Before they went to sleep, Brian and Tony unsheathed their knives and plunged them into the ground near their heads and I saw Dad watch them and do the same.

I lay on my back, the warmth of the fire on one side and Dad on the other, beyond him the sheath knife and the dark bush. Above me the stars flashed between the sycamore branches and I knew this was the time to talk to him.

'Dad?'

'Hmm?'

'I need to ask you something.'

'Mm.'

So I did. I told him what I'd heard in the dark house, and asked if he was 'in'. And if so, was the plot still going ahead? I said I didn't want him to disappear and I was frightened for him and for Mom and me. I told him I was scared Little Harry might be on the border and I still didn't understand why he was there. And I wanted to know what he and Windsor had talked about.

I must have gone on for about ten minutes without stopping, and my voice was steady. Out here in the Wilderness, I had also stopped pretending.

When I'd finished, I waited, holding my breath.

He didn't say anything and I lay there feeling his body rumble until I realised he was snoring.

Air whooshed out of me and for a moment I was lost. It had taken all these months and a journey into the Wilderness to get the words out. And now they had been wasted, just a ripple through the branches overhead.

But as I lay there, Dad murmured in his sleep and shifted position. Then I didn't feel so bad. This was his special time, and I hadn't spoilt it.

One of the dogs stirred, stretched and curled up closer to the fire. The camp was still.

A warm current of air moved up the riverbed and I remembered Millie had asked me to watch for Laika passing over if I got the chance. I focused on the stars between the swaying branches and thought of her lying on her back lawn, looking at the same sky.

When I became sleepy, I rolled over, took my sheath knife out and stuck it in the ground near my head.

19

THE NEXT DAY WE LEFT THE WILDERNESS AND UMFOLOZI and drove home in near silence. I'd watched Dad closely from the moment he'd woken up, but if he'd heard me the night before he didn't let on.

Just as the magic had slowly drawn over us like a cloak when we drove north, so it unravelled with each passing settlement on the return journey. Grass huts gave way to tin shacks, scruffy trading stores and a gradual human thickening.

Durban made itself known long before the strip of beach skyscrapers poked above the treetops, the air red-brown with evening cooking fires curling up from shanties in the bush-covered hills crouched in a semicircle around the city.

Again, we skirted Durban and began the winding climb over the ridges towards Pietermaritzburg. It was well dark by the time we crested the last rise above the Umsinduzi basin and Dad turned off the main road and parked near the drive-in. He switched off the headlights and we looked down at the blinking lights of the town.

He turned to me. 'How is he?'

'The towel is full of kaka and wee, but he seems okay,' I said, folding back the cloth on my lap and stroking the little grey-green head. The monkey opened its eyes, which seemed too big for its face, and closed them again, making a bird noise and burrowing down.

'Dad, what will Mom say?'

'God knows. At least it's not crocodile eggs.'

It had been a typical Harry Mac thing. Driving out on the dirt road from the game reserve, we'd seen a group of boys teasing something on the side of the road. We'd stopped and seen it was a baby vervet monkey with a piece of string around its waist.

Dad asked the *umfaans* in Fanagalo where the baby's mother was.

'*Ufele*,' said the boys.

'They're not lying. She's dead,' muttered Dad, getting out of the car. 'Probably killed while raiding their crops.' He squatted next to the terrified monkey, which ran to the end of its string, screeching, while the boys laughed. Dad stood and dug in his pocket. He hauled out whatever change he had, handed it to the tallest boy and grabbed the string. The little gang took off, skipping and whooping, and chasing the one with the money.

Dad rummaged in the back of the wagon, folded the monkey tightly in a towel and handed it to me.

'What're we going to do with this?' I said.

'I don't know, give it a name. Is it a boy or a girl? Maybe we'll take it to Ben's Den.'

The baby drank some water from our canvas bag then curled up in its towel and slept all the way home.

Now, parked near the drive-in, Dad turned away from the monkey and drummed his fingers on the dashboard, hunched over the wheel and looking like someone shivering on the edge of a cold sea.

'Ah, boykie,' he said and restarted the car.

We drove slowly the last few miles and as we turned into the lane, and the black hedges closed around us, I saw Flash Gordon and Dale with the walls grinding in.

We pulled into our drive and there was Mom silhouetted in the door, and we both knew something was wrong.

Dad switched off the engine and opened the car door, moving in slow motion like a robot. He walked towards Mom.

'What's the matter, Liz?'

'You mean you don't know?' She was teary and speaking in a ragged way. 'Don't you listen to the bally radio while you're running around Umfolozi playing big white hunter?'

'Okay, okay, Liz, settle down. We didn't have a radio. What's happened?'

'Something's happened on the border and there's talk an army boy from town has been killed. And he's up there, Little Harry's up there, I just know.' She sniffled and held a tissue to her nose.

Dad gave her a quick hug, said, 'You don't know that,' and strode into the lounge to turn on the radio.

I held Mom tightly and heard a yelp from the car. I'd forgotten the monkey, who had woken up just as Laika was nosing the strange smell on the seat.

The yelp was Laika's because the monkey had reached out, felt warm fur and grabbed a handful. Laika shook herself but the monkey clung to her neck, making bird noises as Laika took off along the drive and down the lane.

Mom didn't even notice so I said nothing and followed her and Dad into the house. It was still twenty minutes till the news, so we unpacked with the radio turned right up, blaring through every room and across the yard and filling all the space so no one had to say anything. I didn't know what to think. Mom was a mess and Dad had pulled a shield around himself.

Not Little Harry. Please, not Little Harry.

I went out a couple of times and stood in the lane, calling and whistling for Laika, and even told Titch to shut up when he complained about the noise.

At news time we clustered around the radiogram. Mom was clutching a leather wallet and I realised now she had been holding it since we arrived.

'*The government has denied a British newspaper report that the South African Defence Force has clashed with terrorists in the border region of South West Africa. The report, which first appeared in London's* Daily Worker, *a communist mouthpiece with no credibility, said that South African military personnel had been ambushed by SWAPO guerrillas, with an unknown number of fatalities. Although other British newspapers have picked up the report, the prime minister, Dr Verwoerd, said it had no basis in fact. He said the government would never discuss military matters, but it retained the right for South Africa to defend itself wherever and by whatever means.*

'*In other news, the Minister for Justice, B.J. Vorster, said he was confident next week's election would endorse the government's decision to tighten the country's security laws. Mr Vorster said the election gave South Africans the choice between a secure and prosperous future for all races or a catastrophic slide into bloody chaos as evidenced elsewhere in Africa. Mr Vorster accused the nation's English-language newspapers of distorting the reality of a peaceful country where life continued normally, and he warned the press to get its house in order before the government's patience wore out.*

'*And finally, in sport, the Springboks have completed an undefeated season . . .*'

Dad turned off the radio and took Mom's hand. 'Where did you hear this thing about a local boy being killed?'

'Everybody's talking about it.'

He shook her. 'Liz, listen to me. Who is everybody? The Women's Institute? Enid bloody Cockroft? Sandra bloody Lieberman? In these things, everybody is nobody. You don't even know which camp he's in, for Christ's sake! Bloody hysterical women's stuff.'

Mom stepped back, a look of horror on her face. 'You knew. You knew they were sending him there.'

Dad raged out of the room and I heard the fridge door open and slam shut. I sat next to Mom and took the wallet out of her hand. 'What's this?'

Between sobs she told me she had opened an account for Little Harry at a building society which was offering free wallets for servicemen. But she didn't know where to send it or even if she should, now.

'We haven't had a letter from him for ages and then one arrived the day you and Dad left.'

She opened the wallet, where she'd put the letter. 'It's a month old and says we can't write to him and he can't write to us because there's no post where he's going. He's out there. And Dad knew. And it wasn't Sandra bloody Lieberman, it was Mrs bloody Vincent who told me a boy had been killed.'

Mrs Vincent was one of two war widows who lived in the lane. They were both members of the Black Sash, a women's movement that was protesting against the growing number of apartheid laws. We sometimes would see them in town in their sashes, standing silently outside government offices. Some people laughed at them, but Mrs Vincent wasn't a fool.

I went out to the verandah. Dad was sitting in his chair with a bottle of beer next to him and his thick fingers were scrunching his new hat with the grey fur band and vulture feather. After our bush trip, I felt strong enough to stand in front of him and say what I thought.

'It's not fair the way you treated Mom.' And I told him about the letter and Mrs Vincent, and I said it was normal for Mom to worry. In any case, how did he expect her to react when she found out Little Harry had been posted somewhere secret?

He didn't say anything and made a low grumbling sound, but I just stood there looking at him and after a while he got up and went in to Mom.

This was the worst thing that had happened to our family, even though we didn't know the truth yet. I stood on the verandah, looking into the lit room where Dad had his arms around Mom. I was calm. Something had shifted inside me for good. Like I had to behave differently now. I didn't know in what way, but something had shifted.

I walked out into the yard again to look for Laika, calling and whistling down the lane, but she didn't respond. As I was passing the garage I heard bird noises. I went in and switched on the light. They were on the blanket in the cardboard box, the crocodile eggs pushed to one side, the monkey curled up, eyes closed, gripping Laika's collar while she licked him from top to tail. The monkey opened his eyes when I knelt down. He had a long forehead and when he lifted his eyebrows the skin wrinkled, like Nelson Eddy.

I decided to leave it until tomorrow to introduce Mom to Eddy.

20

IT'S FUNNY HOW THE DAY AFTER SOMETHING HORRIBLE has happened, you wake up thinking everything will be all right. But it never is. Things weren't any better for us the next morning. We'd avoided a silence, but Dad's face was grim and Mom walked listlessly around the house, picking up the leather wallet and putting it down. I fetched Eddy from the garage and she shook her head and said, 'Oh, Jesus. I don't want anything to do with it.'

It went on like that for another day. Dad tried to find out more about the British newspaper report but there was nothing on the wires, so we listened to the radio because that's where the government made important announcements. But the SABC ignored the story.

For two nights I stayed up, fiddling with the radio dial in the dark, hoping to hear the hate voice, hoping maybe it would say something, but all I got was scratch and hiss. I walked through to Little Harry's room on the second night and shone the torch on our dogfight. I put down the torch and felt under the bed for the *knobkerrie* he kept there and swung it wildly at the ceiling, feeling it connect, and hearing plastic clatter around the room. I curled up on his bed and stayed there the rest of the night.

•

Mom let me put the cardboard box in my bedroom after throwing out the crocodile eggs, and Laika settled down with her new baby. Eddy wouldn't let go of her, even when she ate her dinner, reaching out and grabbing tiny handfuls of dog food, which he chewed and spat out. So we put a saucer of milk next to Laika's bowl and he was happy with that.

On the third day, Dad called us into the kitchen, leant on the fridge and said he'd rung the army and got through to a personnel officer.

'I am not at liberty to discuss security matters with you,' the officer had said.

'This is not about security, it's about my son—'

But the man cut him off, repeating the sentence. And that's when Harry Mac blew his stack. He swore at the man and told him he was a snivelling little Nazi shit and typical of the heartless robots who ran the state. By the time he'd finished the line was dead.

Mom listened in silence. She didn't care how badly Harry Mac spoke to the army.

The following day, Dad came home unexpectedly at lunchtime in a work car. Mom ran to the door and watched him get out. He was smiling and started talking while still walking up the steps.

He'd been sitting in his office when his secretary put her head around the door and said, 'There's a man on the phone wants to talk with you, but won't give his name or say what it's about. He insists and says please hurry up.'

Dad nodded and picked up the phone. The man didn't introduce himself, but Dad recognised the voice.

'The families were notified a week ago.'

Dad tried to get the army officer to explain what he meant, but the man was frightened. 'I'm just saying that the families were notified a week ago.' He hung up.

Mom sat at the table, dazed, asking Dad to repeat the conversation and explain it.

'Well, it's bloody obvious.'

I pulled a face at Dad and he softened his voice. 'It was the same bloke. And it means that something did happen out in the bush and that the families have been told that their sons were, are—shit, I don't know. I just think it means he's okay.'

'He could be badly injured.'

'Liz, I don't know. I don't know. What I believe is that he's alive. Isn't that enough for you? Just because we haven't heard from him doesn't mean something's happened. For Pete's sake, he could be in some cushy camp, digging ditches. I don't know, for Christ's sake. Please.'

There was a smell of rhino in the room, and tobacco on Dad's breath. A new smell.

We should have felt good after that call but all three of us were unsettled. It was made worse when we heard the *Bosmoedertjie* shriek and sob just before he went to bed to visit his nightmares.

The government had lied about the battle and so how could we believe Little Harry was okay? How could we believe anything anymore?

•

That night, Millie and I visited the *spookhuis*, stopping as usual when we opened the front door to ask for permission to enter. We waited as the cool air reached out and curled around us, and then walked quietly through to the lounge.

I wasn't thinking about the *spookhuis* when we went in and so didn't notice if it felt any different. Millie was distant and moved away from me to stand in front of the fireplace and stare at the empty grate.

The weather was warming and I opened a window and sat on the sill, inhaling the scent of night flowers and waiting for her to speak.

The first thing she asked was, 'Did you watch for Laika passing over?'

'What do you think?'

We compared scars and I talked about the rhino charging the horse, the Wilderness and Eddy. She kept quiet, knowing there was more. I was struggling to put the words in the right order, but I finally managed to tell her about Little Harry.

'I think he's okay.' She said it fast.

'How can you know that?'

'Just a feeling.'

She waited a bit then said, 'Like I've got a feeling something's not right with Sol.'

'Not right? Is he sick?'

She shook her head. 'Tense. And Sandra's being a bitch. The tennis wives have told her about a really good opening with one of the old practices in town, and now she's hassling Sol to talk to them. They're Jews, too. But she's nagged him about this sort of thing before and it doesn't bother him. No, there's something else.'

I waited to see if she would talk about Sol's secrets but she didn't. That was okay, his secrets didn't seem so important to me now.

She changed the subject. 'Like I've got a feeling about this place.'

'The Van Deventers?'

She nodded.

No one in the lane seemed to know much about the Van Deventers. They had arrived a couple of years ago at this house on the corner, half in and half out of the lane, and kept to themselves. Gillian had no friends at school that I could remember and you never saw the parents out in the garden. Mr van Deventer was thin, with swarthy skin and dark, wavy hair, like many of the Afrikaners who weren't huge and blond. That was because some had Dutch blood and some French, we were taught at school.

'Sol went to visit them when they first moved in,' Millie said. 'You know Sol—yakkety-yak. But they had almost nothing to say and didn't talk about where they had come from or anything. He said it was strange because he felt like they were the visitors to the house, not him. They gave Sol tea and waited until he left. I think Mr van Deventer was an electrician or something with the government. Sol invited them to our house but they never came. Thank God, because Sandra would've had a fit.'

'So what happened to the romantic shooting theory?'

She waved me away with a flick of her hand.

'The servants were talking about them one day when they thought I wasn't listening. They really didn't like the Van Deventers. None of the servants in the lane did, from what I could tell.'

It was warm but I felt a chill in the room and had to stop myself from turning around. 'So what do you think now about what I said?'

She turned. 'Huh?'

'About them maybe not having completely gone away.'

'Oh, Tom-Tom. My little Tom-Tom.'

•

No one expected the Nats to lose the election, and they didn't. But the shock was the massive jump in their vote and the near wipe-out of the new Progressive Party, slashed from eleven seats to one.

We knew Dad had started smoking again at work, but now he brought it home. I don't know if it was the election or because we were waiting for word on Little Harry. He'd given up years before because of a cough, but now he was straight back to a packet of Rothmans a day. What drove Mom up the wall was the mess; he was a careless smoker and would leave unfinished cigarettes all over the house, standing them on their butts and letting them burn down, so there'd be these little crumbling pillars of ash on tables, verandah railings and mostly the radiogram.

Mom asked him once to stop but he didn't even answer.

He was also upset by a phone call to the paper from the man who had spoken at the All-in Conference, Nelson Mandela. Mr Mandela was still on the run and would occasionally call a newspaper to make a comment, although they couldn't publish what he said. When he rang Dad's paper he had spoken to the political reporter, Ken Brady, and told him that the English-language press had misrepresented the stay-at-home strike, printing the government line that it had been a failure. That hurt Dad because although he thundered against the government, he had to admit coverage of the strike had been weak.

I heard him talking about it to Sol when we had a rare garden party to celebrate the new pool about two weeks after we got back from Umfolozi. The last thing Mom felt like was a party and she said no one would swim because it was too cold, but Dad said we couldn't put our lives on hold. We had to live normally. He sounded like Vorster.

Dad and Sol were sitting in deckchairs on the new crazy-paving patio where the adults drank and talked while the children splashed in the chilly pool and Haas Cockroft kicked the loose paving flakes, pointing out poor workmanship.

'We English-speakers get all red-faced and blustery about an issue, but when it comes to a critical point, we back off. It's like a fatal flaw,' Dad said.

I was lying on the pool's edge, soaking up warmth from the pavers and easing the cold-water cramps in my leg. Mom sat to one side among a group of women. Sandra Lieberman was doing the talking and Mom's eyes were unfocused and her glass of wine tilted. She had gone a little quieter each day we didn't hear anything from the army, and there was something in her manner that made you feel she blamed Dad. I knew Dad was worried about her because the party was his idea, and he hated parties.

'Well, maybe it's not such a bad thing in a culture,' Sol was saying. 'It's nice to know that there are some societies that prefer a warm hearth to the roar of the cannon.'

'Don't patronise me, Jew Boy.'

Sol chuckled and got up to get fresh beers.

Dad called after him, 'And you're one of us now, remember.'

Sol stopped, turned and looked at his friend, his smile fading. He nodded slowly. '*Ja*, I'm one of you.'

Dad lit up a new cigarette, sucked and exhaled rapidly five or six times then stood the cigarette on its butt on the paving. It was all done in the time it took Sol to return with two cans.

'No, I'm serious,' Dad continued. 'Look at this shower of shit: "The Group".' He pointed at a knot of men that included Haas Cockroft, who was wagging a finger in the air, gold watch glittering, and two journalists from the paper, rat-faced Mr O'Neill, bent forward, head bobbing, and moustachioed Mr Farrar, who kept threatening to throw the women into the pool and who was now massaging his chest muscles.

'Talk, talk, talk, but can you imagine them actually having the guts to do something radical; to see it through?'

This bothered me, because I knew what he was referring to, but I couldn't understand why he was so angry with the men who had put up the idea in the first place. Or maybe, as Sol had said, Harry Mac was angry with himself.

'*Ag!* All The Group is good for is standing in the bioscope to sing the British anthem and turning on fire hoses at public meetings.'

Sol sipped his beer, smiled and said nothing, but Dad wasn't done. 'You know what the latest thing is, hey? They couldn't stop the republic so they ran off to Cape Town to ask the British high commissioner to support Natal seceding and becoming an independent Commonwealth nation.'

Sol had to laugh at that, but Dad was leaning forward, tapping Sol's knee. 'And you know what stuffed them? The commissioner told them Britain would only consider it if Africans were given equal rights in the new country. And I'm afraid, old boy, that was unacceptable to our fearless revolutionaries. And that's the crux. They don't want justice; they want a little British outpost where they can swan about in pith helmets, drinking gin with toffs in plumed hats. No wonder the Afrikaners call them *soutpiele*, salt penises— one foot in England, one in Africa, and their cocks dangling in the ocean. That probably includes you—one foot in Europe.'

Sol leant away, his eyes fixed somewhere else. 'Europe is not home to me. Europe is a grave.'

As though he hadn't heard him, Dad continued to rant. 'The truth is, Haas and his ilk are just shit-scared. It's simple selfishness.'

He sat back and there was a meanness in his eyes I hadn't seen before. He lit up and the cigarette crackled towards his fingers.

Sol stood and put his hand on Dad's shoulder. I could see he was annoyed. 'Take it easy, old friend. Don't be too hasty to condemn.' He walked away and I didn't see him for the rest of the party. Dad disappeared soon after and I knew he'd gone for a lie-down. He always left gatherings early anyway, so no one noticed.

Millie and I swam some more and after a while people called their kids out of the pool, dried them off and started to drift away until there were just the two of us in the pool and Mom sitting in her chair staring at the water.

21

WE DRIFTED ALONG FOR ANOTHER WEEK OR SO, DAD grumpy and worn out at the end of each day with the aftermath of the election, smoking and drinking and heading off early to bed. Mom was miles away, going through the motions, but one day it hit her there was a baby monkey living in the house.

It was Essie who made a thing of it, complaining about having to clean shit and piss from my room.

Mom came and sat on my bed one morning and watched Laika and Eddy curled up together, the little hands buried in the wiry fur. Laika's tummy hair had caked shit in it and she seemed to have lost weight.

Without a word, Mom left the room and came back with Laika's basket from the verandah, a sheet of plastic, newspapers and scissors. She told me to pick up the animals and handed the cardboard box to Essie, who was clucking disapproval in the doorway. Mom lined Laika's basket with plastic, laid fresh newspapers over it and replaced her blanket. She sat on the bed and made me hold Laika's head. She couldn't prise Eddy's fingers open so she cut the fur away underneath and made me hold the shrieking baby while she trimmed the caked hair and checked Laika over.

'Poor girl,' she murmured. 'But you've only got one baby; I've got three.' Laika nuzzled Eddy in my hands but Mom wouldn't return him.

Mom had put on an apron and she tied the leash around her waist and stuffed Eddy, still clutching handfuls of fur, into one of the deep pockets.

And that's where he stayed for most of the day and the few days after, until he got used to being with the rest of us.

'But I can tell you something,' Mom said at dinner one night in a voice that made Dad and I look at each other. 'I'm not having him here permanently. So you can bally well start looking for a home for him.'

Then of course she grew fond of Eddy and started talking to him while she cooked and cleaned and typed up her notes for the Women's Institute and the malnutrition relief organisation of which she was now secretary.

·

One afternoon I came home and was throwing my satchel on the bed when I heard Mom scream and something break. In the past few days, Eddy had started moving around the house on his own and had knocked a few things over, so I thought he'd broken a vase or something.

I went out to see what was going on and Mom was standing in the kitchen, hand to her throat like the women in films, face white.

And in the doorway was Little Harry.

Mom didn't seem to want to move but she stepped forward

through the broken china and touched his arm as if to check he was real. And then tears. Like the Duzi in flood.

Why is it when adults get a happy surprise they sometimes get angry? Mom slapped Little Harry's arm and scolded him for not writing or phoning; for being missing for so long; for making her sick with worry; for being her eldest son.

Little Harry just grinned, although it seemed a bit forced, and his eyes were tight. He was even thinner than before, burnt dark brown, and filthy.

After nearly crushing the life out of him and making Eddy—who was still in her apron pocket—yelp, Mom stepped back, wrinkling her nose. '*Ag!* You stink. What's wrong? You didn't run away, did you?'

Little Harry shook his head. He hadn't even had a chance to put down his duffel bag. But he dropped it now, nodded to me and sank into a kitchen chair. That's all I got. A nod.

He'd been on the move for two days with little sleep. He didn't tell us where he started from but said the lieutenant just walked into their tent and said they had been granted leave and a truck was leaving in thirty minutes. They'd driven for nearly a day along bush tracks until they reached an airstrip, climbed into a Dakota and flew to Joburg. He'd then hitched rides all the way down. He had four days at home before he had to hitch back.

Mom went and ran him a bath while Essie came into the house and went through the same routine as Mom, with the hugs and the tears and the scolding. Little Harry looked at me over her head and raised his eyebrows. I shook my head. No, we'd heard nothing more about Windsor. Essie went back to her *kaya*, dabbing her eyes with the corner of her apron, and I knew she wasn't thinking about Little Harry.

I rang Dad at work and he said it was what he expected and he couldn't understand all the fuss. But he didn't fool me for a second, and within half an hour he was home.

When Little Harry had finished his bath, he wrapped a towel around his waist and unpacked his duffel bag, which stank worse than him. I sat on the bed and watched his hard, tanned body move around the room. The muscles were lean, not like Titch's big puffy ones, and his eyes were still tight. When he bent over I saw a healing cut down his back. I got up and touched it. 'Were you shot?'

He straightened and nodded with a solemn face. Then he pushed me back on the bed, laughing. 'Nah. You get scratched and cut by thorns and branches all the time crawling through the bush.'

Whenever I asked him about where he'd been or what he'd done he just laughed. He unpacked his bag and brought presents out to the dining-room table: a delicate Zambezi teak carving of a duiker for Mom, an ostrich egg for Dad and a single springbok horn for me. He even had a small bottle of seawater for Essie that he'd got from the Skeleton Coast.

He tapped the ostrich egg and said to Dad, 'Uncracked and fresh. You could probably hatch it.'

Dad was delighted but Mom stood firm. 'Uh-uh. We've just got rid of crocodiles and there's a bally monkey in my pocket. No ostrich running around the garden, thank you very much. Drill holes in the ends of the egg and blow it clean. Away from the house. The thought of it!'

With Little Harry home we ate like it was Sunday lunch every day. He would attack his food then stop and push away the plate after only eating half of it. But he made up for it with beer.

Dad pretended it was the most normal thing in the world to have his son home from the *bundu*, but the big furrow between his eyes was smoother and he took every chance to call Little Harry out onto the verandah to smoke and drink beer.

I knew they spoke differently when Mom and I weren't around but I didn't feel so jealous this time. Little Harry was not so much a big brother anymore but another man in the house, a sort of favourite, edgy uncle.

So I sat quietly out of sight just inside the verandah door and listened to them, which wasn't easy because they said nothing for long periods, something I'd noticed before with Harry Mac and Sol. The silence of men.

'It *is* fresh, you know,' Little Harry said. 'We could make an omelette. Just say to Mom we'll do breakfast and then tell her after we've eaten it.'

'Sh!'

They drank a bit then Dad said in a low voice, 'Caprivi?'

I couldn't see them from where I sat, but Little Harry must have nodded because Dad went on. 'Was the ambush story true?'

Silence.

Then Little Harry, voice flat. 'Different unit. Out on patrol. Got four of them. One was a railway apprentice from Fort Napier.' More silence, then he said, 'You sit around for so long doing bugger-all. Just bugger-all. Some of the boys go a bit funny.'

A sigh and Dad's voice. 'I remember.'

'You know, the whole time I was there, I saw nothing, no one. We had to watch this river, you know, just like the *Bosmoedertjie*. Day after bloody day. Hot, dry, nothing to see, nothing to do. You almost looked forward to going on patrol just to get out of the camp. It's beautiful up there when you're not staring at a dry riverbed, and we once saw desert elephants. Our lieutenant said the local tribes had been warned to stay away from the river crossing and we were ordered to shoot anyone that came near. A few of the boys were itching to peg something, targets, game, anything, but it wasn't allowed in case we gave our position away.'

He fell quiet for a moment and I wished I could see their faces.

'And then one day someone saw movement in the bush opposite our position. A murmur went through the unit and we made ready.

"Hold your fire until I say," the lieutenant whispered. Then out of the bush walked a young woman in a beaded skirt and with a clay water pot on her head. Behind her was an old woman dressed the same. We all looked at the lieutenant. "Shoot them!" he hissed. "They could be a cover." But we just looked at him.'

Little Harry's voice had been getting faster and faster and started to crack. He stopped and I heard him swallow then the hollow sound of a beer can on the table. I craned my head around the door and all I could see was Dad's hand wrapped around Little Harry's forearm. I sat back and waited.

A match scraped and smoke drifted into the lounge. Little Harry's voice was quieter and slower. 'The lieutenant snatched a rifle and aimed at the women, but he was watching us out of the corner of his eye. He lowered the rifle, said, "Cunts!" and fired a shot into the air.

'The women screamed, dropped their pots and ran back into the bush. We just sat there. One of the boys started crying. A few days later we were given a week's leave.'

'Are they sending you back?'

Silence, and I couldn't tell if it was a nod or shake of the head.

●

On his second-last day, a Saturday, Little Harry got up late, dressed and walked straight across the lane to the *Bosmoedertjie*'s house. Mr de Wet was in the garden and he and Little Harry chatted and then Mr de Wet pushed the fork into the ground and they went inside.

Little Harry was there for a while before he came out, crossed the lane and went to his room. Mr de Wet didn't go back into his garden, but sat on the verandah, drinking Kool-Aid. I raised a hand to greet him but I don't think he saw me.

I was dying to ask Little Harry what he'd done over there and why they'd gone inside, but he was different now and it was hard to joke about the things we used to.

So I went into his room and sat on the end of the bed and we listened to music. It wasn't even lunchtime yet, but Little Harry was already drinking beer. He tilted the can to empty it, burped and switched off the radio. He lay back with an arm behind his head, looking at the ceiling, and said, 'He just cried. He shouted and hissed and aimed his stick when I went into his room, so I sat on the bed like you are and talked. I talked and talked and he curled up and started crying. Like a baby. Then he went quiet and fell asleep.'

Little Harry swung his legs off the bed and went into the kitchen for another beer.

•

Next morning, Mom stood in the doorway to Little Harry's room, sniffling and blowing her nose while he packed his duffel bag, but they were see-you-later *totsiens* tears, not worry tears, because he had told her he wasn't going back to the bush and would see out the rest of his time as an *ouman*, instructing new intakes.

Dad was the one who looked worried and I got the feeling Little Harry had said something to him privately.

I couldn't work Dad out these days. Little Harry was safe—for now—the Verwoerd plot must be off and he'd been a different man in the game reserve. Yet he smoked and drank heavily and there'd been that meanness in his eyes at the garden party. Something was burning deep inside him and was looking for a way out.

Dad said he wanted to prepare a special breakfast and Mom knew something was up, so she said okay, but watched her husband and eldest son with narrow eyes. Watched them all the way to the garage and watched when they came out with the ostrich egg.

She stood blocking the doorway, arms folded, and didn't have to say anything. Dad shrugged and said fine, they would empty it first into a bowl on the verandah and she would be able to see how rich and wonderful a wild egg was, 'not like that pale rubbish from the supermarket'.

They got out the drill and made holes in both ends so the egg wouldn't crack, then Little Harry put one end to his mouth to blow it through 'like we do in the *bundu*'.

Well, I thought, watching Little Harry hanging over the verandah rail, vomiting into the hibiscus, it was a good thing it didn't break in his duffel bag on the way home.

Mom turned without a word and went inside to cook the bacon and eggs she had waiting, while Little Harry retched and Dad laughed so much he had a coughing fit and had to sit down. Little Harry went inside to clean up, put on his uniform, and have a beer to take away the taste, and I was left with the job of hosing rotten egg and vomit off the verandah and the hibiscus. But it was worth it because Little Harry and Harry Mac were getting a bit smug for my liking.

We finally got going. The plan was to drive Little Harry out to the highway, and Mom insisted on taking him up the steep hill out of town and all the way to Howick where it was flatter and cars were more likely to stop to pick up soldiers. Little Harry said it was just as easy to get lifts downtown, but Mom wanted to hang on to him as long as possible.

As we left the lane, the *Bosmoedertjie* was on his verandah, shrieking, '*Min dae, ouman. Vasbyt!*' Little Harry touched a finger to his beret as we passed.

We did a loop around town and started the long climb to Hilton. We'd passed the last houses and were coming around a curve through the plantations when we saw a car on the side of the road and two men looking at one of the back wheels. One of the men was dressed in a suit, and the other was his native chauffeur in a white coat. They had a helpless look about them so Dad slowed down and stopped. He leant across Mom and called through the window, 'What's the problem?'

The chauffeur, a burly man with a scruffy beard, walked away to the other side of the car and turned his back on us, but the owner came to the window. 'Flat tyre and we haven't got a jack.' He had an English accent and seemed well-to-do. The Austin Westminster was new and polished.

Dad parked in front of their car and he and Little Harry got out our jack and changed the tyre while I stood and watched. I glanced up and the native chauffeur was staring hard at Little Harry in his uniform. He had odd, downward-slanting eyes. When he saw me watching the fierce look dissolved into a smile and I saw that his eyes were sad as much as angry. He looked at me a second or two longer, as if trying to memorise or understand something, then he turned away, scratching at his ragged beard.

The car owner shook hands and thanked us, and we got back in our own car and drove away. Something puzzled me about them, particularly the chauffeur. 'Dad,' I started, but he was giving me a look in the rear-view mirror that meant shut up.

The incident was soon left behind in Mom's chatter and the passing of a tin of crunchies between the front and back. She talked more than usual, brighter than usual, as if words would keep something away.

We neared the Howick turn-off and Dad started to slow down, but Mom said, 'Just a bit further.'

Dad lifted his hands off the wheel and swore. 'Why don't we just bloody drive him all the way to the damn camp!' But Mom was in charge and waved him on.

'There, up ahead,' she said, pointing as the Lions River railway station appeared around a bend. 'There, or at the petrol station. Good place for a lift, and there's shade.'

Mom didn't cry when Little Harry was finally allowed to get out of the car because she had done all she could bar locking him in his bedroom. He had a clean uniform, he was alive and he wasn't going anywhere near the border. That was as good as it got for her.

Dad suggested we go into Howick on the way back and see the falls, but Mom wasn't interested and just wanted to get home.

We'd only driven a few minutes when I saw the Austin Westminster pulled over again on the side of the road. 'God, they didn't get very far.'

'Well, somebody else is helping them this time,' Mom said.

Two cars had stopped, one in front, one behind, and a group of men were standing around the open doors of the Austin.

'Shit!' Dad said. 'Oh, shit! Bugger, bugger, bugger!'

'Harold MacGregor! Language.'

'Oh, bugger, bugger, shit!'

I had an idea why he was swearing but no one could talk to him when he was like this and the smell of rhino was choking.

•

That night the black car visited the lane. I heard it change gear as it emerged from the valley and started to claw its way up the gravel. I thought about Mr Lambert and his house arrest, and wondered if he was safer that way. It was probably my imagination, but the black car seemed to stop and idle further up the lane this time, closer to our house. If they put Dad under house arrest he'd be safer, too, and wouldn't disappear in the night. But Harry Mac would be like one of those rhinos that fight their cage until they drop dead. I pulled the curtain closed and waited until the black car ground its way past, turned and accelerated up the big road.

22

THE NEXT MORNING IT WAS IN THE PAPER. THE downward-slanting eyes were unmistakable and although the beard wasn't the neatly trimmed one he'd worn at the All-In Africa Conference, and he was wearing a chauffeur's coat instead of an expensive suit, it was him. And now the police had him.

Although the newspapers all ran excited headlines saying the Black Pimpernel had been caught, the Special Branch and the government behaved like a rugby team that was so far ahead in the score it didn't matter.

Nelson Mandela was taken before a magistrate in town and then sent back to the Transvaal and that was the last we heard of him for a while. But you got the feeling of a net tightening slowly around the whole country.

I was reading the paper every day and asking Dad to explain what was happening. The re-elected government was growing stronger all the time and there were so many arrests, banning orders and threats that it had a curious effect on people. Dad said some were frightened and tried to get on with the normal lives the government encouraged, but many were relieved, believing the government was all that stood between us and the communists and terrorists.

Dad also said that there were so many laws now that the government could arrest anyone they liked and then choose a charge to suit. Like with the lawyer, Mr Mandela, who they later sentenced to five years' jail just for leaving the country illegally and urging people to strike.

At the paper, Dad spent a lot of his time working out what they could and couldn't report, but he didn't let up in his leading articles, and nor did the Sunday papers, which were almost at war with the government. I asked him why the government didn't simply shut the papers down and he said they would like to but it helped them pretend to the world that we were a normal democracy with a free press. But a time would come.

Dad came home every day exhausted, and as the weather warmed up, he took to putting on his swimming trunks and thrashing up and down the pool. He'd then sit on the patio and suck down cigarettes and whisky.

We got a letter from Little Harry saying he was being posted to the artillery and would be based in Potchefstroom. So it appeared he told Mom the truth when he said he wasn't going back to the bush, but I wondered what he'd said to Dad in private to make him look so worried.

Then my world heaved over again, twice in quick succession.

•

Dad came home from work one day, put on his trunks but didn't launch into the pool. He sat on the patio and smoked and drank and then said to Mom, casually, 'Verwoerd's coming.'

It didn't matter to Mom one way or the other, but I clutched the side of the pool and stared at him.

'They're so cocky now, he's coming to the heart of the English-speakers on Dingaan's Day to lecture us on God's will.'

A few weeks ago, Mr de Wet had told Little Harry that Dingaan's Day was sacred to the Afrikaners. It was the conclusion to the Piet Retief story we got at school. When the Voortrekkers set out to avenge the slaughter of their families by Dingaan's *impis*, they made a vow that if they defeated the Zulus they would keep the day holy and build a church. After their victory at the Battle of Blood River in 1838 they built the Church of the Vow in our town and 16 December later became a public holiday. Now Verwoerd was coming to lay a wreath and address a public meeting.

My nightmares returned, the walls moving closer and closer.

When news of Verwoerd's visit was announced in the paper, Haas Cockroft hung close to our fence with a hose—watering God knows what, because he'd trampled the petunias and cut down all the trees—waiting for Dad to come home. But to my relief Dad ignored him. At the garden party, he had been vicious about Haas and his pro-British crowd, calling them gutless and selfish. But it was confusing because they were the ones who'd hatched the plot. All I had to fall back on were Sol's comments about Dad's frustration with life and himself. And that didn't help me work out what Dad planned to do.

●

I'd once asked Sol how people could carry on with normal lives if things were so bad in our country. He'd said it was like car accidents. The road toll was horrendous but everyone believed crashes only happened to other people. I thought about that. Maybe I was going too far the other way, seeing a crash around every corner. Seeing things that just weren't there.

Then one night we were sitting down to dinner when we heard Essie scream. Even I could tell that this was something much worse than finding a snake in her room or even a *skabenga* stealing her things.

The scream was torn from somewhere deep inside, and the three of us sat frozen at the table.

Mom was the first to move. Maybe she heard something only a mother could.

She was at the back door before we had even stirred, and then it was all action, with Dad calling for Mom to come back so he could check it out. But she beat us to the open *kaya* door, which threw a yellow glow across the strip of lawn next to the patio.

I was just behind Dad, ignoring his yells for me to stay inside, and the first thing I saw was a smeared bloody hand print on Essie's window.

There was more blood on her door and blood splotches across the floor, all the way to Windsor lying on her bed, gasping and bleeding. Essie stood against the back wall, hands to her face, staring at her son and babbling to herself.

Mom went straight to Windsor and knelt by the bed. In the dim light of the paraffin lamp, one side of his face had a melted look and the skin was hanging in strips, the flesh pink-red against his dark skin. But the blood was coming from his left hand, seeping and dripping through the handkerchief wound around it.

A biting, choking smell filled the room, forcing me back to the door.

Windsor was shuddering with pain, his eyes rolling, and Mom took charge. She chased all of us out of the room, including Essie, and ran back to the house, shouting over her shoulder, 'Don't touch him. Sulphuric acid.' How did she know that?

She came back with a jug of water, which she poured over Windsor's face, forcing out a scream and a mad clawing at his skin.

Dad and I waited at the door, but Essie followed her back in, still babbling. Mom turned, grabbed her by the shoulders and shook her. She gave Essie a pair of rubber washing-up gloves and told her to take off all Windsor's clothes and throw them out the door, then call the rest of us back in.

'*Checha! Checha!* Hurry, Essie!'

Outside the *kaya*, Mom sent me to fetch a torch. Dad was told to bring over the garden hose and a bucket while she went inside for medicines.

By the time I returned, Windsor's clothes were in a stinking heap on the patio and he was writhing under a sheet on the bed. Dad had moved Windsor to the edge of the bed and while Essie held his head, ran water from the hose over his face and into the bucket. He stopped struggling under the flow of cool water and Mom beckoned for me to shine the torch on his hand.

'Jesus!'

The handkerchief came away to reveal three bleeding stumps and a shredded index finger and thumb.

Mom poured water and Dettol into a large bowl then, with Dad, Essie and I holding Windsor down, she plunged his hand in. Windsor was so far gone he barely flinched.

'Okay, good,' Mom said. 'Now we've got to stop the bleeding.' She looked through the medicines she had brought, thought a moment, then picked up a jar of ichthyol, which was used for everything in our house that couldn't be treated with mercurochrome or gentian violet. She patted Windsor's hand dry and with firm movements smeared the thick black ointment over the stumps and cuts. Windsor had stopped shuddering and was moaning and trying to touch his face. Mom tore open a new bandage and wrapped it tightly around his hand.

She stood up, arched her back and pulled the sheet down to Windsor's waist. His chest was pocked with tiny holes, which she wiped clean and dabbed with mercurochrome.

When she was finished, she stepped back and ran the back of her hand across her forehead, leaving a red smear in the blonde hair. She gave a shy smile when she saw Dad and me watching her. 'Not just a housewife, hey?'

She nodded towards Windsor. 'That'll do until we get him to hospital. Harry Mac, you'd better call the ambulance.'

Windsor snapped upright, the undamaged side of his face twisting, his voice a croak. 'No ambulance! No hospital!'

Mom started to argue, but Dad took her by the arm. 'Liz, why don't you gather up your things and take Essie inside. I want a quick chat with Windsor and then we'll sort this out.' He looked at me. 'You too, *Wagter*. Inside.'

Dad had stood back when Mom was bandaging Windsor, his eyes tight and one hand in his trouser pocket, holding something heavy. Now he waited until we were out and then closed the *kaya* door, but I just turned and stood next to the open window.

'You're in a bad way, Windsor. You'll bleed to death.'

Silence.

'You've done something stupid, haven't you?'

Oh, good one, Harry Mac. Half his face and hand gone and you're giving him hell.

When Windsor spoke, his voice was calm, but gritty with pain. 'I don't have to listen to the likes of you.'

'You came to my house.'

'My mother's room. Anyway, doesn't give you the right to question me or criticise.'

'A few months ago you wanted my opinion.'

'The time for talking is over.'

'Christ, Windsor, you sound like a cheap novel.'

'And you, what do you sound like, Mr MacGregor? Or is it all sound?'

Dad's turn to be silent.

Then Windsor again, bitter. 'Go back to your soft bed, Mr MacGregor.'

A sigh from Dad and a creak as he got up off the bed. 'You can be a real shitehawk, Windsor. I'll get Dr Lieberman; he won't say anything.'

And that's when the police arrived.

23

TWO VANS, FOUR WHITE POLICEMEN AND HALF-A-DOZEN native constables. They'd parked in the big road and crept down the lane on foot. The first I saw were two constables climbing over Haas's fence and into our yard, then another two appeared at the bottom of our garden and the rest walked up the drive and around to the *kaya*. Leading them, pistol drawn, was the Special Branch sergeant, Viljoen.

As soon as I'd seen the men climbing the fence I'd run back into the *kaya*, but I'd hardly said a word when the police shoved open the door, guns pointing. Dad pushed me against the wall and stood in front of me, while Windsor reached under the sheet, scrabbling around with his good hand.

He caught Dad's eye as the native constables rushed him and pinned him to the bed.

Windsor's one good eye was bulging, fixed on Dad. His scream was one of fury and frustration. 'You had no right! This is my fight. You had no right!'

The room was full of police, swarming over Windsor and ransacking the *kaya*, monstrous shadows lunging across the walls. He screamed when they grabbed his bandaged hand and wrenched him upright. He stood there naked, blood starting to stain the white bandage.

Dad stepped forward. 'For Christ's sake, Viljoen, have some common decency.'

The sergeant swung on him, his face bleak. 'You think what he was planning was decent?'

'The man needs urgent medical attention.'

'He'll need even more urgent medical attention where he's going,' one of the policemen said, and some of them laughed.

They handcuffed Windsor and frogmarched him out of the *kaya*. Dad threw the bloody sheet over his shoulders and the police ignored it.

Up on the verandah, Mom held on to Essie, who sagged against a post and watched them drag her son away. Dogs were barking up and down the lane and all the house lights were on, people thinking it was another *kaya* raid.

Sergeant Viljoen stopped at our gate, turned and shone his torch full in Dad's face. 'Now you're in deep *kak*.'

On his last visit to the Kolonel, Dad had threatened that the next time Viljoen set foot on our property it would be the last. I felt for Dad's hand to tug him away, but he stood there and did nothing. There was nothing he could do. His hand closed around mine and crushed it until they'd all left and we heard the sound of the two vans pulling away down the big road.

'Go to your mother,' Dad said, releasing my hand and pushing me on the shoulder. He went into the house and came out with the car keys.

'I'm coming, Dad.'

He shrugged and we got in and drove slowly out of the lane with our lights off. He stopped at the big road and waited several minutes, looking both ways along the dark street, before easing out. He turned on the lights and we headed towards town before turning off into the valley, winding our way down towards the sewerage farm, Dad checking the rear-view mirror all the way. We parked at the causeway where we came every summer to watch the Duzi Marathon canoeists go by. Dad turned off the lights and we sat for a minute or two before getting out. He held my hand and we walked along the riverbank, not even shining a torch to check for night adders. He stopped, dug in his pocket and pulled out the heavy object I'd seen him holding in the *kaya*. With a handkerchief he cleaned the revolver, even taking the bullets out one by one, wiping them and tossing them into the river. When he was satisfied, he held the revolver in the handkerchief and hurled it far out into the night, listening for the splash.

•

Mom and Essie were at the kitchen table drinking tea when we got back, so we joined them. Mom was still in charge, giving us little jobs like turning off the hose and emptying the bucket. Her eyes flicked between Dad and Essie and I think she was keeping things steady in case Essie collapsed or Dad exploded.

Essie was spent, beyond tears. She looked up at Dad with a collapsed face. 'What will they do to him, master? He must see a doctor.'

He shook his head. 'I'm not sure, I—look, Essie, he had a gun under the sheet. The police didn't find it.'

At the time, Dad's behaviour in the *kaya* had puzzled me. He had known Windsor from a small child and he himself said there was a bond between them. I had expected a violent reaction when the police grabbed Windsor's injured hand. But for once, Harry Mac had kept his self-control.

Essie stared at him. 'But Windsor is a good boy.'

'Essie!' Dad's voice hissed like a whip. 'Sorry. Essie, Windsor is lost to us now. To you, to all of us. But they didn't find the gun and that might save his life.'

She kept looking at him, not understanding, not believing, saying softly to herself, 'A good boy.'

He leant across and took her hand. 'He was making or carrying a bomb, Essie. It must have gone off in his hand. The police will take him to a doctor because they will want to ask him about the bomb and who he was working with. Someone must have driven him here and dropped him off. The police will come back and they will ask lots of questions. Be careful. Tell them your son has been missing for many months and this is the first time you have seen him. If they ask you who his friends are, say you don't know. Don't try to think of anyone and don't give them names, understand?'

I don't know if Essie was in a state to understand, but she nodded.

'The police will want to question me, too, so I will go and see them tomorrow.' He turned to me. 'And if the police come nosing around here while I'm at work, do what you do best—watch and listen. And keep your big mouth shut.' Which I thought was unnecessary because I hadn't done anything wrong.

●

Dad got Mom to drop him off at the Special Branch headquarters first thing in the morning. He asked for the Kolonel, but they ignored him and sent him through to Sergeant Viljoen.

Dad told us later the sergeant wasn't threatening like before. He was cold and practical, and this made Dad careful. He was there for an hour, answering questions and giving his statement, and then he was left in the room on his own. He was beginning to think maybe he should have told the Old Man at the paper where he was going, when a secretary put her head in and said to follow her.

She led him to the Kolonel's office, tapped on the door, opened it and stood aside.

The Kolonel was reading something on his desk and didn't lift his head. When he'd finished he held up Dad's statement between his thumb and fingertip. 'This is going to make your life really difficult.'

That would normally be the trigger for a Harry Mac retort, but he kept silent and waited.

'Ah,' said the Kolonel. 'Don't want to antagonise us. Worried about your little friend, hey?' Dad said there was no mocking in his voice. It was official, as though they had passed a certain point and nothing between them would ever be the same.

The Kolonel, out of habit, stood up to cross to the window, but sat back down. 'I'm not playing any more games with you. If you're withholding anything, it'll be the worse for you. We'll find out because he will talk, or someone will.'

'What's the charge and where are you holding him? We'd like to arrange legal representation.'

'He hasn't been charged yet, but the nature of his injuries speak for themselves, don't they? And save your money; there's always some Jew waiting to defend these terrorists.'

The bitterness wasn't deliberate. It was a deep rot, Dad said, needing to burst out like a worm through apple skin.

Mom and I were sitting silently holding hands, listening to Dad. I was glad Little Harry wasn't there. Something had changed and we all knew we had to be very careful from now on.

Dad, shocked by the Kolonel's outburst, had leant forward and put his hand on the desk. 'I give you my word of honour I know nothing about this. All I ask is that you treat him like a human being.'

The Kolonel had gathered himself. He opened a drawer, pulled out a sheet of paper and slid it across the desk. It was headed: *SAP press release—DRAFT ONLY.*

Dad read:

Acting on a tip-off, Pietermaritzburg police last night arrested a dangerous terrorist who had been on the run for more than a year.

Windsor Khulu Dlamini, 19, was arrested in his mother's kaya at the home of a prominent citizen, where he had gone to seek help for injuries sustained when an explosive device detonated at a house in Sobantu Village. It is believed the Sobantu house, which had been under police surveillance, was being used by a terror cell to assemble bombs.

The other members of the cell fled when the device exploded, but police have strong leads and expect to make arrests soon.

Kolonel L.C. Engelbrecht said police were confident the terror cell had been destroyed and any danger of a bombing campaign averted. But the incident demonstrates that the public need to be aware there are those operating among us who wish to destroy the peace of this country.

Police are investigating any possible link with the prominent citizen on whose property the terrorist was arrested.

Dad pushed the release back across the desk. 'You were watching them?'

The Kolonel shrugged. 'Your boy's incompetence with bomb-making meant they all fled before we could close in. But we know who they are, and we'll get them. We always get them. All of them.' The Kolonel said it as a statement of fact.

Dad got up, nodded to the Kolonel and turned to go. There was nothing left between them.

'Harry Mac.' The voice was quiet, neutral. Dad turned and the Kolonel picked up a pen and crossed out the last sentence of the press release. 'I don't want to see you here again.'

•

We spent the next few days pulling ourselves together, mainly settling Essie down and waiting for the police to come calling.

Mom stayed at home and they turned up one morning while Essie was hanging out the washing. They didn't come to the house, but walked straight down the side to the *kaya*, and when Mom heard voices she went out. There was just the one white constable who touched his cap to Mom and then worked through a list of questions from a notebook. He didn't seem to mind Mom standing right next to him, arms folded.

He took down Essie's name, checked her passbook and got her to tell him everything about Windsor's visit. He was most interested in whether Essie saw or heard who dropped him off, whether Windsor mentioned any names, and then he pumped her for the names of Windsor's friends. Dad had been right about that. The policeman read out a list of names and watched her face when he asked if Windsor had ever mentioned them or if she knew them.

Throughout, Essie stood rigid, wringing a pillow case between her hands, eyes down and answering in a soft voice, '*Ayikhona*' and '*Angazi, baas*'. No. I don't know.

Dad waited a few days and then rang the police. All they would tell him was that Windsor had been taken to Pretoria and they had no further information. Everything he tried came to nothing. A door had been closed and this was one Harry Mac couldn't open by charging at it.

•

While we waited, our home routine crept back. Eddy shared his time between Laika's back and Mom's apron pocket, and in the evenings Dad would have his swim and then let Eddy clamber around the garden.

Eddy was wary of Dad. He liked to be around him, poking through his hair, but always ready to flee with chattering cries. His favourite game was to perch on Dad's outstretched feet and play with the twiddling toes. It settled Dad, and he would stare out across the pool, forgetting to smoke.

He was quieter in these days after Windsor's arrest. He always had a glass in his hand, although he didn't actually drink more. But he made up for it with smoking, and as the upright cigarette butts with their towers of ash rose on surfaces around the house, including on the half-read Westerns, it was like living among crumbling miniature ruins.

Dad eventually rang one of his old friends from the *Sunday Express*, where he'd worked briefly after the war. A couple of days later the reporter called him back. Windsor was in Pretoria Central with the growing number of activists being rounded up. The police were in no hurry because they wanted to charge him under the Sabotage Act, which hadn't been passed yet, but which would be backdated.

'That way they'll get the death penalty,' the reporter said. 'Sorry, Harry Mac, but your man is finished. And don't worry about getting a lawyer. Apparently that's already been arranged.'

Dad said none of this to Essie. He told her only that Windsor was alive and in Pretoria. It meant his injuries were being treated, and that gave Essie some hope to cling to.

But it was the last thing the *Express* reporter told him that hit Dad the hardest—someone else was arranging Windsor's defence. It was none of Dad's business. Not his fight. Something from one of his leaders jumped into my head again, about peanut-sellers on the sidelines. I was starting to understand how Dad felt.

•

The day after the phone call from his old friend, Dad slipped into a silence. But this one was different. He wasn't angry. He just didn't want to talk.

Mom wasn't so upset by this silence. She kept out of his way and didn't try to start conversations. But it worried me because it *was* different and I couldn't tell where it might lead. I wanted to let him know I was starting to get it, but every time I tried to talk to him, he would go, 'Hmm,' and give me a half-smile.

One afternoon, Dad was out by the pool twirling his toes while Eddy pounced and tumbled around his feet. There was a sharp cry and Eddy fled inside screeching and hopped into Mom's pocket, his eyebrows shooting up and down. Out on the patio, Dad clutched his bleeding toe and hobbled over to the tap, calling for bandages. Well, at least it ended the silence.

We all looked at Eddy. He'd moved on from milk and was trying his teeth out on anything that took his fancy. He cowered in Mom's apron pocket, but he could barely fit now.

After Dad's toe had been patched up, he put a call in to the Parks Board and within a few days Eddy was gone. The men who came with a van and a cage said he wouldn't survive in the wild and would go to a zoo in Bloemfontein.

Mom was the only one who really missed him. Laika sniffed around the house for days after Eddy left, but I was happy to have her back on my bed again and not caked with monkey shit.

Strangely, it took something out of Dad, and the Saturday morning after Eddy went away I saw him standing in the garage holding the ostrich egg which Mom wouldn't allow back in the house until the smell was completely gone. Something about the way he was looking at it made me not want to interrupt him. As I walked away I heard a crack and, turning, saw the egg in pieces on the garage floor and Dad looking down at it. He lifted his head and saw me watching him and there was such misery in his face

I turned away. And I couldn't tell whether he'd dropped it on purpose or not.

He never mentioned the egg again, not even when Little Harry came back from the army for the last time a couple of weeks later.

•

Mom was almost her old self again when Little Harry moved back into his room. Dad brightened a bit but he was still quiet and I knew something was brewing. He asked Little Harry what he would do now, but apart from getting a job on the railways to earn quick money, he had no plans. Or none that he told us.

From the day he returned, Little Harry let his hair and beard grow. He started paying rent, got up early for the railway job shovelling coal on the goods run between Maritzburg and Durban, came home after working overtime, had a bath and dinner and then went out.

I knew he drank every night, and from what people at school told me he was getting a reputation as a street fighter. He drank with his close friends, and when everyone went home from the pub, Little Harry would cruise over to the Market Inn or the Pie Cart looking for fights. He always wore old jeans and took off his T-shirt to fight, and he told Mom the cuts and bruises were from the dangerous railways work.

But Essie knew what was going on, clucking and shaking her head when she was handed the bloody T-shirts that he had soaked overnight.

I thought when Little Harry came back from the army the family would close up again and it might make Dad less tense, but it didn't happen that way. Mom must have known things weren't right with Little Harry but she said nothing, and Dad was so distant I don't think he noticed anything.

24

SUMMER CAME EARLY AND THE JACARANDAS WERE blazing away again when I walked up the Liebermans' path. An angry voice from inside the house stopped me dead, so I waited on a garden bench until it was quiet then walked up and sat on the verandah. But she must have been reloading because she went for it again full-bore in the lounge right behind me. I had my back to them and slid down in the canvas deckchair. I might be a watcher and a listener, but I didn't want to get caught by Sandra Lieberman.

The lane servants called her *Mfezi*, spitting cobra, and they would freeze when she scolded them, rearing back, her eyes flashing, and shooting out little jets of spit. Her eyes were the colour of dark honey and they glittered, unlike Mom's, which were pale blue and so clear you felt you understood her straight away.

'You owe me more than this. You may enjoy spending your days with cretins, but this is my only life. Haven't I got the right to enjoy it, to choose stimulating company? That was what I was raised with in Cape Town. Music, conversation. Not . . . not dribbling and leering—and that's just the bloody no-hope doctors and nurses you work with.'

Poor Sol. I heard his soothing voice slip into the gap as she paused for breath. 'Sandra, it's only the Christmas party. Once a year, for pity's sake.'

But she had gathered her coils for another go. 'It's always the same people we have to socialise with. Dull provincials. And if it's not the bloody loony bin, it's those creepy political do-gooders you find so enchanting.' There was a sob in her voice now, but an angry one. 'Bad enough this bloody government making us international pariahs. Arrests, disappearances—look at what the papers are full of: condemned by the UN, can't travel to this or that country, kicked out of this international movement, can't read this bloody book or watch that damned film. I'm sick of it, do you hear? Sick of it. I didn't ask to be born into this madness, and I refuse to let it dominate my life. Ruin my life. People in other countries have full lives; why can't I? And why can't you, Sol? Why can't you at least get out of that dump and join decent society?'

Now Sol's voice grew hard. 'I've been an outsider for two thousand years, and so have you. Do you think having a privileged family and playing Beethoven makes you any less of a Jew? Huh? Do you think that if I join a private practice and become rich prescribing sedatives for Maritzburg matrons that—hey presto!—I will suddenly belong? I'm an outsider working with lunatics, and I'm comfortable with that.'

At that point I felt a hand on my head. I jerked around and it was Millie, the frog mouth all twisted.

I sat up and Mrs Lieberman saw me. 'Oh, for God's sake!' she said, and spun out of the room.

Sol saw me too, and tried to smile. I wanted to run, but Millie pressed down on my shoulders. 'Stay. You'll stop them killing each other. Or me her.'

Sol came out onto the verandah like he had weights tied to his legs and flopped into the chair next to me, eyes closed. He lifted a hand. 'Millie. Please.'

She went inside and came out with a tray of ginger beer and glasses. She poured and we drank in silence, around us the buzz of the Christmas beetles, which had been arriving in the lane in numbers, crashing into insect screens and forming brown rafts in our pool.

'I think she married me because I was the only young man who could pronounce Beethoven.' He caught himself. 'Sorry, Tomka. Any news of Essie's boy?'

The whole lane knew about Windsor's arrest and I'd kept Sol and Millie up to date. But no, there was no news of Windsor. Sol nodded: of course.

'And how's the zoo?' Sol loved the idea of a monkey living in our house and his face lit up with each little Eddy story, but now I told him that Eddy was gone and Harry Mac was sad. I also told him about the ostrich egg breaking on the garage floor.

He nodded vigorously and sat up. '*Ja, ja.* You see what I mean? Sandra and Harry Mac both want an outside life, a bigger, better one.' His voice dropped and he was talking to himself. 'But there is a difference. Harry Mac is not thinking only of himself. He wants to share this better life.'

His face sagged and with an effort he lifted a hand. 'These animals, Tomka—these crocodiles, rhinos, monkeys, ostriches— they are his lifeline to that other world. It's a folly that keeps him sane.'

'But why break the egg?'

He snorted. 'Harry Mac would not be happy with an empty shell.'

I looked at Millie, and she shrugged and gave me a sweet smile.

•

That night we visited the *spookhuis*. We sat in the window and listened to Titch. He grunted more on these warm evenings and every now and then let out a big whoosh. It didn't matter whether he failed or not this year. In a few weeks school would be over for him, and he was nervous about the army. Haas was in a bind because he could hardly put on his own reservist uniform and go down to the drill hall on Friday nights and tell the officers' mess that he had arranged a cushy posting for his son. As for Titch, what Olympic hopeful could find a way to fail the army medical? Their family would just have to go through with it like everyone else.

The garden hummed with Christmas beetles and a few made their way past us into the *spookhuis*, where they ricocheted through the empty rooms. It was the first time in a long while there had been anything alive in the *spookhuis* apart from Millie and me, and it was unsettling to hear the scratches down the corridor.

Millie and I hadn't said much in the *spookhuis* that night and there was a reason for it. Next year we would be starting high school and we could feel something between us starting to change. We couldn't put words to it and I think we were a little afraid to try.

I filled the silence with a new theory about the Van Deventers: they had been nasty to their maid, so the lane servants got a witchdoctor to curse the family, and . . . and my story dribbled away when Millie didn't respond or come up with anything of her own.

So we told each other how much we were looking forward to the end of term and the beach holiday our families had planned—the MacGregors in the caravan and the Liebermans at the hotel. But again it sounded like we were looking for things to say, and our voices faded.

We sat in the scratching dark, shoulder to shoulder, and then Millie spoke. 'A few months ago, Tom-Tom, I said that one day you and I would remember all this differently.'

I looked at her and nodded, waiting. She turned and rested her forehead against mine and whispered, 'It's starting to happen.'

25

AT HOME IT WAS LIKE WE WERE FOUR PEOPLE LIVING separate lives in the same house. Mom held the centre, the engine keeping things moving, while Dad brooded around the edges, spending a lot of time on his own on the verandah with his cigarettes and the phlegmy cough he'd developed. Little Harry orbited the house, swinging by every now and then to eat, bath, sleep and spin off into the dark again. He looked different, spoke in grunts and worked long hours, depositing his earnings in the new account Mom had opened and keeping back only enough to get drunk on. Essie had lost all her sparkle and did her chores on automatic, waiting, waiting. I stayed close to Mom but kept a sharp eye on the rest, particularly Dad.

I hadn't forgotten about Verwoerd's visit on Dingaan's Day, and it was only a few weeks away. I hadn't seen Dad talk with Haas Cockroft recently, but the sense of something building grew stronger. And although Dad was quiet at home, his leading articles moved into a new, dangerous, zone.

He wrote that it was two years since the British prime minister, Harold Macmillan, had stood in our parliament and given his Wind of Change speech. But, Dad wrote, while that wind had brought independence to seventeen African countries in one year alone, the wind had died at our borders. He argued that the Opposition parties had been all but wiped out in the recent election because the Nats had frightened everyone, and he wondered how many people realised or cared that this was the first election where black people had lost all political representation.

But that wasn't the dangerous stuff. It was his last sentence: *Is there any wonder then that black African leaders talk of bypassing the political process altogether and turning to violence to achieve their ends?*

It was the first time I'd heard Dad support violence in any way, and it came just as Verwoerd was about to visit. It also made me think of something Sol had said: that the law was now plasticine in the government's hands and they could shape a crime out of any criticism if they felt like it.

•

Dad then did something odd. For a man who loved staying at home and who hated what Mom called 'socialising', he took up playing cards in Sol's rondavel on Friday nights. Not every Friday, but most, and Millie and I were banned, even though we could play all the games they knew.

'Adults only,' said Sol with that little chuckle that drove Millie up the wall.

Mom didn't like cards but she was glad that Dad was doing something other than brood, smoke and cough. And on Saturday mornings after a night of cards Dad was in a better mood, giving Mom a sloppy kiss before she drove into town to do her shopping.

This went on for a while, and then one Sunday evening in bed I was turning my radio dial when I heard the '*da-da-da-daaa*' V for victory signal, followed by a woman's clipped voice.

'*This is Freedom Radio—the voice of Natal. The voice the government can't silence. This week, we examine the historical connections between the Nazis and members of the current South African government. As a starting point we will look at the government's 1936 Commission of Inquiry, which revealed that Nazi political cells were operating in this country, as well as Hitler Youth groups and other covert operations under the guise of labour and support organisations.*'

I wasn't interested in the program and kept searching until I found my music station, but there had been something familiar about that woman's voice.

I didn't think about it until I was going through the paper at breakfast a couple of days later and saw a story about a new radio station that had popped up. There was a report on the program I'd heard—the one about the Nats and the Nazis—and the paper quoted the local police chief saying that the station was unlicensed and was spreading communist propaganda and outright lies. Those responsible would be arrested and charged under the Suppression of Communism Act and for operating an illegal broadcasting station.

'Hey, Dad. This radio station. I heard it the other night.'

He put his fork down. 'Oh yes? I wouldn't think that would interest you.'

'No it didn't, but the lady who spoke, I've heard her somewhere before.'

He shook his head and carried on eating. 'I don't think so. Imagine how many middle-aged women speak like that.'

'Oh, so you heard her too?'

'No, I—yes, of course, we taped it at work to do the story. These people, this Freedom Radio, put up a notice on the door of St

Saviour's saying they would broadcast on Sunday night, so we got Ken Brady to record it and write a story. Cops are mad as hell about the whole thing.'

The next Sunday night, I tuned in again to see if I could work out whose voice it was. She had just started talking about the arrest of Nelson Mandela when we had a power blackout. I switched the radio to battery and listened to the woman in the darkness. She was going on about how the American CIA might have been involved in capturing Mandela. An American news report said the CIA had an agent in the African National Congress, who was feeding the South African police. I couldn't place her voice and I fell asleep. Next day, Dad came home from work and sat by the pool with Mom. I was in my room, finishing homework, when I heard them giggling. Dad was not a giggler, so I got up and went outside, but they stopped when I walked out and Dad became over-friendly and pretended to throw me into the pool. I didn't find it funny and we all knew they had shut me out of their joke.

Dad was in a good mood all week and of course it lifted us— well, only Mom and me, because nothing could cheer up Essie, and Little Harry was never there.

And then, out of the blue, Little Harry came home early from work one night and had dinner with us. He ate in silence and when he'd finished he announced he was going overseas. Just like that.

Mom's mouth dropped open, but Dad nodded.

'I've saved all my army pay and most of the railway money. Martin and Jacques and I have got enough between us to get to London.'

He said it like he was popping down to the tearoom with his friends to have a milkshake.

'And then?' Mom's voice was sharp, the way she spoke to us when we told her things we hadn't thought through.

Little Harry shrugged. 'There's jobs in London—furniture

removal and so on. We've already got enough to buy an old car and we'll go see Europe.'

Dad leant back and drummed his bare stomach with his fingers. 'Buy an old car and go see Europe. Wonderful.'

But Mom would have none of that nonsense. She pointed at Dad. 'You keep quiet.' Then she turned back to Little Harry, who was also smiling. 'Just like that, hey? Just like that. What are you going to live on? What are you going to do after you've "seen Europe"? What about your studies?'

I think she stopped just short of saying, 'What about me?'

'It's okay, Mom,' Little Harry said, holding her arm and speaking in a drawn-out way like you do to a child or an idiot. 'It'll be fine.'

'Have you asked the army?'

Little Harry dropped his eyes. Ha! The idiot had him.

Dad had stopped smiling, too, and now I remembered the worried look on his face the day Little Harry went back to the army from leave. He must have told him then he would be going away when he'd finished his service. Even a short holiday required permission from the army because the servicemen had to attend annual camps and remained on permanent call-up for years. It could only mean one thing—Little Harry was planning to stay away a long time.

Little Harry lifted his head. 'Don't worry, I'll sort it all out. It'll be fine.'

•

Mom got over it pretty quickly in the next couple of days because she didn't know exactly how the army worked and she knew Little Harry needed a holiday, but she insisted on taking him shopping for a duffel coat and gloves because it would be freezing in London. She even tried to give him the fifty rand she'd won on Kerason in the July Handicap, but Little Harry refused it.

The next Friday night, Dad invited Little Harry to play cards with him and Sol, while Mom and I were expected to sit at home like spare thumbs. So when Mom asked me to go to the bioscope with her I accepted, forgetting to ask what the film was.

It turned out there was a Fred Astaire festival on and that night they were showing something called *Roberta*. The film was terrible and I fell asleep when the woman with the high voice started singing, and didn't wake up until Mom shook me and asked didn't I think it was wonderful.

All the way home she sang in exactly the same voice as the woman in the film. 'I'm singing to keep you awake,' Mom said. But I wasn't the one who was driving.

When we got home, she tucked me in and kissed me. 'You and I must do more things together, my little Fred Astaire.'

No thanks. And don't call me that.

But she bribed me into going with her to do her Saturday shopping the next morning with the promise of a baked custard tart from Kean's Tearoom.

Dad gave Mom a kiss when we left and she seemed nervous as we backed out of the drive, and she didn't try to sing once on the way into town, which was some sort of record.

We called in at the men's outfitters and Mom was fidgety and kept looking at her watch while I was being measured up for my next year's uniforms. We hadn't even made it to either of her favourite dress shops when she said it was time to go to Kean's because she was hungry. We parked and went inside and found a table where Mom sat and faced the door. Something was going on. She ordered tea but nothing to eat and wasn't interested even when I offered her some of the custard tart I knew was her favourite ever since she came here as a little girl. She kept watching the door, clicking and unclicking the clip on her handbag, and she grew even more fidgety when a man came in, glanced at her and sat at a nearby table.

I'd finished my tart and was getting bored, so I started watching the people pass in the street. 'Hey, there's that nasty Viljoen,' I said.

'What? Where?' Mom nearly jumped out of her seat.

I pointed out the window. The sergeant, dressed in a safari suit, had come out of the post office over the road. He stopped, lit a cigarette and leant on a post box like he was waiting for someone. He smoked, glancing up and down the street.

'Let's go,' Mom said, grabbing my arm. The man at the nearby table rose and looked like he was going to say something, but Mom ignored him and dragged me out the side entrance which opened onto a narrow lane.

'But Mom, our car's back there.'

'Keep walking.'

'But Mom—'

'Shut up!'

The town centre was crisscrossed with these little alleys, and we threaded our way through the block until we came out onto the street further up. Mom looked down the road. 'Okay, he's gone. Come on. I'll tell you about it when we get home.'

We slipped into the car and headed out of town, Mom's face set, and I knew to keep my big mouth shut.

We'd just passed the Voortrekker cemetery and were coming up to the bridge over the Duzi when Mom slammed on the brakes. 'Shit!'

Up ahead, vehicles were blocking both lanes of Victoria Bridge, and the blue-grey uniforms of white policemen and the heavy khaki of black constables swarmed around, waving cars to the side.

Mom got the car going again, crawling forward while she dug a flat packet out of her bag and tried to push it down the front of her Capri pants. But they were too tight. She looked at me, 'Here, quick, shove it inside your shorts. Quick, Tom, for Christ's sake! They're looking at us.'

And they were. Police lookouts were watching for cars that stopped or tried to turn back, and now a white constable was jogging towards us, motioning for us to pull over.

I jammed the packet inside my shorts as Mom stopped the car and got out. She leant against the door and waited for the young policeman.

'Good morning, Constable. What's going on?'

The policeman's eyes ran over the car and then ran over Mom. She smiled and he turned red, dragging his eyes away from her Capri pants.

'I'm sorry, *mevrou*, but we have to search your car. Please open the bonnet and boot and give me your handbag. Your son will have to step out of the car, too.'

'My son has polio and can't walk.' Mom's voice had a little break in it. The policeman stuttered an apology and Mom turned and leant into the car to fetch her bag, the Capri pants stretching across her bottom, and the policeman's face looking like it might burst.

He hurriedly checked Mom's bag and looked under the bonnet and in the boot. He felt around under the seats, opened the cubby hole and then apologised to me, patting me awkwardly on the head. Mom followed him around the car and I thought of Dad's description—'sashaying'. He gave Mom a salute and waved us on.

After we crossed the bridge, Mom let out a little whoop and grinned at me. 'Thank God you wear baggy shorts.'

'I do not wear—'

'Shush! Save your energy, my poor little cripple.'

It was like she was drunk. Her eyes glittered and she was being really silly, and there was I with that damn packet squashing my willy and the policeman treating me like I was soft in the head, and no one telling me what was going on.

But the way Mom had reacted when I saw Viljoen and again at the roadblock, told me this was connected with Haas Cockroft and the plot against Verwoerd. Mom was doing something for Dad and so she must be part of it.

Dad was on the verandah, smoking and waiting for us when we got home. Mom ran up the steps and hugged him and let loose a flood of words, speaking faster and faster and making less and less sense. Dad sat her in a chair and got me to stay with her while he made her a gin and tonic. She drank half of it down and then slumped into the chair, and tears weren't far away.

'Dad?'

He turned and realised I needed an explanation but you could see he didn't want to tell me the truth. 'Tom, I—'

'Don't tell me crap, Dad.'

'Okay, okay. All right. Look, I'm not going to tell you what it is. I will tell you. One day. Maybe soon. Soon. But I'm not going to tell you now, okay? That's all there is to it. Please, Tom. Okay?'

'Does Little Harry know?'

'Oh, for Pete's sake! Tom, just bloody grow up. Grow up and shut up. You do not talk about this.'

It was like a slap in the face. Mom looked up and said, 'Tom, put the packet in my bag.' I ignored her and stumbled to my room, stung by the way Dad had spoken. Dad and Haas Cockroft had a secret, Little Harry had secrets, Sol had secrets, the *spookhuis* had secrets, and now Mom had secrets. Even Millie knew things she wouldn't talk about. Windsor had had a secret and it was now about to cost him his life. The whole bloody lane was this dark tunnel of secrecy.

Eyes smarting, I rolled over to press my face into the pillow and felt something hard against my belly. The packet.

I rolled back, pulled it out of my shorts, threw it on the bed and stood and looked at myself in the mirror. So what? Dad wore baggy shorts, too. I sat down and picked up the packet. It was brown paper, sticky-taped together. Whatever was inside was flat, round and hard.

One secret less, I said to myself and tore it open. Inside was a metal tin and inside that was a spool of tape like the ones on the recorder Dad brought home from work.

Not much of a secret. I tried to rewrap it, wishing I had undone the sticky tape rather than tear it. I was not getting anywhere when I looked up and saw Dad watching me from the doorway.

He walked in, grabbed the tape out of my hand and left the room. He stopped in the doorway and pointed at me, giving me the full black eyebrow thing. 'One word about this and I'll knock your bloody block off.'

26

DAD AND MOM WERE BOTH STRANGE FOR THE REST OF the weekend, edgy and talking quietly to each other. Mom had promised in the car to tell me what was going on, but now she gave me such a look whenever I approached her, I didn't dare ask.

On Sunday morning they had a row and the feelings in the house were all jumbled up. They weren't angry with each other, but with something separate, obviously something to do with the tape and the plot.

Then there was the fact that Little Harry was leaving the next day with Jacques and Martin, being driven to Durban airport by one of the other parents.

Even Millie had changed, talking gobbledegook about remembering things differently and that it was starting to happen.

We were all breaking into pieces and flying apart and no one was doing anything to stop it.

I stayed in bed, reading. I didn't tell anyone but my leg had started cramping, and when I dozed off I found the walls had closed in to the point where I could touch them with my arms stretched out.

Late in the afternoon, Dad and Mom argued again. I couldn't make out the words, just the tone; Mom worried, Dad reassuring.

Then his shape filled my doorway. He coughed wetly into his fist and looked at me. 'We're going out for dinner tonight.'

I wanted to ignore him, but this was too unusual: our family didn't go out for dinner. I didn't look at him, but nodded, lowering my book.

He patted his pockets for cigarettes, thought better of it and sat on my bed, elbows on his knees.

'There's something I want to talk to you about.'

Here it was. But for some reason I didn't want to hear him say it. I blurted, 'I already know.'

'You know? How?' There was a small smile on his face. How could he smile about something like that?

'I heard you and Haas. Don't do it, Dad.'

He straightened, frowning. 'Now hang on, boykie, it's not that big a deal. Haas? Haas has nothing to do with this. Haas? Still, I meant what I said; you mustn't talk to anyone.'

And then he told me about Freedom Radio.

At first I wasn't listening properly because I was confused and relieved and frightened all at once. This wasn't about the plot. Good. But it was something he wanted to keep secret and that was scary.

I forced myself to concentrate on what he was saying. It wasn't your usual Harry Mac story with waving arms. It was quiet and serious. He said Freedom Radio had been around during the 1950s when opposition to the Nats was more bold—even humorous, because no one knew things would get so bad and a lot of the English-speakers scorned the Nats, made jokes about them, thinking they would run out of steam. But by the time of the Sharpeville massacre and the political bannings, arrests and new apartheid laws, it was clear the Nats were here to stay. So Freedom Radio started up again. They'd approached Dad to write scripts but he turned them down because he didn't like what he called their British jingoism. But something had made him change his mind, although he wouldn't say what. I guessed it might be his frustration, the clampdown on newspapers and maybe, finally, the arrest of Windsor.

'So what were Mom and I doing in town yesterday?'

He turned away and scratched Laika's ears. 'Sorry about that. I think the Special Branch is watching me, so we get Mom to deliver the tape to someone when she goes shopping.'

The man in Kean's tearoom, who looked surprised when Mom got up and walked out.

'So you're not playing cards on Friday nights?' Well, at least there was a good reason for Millie and me to be shut out. But it meant Sol was involved. That was new.

Dad must have been following my thinking. 'Sol's not part of this. You know Sol, he doesn't want to get involved—bearing witness and so on. But he agreed to let us use his rondavel for the taping. Mrs Vincent reads the script. She's got a neutral voice, hard to trace.'

Of course, Mrs Vincent, the Black Sash lady.

To think all this was happening just down the lane. I wondered if you could hear Titch's weightlifting grunts and the chink of the barbells in the background on the broadcast. What would the Special Branch make of that?

I smiled at the thought and Harry Mac frowned at me and continued, 'The government is furious about Freedom Radio. It's not much of a threat but they can't stand having something happening under their noses that they can't control. So the local Special Branch is under pressure from Pretoria to find the radio station.' He chuckled. 'Remember that power blackout last Sunday? The Special Branch hit on this idea that whenever there's a broadcast, they would start shutting off the power to different parts of the city, bit by bit. If the broadcast stops, they can pinpoint where it's coming from.'

He laughed again, and it was good to see. Even though it was dangerous, he was actually doing something, and that's what Harry Mac liked. I felt good, too, because at last he was talking to me. One secret down.

'What will happen if you're caught?'

'Don't worry about that. Now listen, I need to talk to you. The reason the Special Branch can't trace the location of the radio station is because it lives in a suitcase—two suitcases, actually: one for the tape recorder and one for the transmitter. It runs on batteries and we—they—record from a different location every time so the police can't get a fix.'

'Is Haas one of them?'

'Haas? What's the fixation with that baboon? No, of course not. Now listen and stop interrupting. I don't think Sergeant Viljoen's presence near the tearoom was a coincidence. The Special Branch has obviously been tipped off about the tape handover. People blab, they can't help themselves, and that's why you need to keep your trap shut. Mom did the smart thing by getting out of there, but now we're stuck with the tape and we have to deliver it for tonight's broadcast. I'm asking if you'll come along to the handover. It'll look less suspicious if we're just a family out having a farewell dinner for our son.'

'Where are we having dinner?'

'Crossroads Hotel. There's nothing to be afraid of. Mom wasn't happy but I think she's okay now.'

●

The police had starting setting up random roadblocks around town on broadcast nights, and Little Harry made a huge thing out of me needing to wear my baggy shorts to hide the tape, and he said they could hide the tape recorder suitcase in there too, and he went on and on until even Dad told him to shut up. Crossroads was on the old highway which wound steeply up the range behind town. It was a hot early summer evening and the air cooled as we climbed out of the Duzi basin, higher and higher through the trees.

No one spoke much. Little Harry was thinking about getting away to London and hadn't wanted a fuss on his last night. Dad drove, fingers drumming on the steering wheel, thinking God knows what. Mom seemed calm but I knew her mind was flitting between Little Harry's departure and the flat metal tin tucked under her girdle.

But the roads were almost empty with not a police van in sight, and we all relaxed when we arrived at the hotel.

The dinner was an easy one and Dad and Little Harry drank a lot of beer and talked about London and what sort of car to buy for Europe, and Mom made jokes about English girls and said they'd like him more if he cut his hair and trimmed his beard.

I thought we were delivering the tape to someone at the hotel, but no one came to our table and when the meal was over we climbed in the car and headed back down the range. We'd only gone a short way when Dad slowed and turned off onto the World's View road.

He shifted in his seat and hunched over the wheel. World's View was a good transmission site, part of the Swartkop Range towering more than a thousand feet above the city. But there was only one road in and out.

We could feel the dark trees pressing either side as we drove in. No one spoke until we cleared the trees and found ourselves at the edge of the bluff. We parked, got out and sat on a log looking out, lining up like we did on the lawn at home, Dad and Little Harry on the outside, Mom and me in the middle.

The city lay silent far below us, spread out 'like a carpet of jewels', Mom said. The storm season was flickering to life along the distant coast and I could feel the air being drawn towards it, sighing as it passed through the plantations.

Nearly a year ago, Millie and I had sat in the window of the *spookhuis*, watching this summer light show and telling each other secrets. Well, at least I had. After all these months, I still didn't know what Sol carried inside him or why Mr van Deventer killed himself and his family.

And Verwoerd's postponed visit was now only two weeks away.

I looked sideways. Little Harry's arm was around Mom's shoulders, Mom held my hand, and I was tucked inside the big animal shield that surrounded Dad. And then I sensed something pass between us; a feeling of something that wouldn't come around again. It was different from my pale sun. That was about things lost. This was something we were hanging on to.

There wasn't another soul around, and I thought of the Panga Man. But he didn't operate up here, just down there in the dark patches of the jewelled carpet.

A low whistle from below, and Dad stiffened. He whistled a different set of notes back and, after a while, two forms emerged, making their way up the old Voortrekker wagon road which curled around the bluff. Mom had taken the tape out in the car and Dad held it, ready to hurl it away over the edge if he had to. The two forms stopped below us and Dad walked down to meet them.

He handed over the tape and we all got up and returned to the car. Everyone was still tense as we drove out of the plantation, but once we reached the old highway, Dad let out a big beery breath and turned the car's nose down the hill.

'The police may have roadblocks into town but they'll probably only set them up after the broadcast to try to catch the men returning from the transmission. The boys will hide the suitcases up there because they believe someone is tipping off the police.'

He leant across and clapped the palm of his hand on Mom's thigh, making her jump. 'But we're okay, just a normal husband and wife out for dinner with a hairy baboon and a boy in clown pants.'

I punched him on the shoulder and he hooted and slapped the dashboard.

The drive home was uneventful and there were no roadblocks. As the justice minister, Vorster, kept telling us, everything was normal.

We passed through the centre of town, where couples and families strolled the streets, window-shopping for Christmas, and Dad gave Little Harry a sly grin and turned off at Church Street, looking closely at passing cars. He checked his watch. 'They would have started broadcasting by—'

'There it is!' said Little Harry, cutting him off and leaning forward to point through the windscreen.

Dad slowed down as a grey van turned the corner from Chapel Street and came slowly towards us. As it passed, I saw it had an unusual looped antenna on its roof.

'Slow down, Dad. Watch! Watch!'

The van reached the intersection and stopped before turning into Commercial Road and continuing around the main block.

'Go round, Dad. I bet it'll be coming up Longmarket Street.'

Little Harry was more excited than I'd seen him in ages.

'All right, you two, what's going on?' Mom said.

'Your son has been a bit brave and very clever. Well, actually, he's not the clever one,' Dad said, looking in the rear-view mirror, 'It's Jacques, isn't it?'

Little Harry's friend Jacques had left school early and gone to tech college. He was now a third-year apprentice electrician. When the Freedom Radio people told Dad that the Special Branch had brought a post office detection van down from Pretoria to find the transmission site, the first person Dad thought of was Jacques.

As something of a farewell gift, Jacques and Little Harry had scaled the wall of the post office yard on Saturday night and Jacques had doctored the antenna.

We drove around the block into Longmarket Street and sure enough, there was the detection van doing another circuit.

'They're pretty sure they're on to the site, but the signal changes a bit each time,' said Little Harry. 'They'll go round and round the block until eventually it'll tell them the transmission is coming from the Police HQ directly behind the post office. We could hang around to watch the fun.'

'Not on your nelly!' Mom had had enough adventure for one weekend. 'Harry Mac, home.'

We left town and crossed the Duzi, Little Harry boasting and laughing like a schoolboy. Everyone was still chattering when we pulled into our drive and Dad turned off the engine. In the sudden silence, Little Harry leant forward and put his hand on Mom's shoulder.

'Mom, there's something I've got to tell you.'

She stayed facing the front but put her hand over his. 'You're not coming back.'

Little Harry stiffened. 'How did you know?'

'*Ag!* Please. I'm your mother.'

Little Harry wrapped his arms around her and buried his face in her hair. Dad got out of the car and went inside. I sat, stunned, but started feeling spare, so I got out and followed Dad inside, leaving them in the car like that.

It seemed I was the only one who hadn't known.

•

I lay in bed in the dark, ear to the radio, hoping to hear Titch's grunts on Freedom Radio so I could tell Millie, but I only caught the end of the broadcast. It was wrapping up when I heard Little Harry's footsteps coming to my room and for some reason I rolled over and pretended to be asleep. But he walked right up and switched on my bedside lamp. 'Don't be a fucken idiot.'

He sat and lit a cigarette, blowing smoke rings towards the window. 'It had to be a secret. The army would stop me. I'll write to you. Keep the letters. They'll be valuable one day.' He slapped my bum and blew smoke in my face. 'I'll see you in the morning before I go.'

He got up and flicked the cigarette butt out the window, turned and sat on the sill, giving me a long look. 'It's an engagement ring.'

I frowned. 'What?'

'In the *Bosmoedertjie*'s box. The one on his lap. He showed it to me. The jewellers were offering a fifteen percent discount to soldiers if they bought an engagement ring. So he bought one. He wanted to get married after the army.'

'But he didn't even have a girlfriend.'

Little Harry heaved himself off the windowsill. 'Makes you feel like shit, doesn't it?' He left the room.

The smaller secrets were leaking away. The *Bosmoedertjie*'s box; Little Harry leaving, maybe for good; Mom and Dad involved in Freedom Radio. But some remained: the *spookhuis* and Sol. And, of course, the big scary one that had chewed away at me for more than a year: Haas Cockroft's plot against Verwoerd.

●

The house was awake early, Mom frying up a big breakfast for Little Harry, and Essie touching him all the time, like she was about to lose another son. I went to Little Harry's room but stopped outside when I heard him and Dad speaking in their men's voices. Through the crack in the door I saw them standing face to face and Dad had him by the beard and was slowly headbutting him.

'There'll just be different problems over there, and you won't solve any of them with your fists, *bobbejaan*.'

'Look who's talking,' said Little Harry, unclenching the fist from his beard and eyeing our father from a couple of inches away. They were the same height now and reminded me of a wildebeest family I once watched at a waterhole: The old bull's herd had grown up around him and he singled out the biggest of his male offspring and mock-charged him again and again. The young bull didn't understand and would squeal and circle around to hide among the cows. But the old bull never let up, gouging his horns in the mud, pawing and snorting until the younger one finally turned and walked off alone into the bush.

But there was a difference here. Little Harry was leaving before he was pushed. Maybe he'd seen a collision coming and wanted to get out before it happened. Once, in his last year of school, he had stepped between our parents during an argument and had stared Harry Mac down. I thought Dad was going to knock his block off but he breathed heavily, looked around at all of us watching him and left the room. It didn't change Harry Mac, but I think it changed Little Harry.

Now he held his father's fist in his own. There was no smell of rhino and they were both relaxed. Little Harry smiled. 'You've had more fights at the Pie Cart than I've had breakfasts.'

'Well then, learn from my mistakes. Treat your upbringing as a cautionary tale.'

And then they hugged. A first.

As I turned away, I heard Little Harry whisper, 'Ease up on Mom.'

And an hour later when he climbed into Jacques' parents' car, he had no final words for me. Just a handshake and a punch. But I knew he'd write.

His departure left few ripples on the surface of our family because we were so used to his absences, but you could see that there was a part of Mom that had been lost and would stay lost forever. It was a first for her, too, a child leaving home for good. This was her pale sun.

27

MILLIE AND I SPENT A LOT OF TIME TOGETHER NOW because of the uncertainties of the New Year. Sol had often told us that nothing lasts, and I had a sense that what we had shared all through our childhood was running out of time. Sol seemed to sense the coming changes too and started reading again from the Greek myths and Primo Levi, which he hadn't done for a while. Millie was more tolerant of his long talks and there was an odd feeling among the three of us. Close, but trying too hard.

The day after the broadcast I hung around the Lieberman house with Millie, but really waiting for Sol to get home so I could talk to him about Freedom Radio.

The copy of Primo Levi's *If This Is a Man* lay on the verandah table. I picked up the morning paper lying next to it and glanced at the front page. The usual arrests, bannings and disappearances. In Cape Town, a university lecturer who campaigned against apartheid was shot when he answered a knock at the door. I turned the page and reread the latest report on Freedom Radio. Ken Brady must have worked late, taping the show off the office radio and then writing up his report.

You could tell Dad's writing style in the parts that were quoted and it seemed reckless of him. The Special Branch weren't that stupid.

The title of the latest broadcast was 'Watching for the Dawn'. Freedom Radio warned people that you cannot go into the *laager* with the Nats because it would be a desperate act that would end with *bloodshed, and chaos, and violence.*

It looked like Dad was the desperate one because his script then suggested that the last decent thing in our country was the legal system and so the people working in it should quit: *Resign en masse. Every magistrate. Every judge. Every court official. Resign. Refuse to legitimise apartheid. It may be our last chance before the bloodbath.*

There he was again, going on about a bloodbath. The government wouldn't let him get away with that in a leader, and they must by now know that he was writing the radio scripts.

'I admire his courage and sentiment, but can't see the judges tossing away their wigs and gowns. He he!'

I jumped when I felt the hand on my shoulder, then heard the voice and the deep, slow chuckle. Sol drained half the tall glass in his hand and reached for the ginger beer bottle. The glass was near my face and I could smell gin. Millie said nothing.

'Did you write any of this, Dr Lieberman? I thought you didn't want to get involved.'

'Oh, no no no no no,' he said, taking a seat next to me. 'I am merely the host and the shuffler—we do actually play cards, you know.'

Sol was restless. He looked at his watch, got out of the chair, walked to the verandah rail, came back and sat. I noticed he didn't kick his shoes off this evening. He emptied his glass, went inside and came out with the gin bottle, poured another drink, gulped at it and flopped down. His face was a waxy yellow. Millie's eyes never left him and the frog mouth was soft.

Sol leant across and tapped the newspaper report of Dad's radio script.

'It's funny—well, not really, it's more of a sad coincidence—that the Afrikaner metaphor for a place of strength and comfort is the *laager*. They draw the wagons into a circle, block the gaps, and the outside world disappears. Foof! Like the Roman *testudo* formation, the tortoise, with the legionaries' shields encasing them in a shell.'

Sol was getting carried away, so I said nothing while he drank again and raised that finger.

'You know, the Nazi concentration camps were also known as the *lager*, slightly different spelling, and most certainly not a place of comfort and security.'

His eyes slid over to Primo Levi. 'You see, Tomka, it's all about survival. Remember that. For every one of us, including the Afrikaners, every day of our lives, in big ways and small. But sometimes survival comes at a terrible cost. Levi is struggling with it and with what man becomes in order to survive.'

Sol, despite the chuckle and the jokes, always had a sadness about him and Millie, as usual, had found a word for it, 'lugubrious'. But it was getting worse, like he was touching the bottom after a slow glide down through the water.

'I talk a lot about the Nazis and the camps, Tomka, because it is what I carry with me every day. It's where my parents were—are. I cannot bring myself to visit the camps for fear that the soil I crush under my shoes may contain their remains.

'And this government brings it all back with what Levi calls the insolent logic of the oppressors. The twisted reasoning they bring to bear to justify their treatment of fellow human beings.'

I couldn't tell if Sol was making a point for us or whether he had slipped into his own world. There was an intensity about him today and so I tried to stay with him. He prodded my arm to make sure I was listening.

'And so everyone ends up in the *lager* and the *laager*—oppressed and oppressor. White and black. And in there too are the accomplices, we who wring our hands and tear our hair. There is no such thing as an innocent bystander. We are the German public who turned a blind eye while the Nazis murdered. Do you get what I'm saying?'

I was struggling. I got survival. He was leaning into our faces now. Too close and with gin breath.

'Look at this last election. The Nats went into it with laws that had even the white people by the throat, and yet those same people gave them more votes than ever. Why? Eh? Why?'

Sol's voice was shaking. He picked up *If This Is a Man* and brandished it at us.

Millie pulled her chair closer and placed a hand on his shoulder.

'Children, you must understand this. Levi tells us that in the *lager*, the moral code is warped. We shed our human skin and are mute beasts, doing whatever we can to survive. You know this, Tomka—*Wagter*—yes, I know what your father calls you. You, my boy, you watch in order to survive. We all have to focus on something or the reality will fill our eyes and blind us.'

The day had faded and I thought I heard Mom call my name from up the lane. I wanted to go home but I knew Sol needed us there tonight. Millie had moved closer again and was gripping Sol's hand, but he was coming down the other side now.

'I work with insane people. In their way, they survive, and I take some twisted comfort from watching their small obsessions while the world swirls madly, unheeded, about them.'

He let go of Millie's hand and jumped up, walked to the end of the verandah and came back to stand in front of us. He looked at his watch. 'Sorry, I may have to go back into the hospital tonight. Difficult patient.'

His hands were shaking as he poured another drink. Millie put a hand over the glass to stop him, but he gently lifted it off and tilted the gin bottle.

'I'm going to tell you children something. I wasn't going to. This is breaking patient confidentiality, but . . .' His free hand made a helpless gesture. 'And it's got nothing to do with tonight's patient.

'You know I also treat Africans? Well, a few months ago I took on a young Zulu outpatient who was having recurring nightmares that were affecting her life. She was a domestic servant, and had started to become overprotective of her employers, an elderly couple up at Hilton. She was acting strangely—she wouldn't go into certain rooms, for instance.

'The old folk were decent people and knew something was wrong. They tried to talk to her but all she would say was that she had bad dreams of her previous job, and she wouldn't discuss it. Her church prayed for her and, being a Christian, she would not go to a witchdoctor. So her employers finally contacted me at Town Hill.

'Her name was, is, Triphena. Triphena Zungu. You probably didn't know her, but she once worked for the Van Deventers. Yes.'

Millie and I were straining towards him. Millie was usually so cool during Sol's stories but her mouth hung open like Titch's.

'I won't go into details, but Triphena was the one who found the family.' He took a hankie out of his trouser pocket and blew his nose. 'And she told me what the servants in the lane knew, and why they disapproved of the family. The Van Deventers were mixed blood. Cape Coloureds. But, like so many other swarthy Afrikaners, their family had for one, two hundred years, lived as whites. When this government came to power they brought in the *Population Registration Act*, classifying people into separate racial groups. Then they started saying which group could do what jobs, where they must live, who they could marry, and so on. The Van Deventers found themselves classified white. Jackpot.

'But they lived on edge because Mr van Deventer had a good job as a government electrician. So they lay low and moved house when things became uncomfortable. When they arrived in the lane, they thought they were safe at last. I remember when I visited them and commented on the lovely garden, Mrs van Deventer smiled and said, "*Ja*, it feels like we've come home."'

Sol walked away, blowing his nose once more. Millie was a statue, eyes fixed on him. Sol turned to face us.

'And then, out of the blue, the Van Deventers received a letter from the government. They had been reclassified. Mr and Mrs van Deventer and Gillian were white, but the little boy, Theo, was coloured.'

Sol shook his head. 'I've heard how it happens. They do these reviews and someone in an office looks at a photo and puts a tick or a cross against it. That's it. No appeal, nothing. A four-year-old boy is no longer entitled to live in the same house as his family in a white area, go to the same school as his sister, ride at the front of the bus next to his mother. The family would have to sell up and move to a Coloured township if they wanted to stay together. Mr van Deventer would lose his job. Their chances of survival were slimmer. So he wiped out his family. He could not stand the shame. His survival had come to an end. He died of shame. That's what apartheid does to people. The moral code is warped.'

Sol's voice broke on the word and he kept repeating it, trying to get it right. 'Shame. Shame. Shame.'

Millie got up and pulled him back to the chair. She poured a drink with a splash of gin, handed it to him and sat close.

He stared out into the night. 'I know all this because Triphena found the government letter in his hand. She's a smart young woman and knew what it was. On some whim, she hid the letter when she raised the alarm. She still has it, and that's one of the things that troubles her.'

Mom was definitely calling me now.

Sol fumbled for my hand in the dark, and for a moment the three of us were joined. He turned to me and spoke with difficulty. 'Tomka, your father is trying to survive. He needs to breathe the oxygen of wild nature before diving back into this . . . this . . . His writings and broadcasts are a great howl.

'And I am trying to survive guilt over the death of my parents.'

His grip relaxed but he held on and his voice was calm, almost happy. 'You know something, *Kinder*? I dipped into Levi again last week. You know how I keep going through it, looking for a clue about my father in the *lager*? Well, again, there was nothing. I closed the book and it hit me. It was obvious. He did write about my father. And my mother.'

We sat in silence and my question came from nowhere. 'So when Windsor decided to make a bomb, was that surviving? What about Gandhi at the railway station?'

'So you were listening, hey? Ay ay ay, Tomka. Kvestions, kvestions.' He was smiling now. He squeezed my hand. 'Keep listening and watching, *Wagter*. Go now—your dinner's ready.'

•

I had no time to think about what I'd just heard because when I got home things were not good. The Security Branch hadn't wasted time. Whether because of Dad's latest script about bloodbaths and judges resigning, or their frustration at not being able to locate the radio station, they had simply banned any reporting of Freedom Radio in the press.

They went further and raided Ken Brady's flat, confiscating his radio recordings and transcripts. There was nothing anyone could do about it. Even the Old Man was worried now. Vorster, the justice minister, had again warned newspaper owners to get their house in order. The Old Man suspected Dad was writing for Freedom Radio but would never ask him outright. He didn't care. He just didn't want his newspaper shut down.

I checked Dad's mood over dinner: grim, but at least talking to Mom. Her involvement in Freedom Radio had brought them closer, even though Mom hated politics. After dinner they sat out on the verandah, and the more Dad drank, the less Mom did, as though she might cut down the overall effect. So I left them there and walked out into the lane.

Millie was waiting. We hadn't made an arrangement but I knew she would be there. I took her hand and we walked to the *spookhuis*.

At the front door we asked permission to enter, wondering if it would be different now we knew the secret. We walked through the entire house but the same feeling was there, just as strong. This time we sat on a different windowsill in one of the front rooms facing the big road.

The Van Deventers had perched in this corner house, neither part of the lane nor the big road, always ready to pack up and leave.

The sound of young voices piped along the road. Our heads jerked up, as though amazed there were other children in the world. It was one of those summer evenings when the temperature is just right, and the adults sit on their darkened verandahs after dinner with the lights off, the doors and windows open to cool the house, sipping at long cold drinks and listening to the radio. The children are sent out with torches to play in the gardens and streets, and the younger servants gather in knots to laugh and tease each other under the streetlamps.

'Theo, hey?' I said. 'Did you know that was Gillian's brother's name?' Pressed against me, I could feel her head shake, but she said nothing.

'I don't know what to think about all that stuff your Dad said.'
Another shake.

'Hey, guess what Little Harry found out?' I told her about the *Bosmoedertjie*'s engagement ring and she answered in a small voice, 'That's sweet.'

'Millie?' I felt her turn but her hair covered her face. 'Are you scared? Not about the Nats and that, but about how things will be different next year; you know, high school and that?'

She didn't say anything, but twisted her body and pushed her face into the side of my neck.

We hadn't noticed the engine strain and gravel crunch of the black car until it pulled up right outside the *spookhuis* and sat there idling. Millie straightened and we watched it. It was too late to hide. Even with the corner streetlight shining on it you couldn't see through the dark windows. I don't know about Millie, but I felt strong. Whatever was inside that black car, if it wanted to come for us it would have to enter the *spookhuis*. And now we knew the secret. And I also knew, just knew, the *spookhuis* was on our side. We held our breath for what felt like minutes until the black car pulled away, unhurried, and purred down the big road.

'Millie!' It was Sol's voice calling up the lane. 'Come, my girl.'

Millie shook back her hair. 'Gotta split, Tom-Tom.' She held my face in her hands and searched me with her eyes, then kissed me on the cheek. She smelt of soap. 'See ya later, alligator.'

She hopped down into the garden and walked out the gate. She had to turn her whole body to wave, and the frog mouth was soft and beautiful under the streetlight. The smell of soap stayed on my cheek as I watched her turn the corner and head down the lane.

•

Lying in bed, I thought about everything Sol had said. There was the *lager* and the *laager*. All in it together, becoming beasts. Something about a warped moral code. The stuff about survival kept popping up. Was that all we were doing: just surviving? The Kolonel, Windsor, Harry Mac—all of us? I would have to talk some more with Sol, get him to go over it more slowly when he wasn't so upset.

And Millie. She had been so worried about Sol's heavy drinking and his emotional outburst. They were a funny family. Kept things close. Millie never said much that told you what she was really feeling, and, like Sol, she joked away difficult topics. I would have thought as we got older it would be easier to talk, but it was actually harder. I touched my cheek where she'd kissed me. What was that about?

28

AT BREAKFAST THE NEXT MORNING I ASKED DAD IF HE would continue with Freedom Radio now the newspaper reports had been banned.

'We'll see. Mouths shut. Watch, don't talk.'

After school I did a bit of homework. This late in the year, the teachers were only giving us reading—to prepare us for a lot more of it next year, they said.

It was well after five when I walked down the lane to the Liebermans', but they were out. I waited for a while then went round to the *kaya* to ask their servant, Betty, when they would be home.

'I don't know, *nkosane*. Out all day. The madam she will be angry because the dinner is not started. But I don't know what she wants.'

There was no point in hanging around so I went home.

We were just finishing our own dinner when Essie came to the dining room and called Mom into the kitchen. Mom came back almost immediately and beckoned to Dad. I went with him and saw Betty standing at the back door, twisting a corner of her apron.

'What is it, Betty?'

The Liebermans were still not home. Betty hadn't seen them in the morning and there was no list of jobs for the day. There was always a list of jobs. Betty was young and quite frightened of Sandra Lieberman. She had two children to support and did not want to lose her job.

Dad looked at me. 'Were they starting holidays early?'

I shook my head.

He turned back to Betty. 'Well, what's the problem? They're just late. Make sure you lock up the house.'

'No, master. It is not right. They do not do this. The doctor, he always say when they go. No, master. Please.'

Mom stepped in. 'For heaven's sake, Harry Mac, just go over and check everything is okay.'

Dad said it was absurd and grumbled about intruding on people's privacy, but we followed Betty down the lane and up to the dark house.

'Have you been inside today?' Dad asked her. She nodded, took out a key and unlocked the front door. We stepped inside and Betty went through the house, switching on lights. Everything was normal; opened mail on the sideboard, a cardigan on the back of a chair. Dad refused to go into the bedrooms, but Betty said they were the same as usual and the beds had been slept in the night before.

'No notes?' he said, checking the sideboard and tables. Betty shook her head.

'Okay, lock up. I'll come back and check in the morning.'

•

But the Liebermans weren't back by morning. Mom told Betty to carry on with her housework and to let her know when they returned. Mom thought we should do something, but Dad said,

'What? You can't go pushing your nose into people's business. Sol's not an idiot. Imagine how you'd feel about Sandra Lieberman poking through your things because we'd decided to go away and hadn't told anyone?'

Dad was impatient to get to work. Things were, as he said, 'getting ugly'. Verwoerd would be here within a fortnight and the political atmosphere in town was tense. There had been a brawl at the Pie Cart between university students and railway workers, with political insults, boots and fists flying, and swastikas had been painted on the office door of an advocate known for representing people arrested under apartheid laws. The newspaper's police reporter said he'd heard there would be dozens of extra police in town for the prime minister's visit. Plainclothes officers from Pretoria had already been here for some time and were starting to round up known activists.

I was still packing my school bag on the dining room table when Dad left for work, and through the open door I saw Haas Cockroft hurry to the fence to talk to him as he climbed into the car. It must have been intense, because both their shoulders were hunched and their heads jerked.

I decided that I would ask Dad straight-out that evening what they were talking about.

But other things got in the way.

The first was a visit by a constable during the morning. Mom and Essie were home when the policeman knocked. They thought it was about Windsor, but it was Little Harry he was after. Mom had hesitated and the policeman said, 'Ma'am, we know he is out of the country.'

Mom then told him that Little Harry had gone to London for a holiday and she expected him back within a few weeks.

He had nodded and said okay, but that it was important for Little Harry to report to police when he returned. He touched his cap and left.

Mom was still shaken by the visit when she fetched Dad from work. They sat on the verandah and agreed it was best to stick to that line: Little Harry was on a short holiday.

They were talking about it when Betty arrived at the bottom of the stairs. There was still no sign of the Liebermans.

'Okay, okay, let me think about it,' Dad said.

Mom told Betty to go home and she would be in touch.

Dad sat a while with his eyes closed then went inside and rang Town Hill hospital, asking for the superintendent. Mom and I sat nearby, watching his face. He got through, asked about Sol and then listened, nodding and grunting.

When he put the phone down, his face was grey.

He walked straight back to the verandah, while Mom quickly refreshed their drinks and joined him. He took a long pull at the gin and tonic and lit a cigarette.

'I don't know what's going on, but Sol didn't tell anyone at Town Hill he was going away. They've been ringing his home for two days now. There's also been some sort of drama up at the hospital. A patient disappeared two nights ago when Sol was on call. The superintendent doesn't know if it's connected and obviously doesn't want to talk to me about it.'

He sucked on the cigarette and stood it on end. He spoke deliberately. 'But this is a private matter. Nothing to do with us.'

Mom frowned. 'Maybe I should ring the school and see if the Liebermans asked permission to take Millie out early.'

'No. It's the Liebermans' business. What they've chosen to do is their own affair.'

'What about Betty? The house?'

'What's it got to do with us? Sol will be in touch.'

'Yes, but Betty's got to be paid. It's Christmas. She's got kids—'

'For Christ's sake, Liz! Will you leave it alone?'

'Come on, Dad. That was uncalled for.' I stood up from my chair and stepped in front of Mom. I'd acted without thinking and was now trying to work out how Little Harry would do this.

He looked at me, eyebrows lifting, and I couldn't tell which way this was going to blow. He snorted and sat back. 'All right, all right. Tell Betty to carry on as normal until we hear from the Liebermans. And tell her she'll get her pay at the end of the month, whether they're back or not.'

I looked at Mom. She was smiling. At me.

That night I was scared to close my eyes in case the walls moved. I eventually fell asleep and woke up late, screaming, with Mom at my side stroking my head.

•

We found the Liebermans' absence too difficult to talk about, and the days went by with no word.

On break-up day, school closed early for us, the final-year pupils, to allow time for assembly, tears, promises and gifts to teachers, but as soon as the last bell went, I walked out and rode my bike home.

Every day, I visited the Lieberman house, once in the morning and again just on dark. Betty aired the house each day, washed all the bedding and started on the curtains. As the days dragged by she rolled up the rugs and spread flea powder. In my sunset visits I would sit for a few minutes on the verandah and watch the garden wilt under the summer sun. Mrs Lieberman's pot plants along the verandah were dying and I wondered if I should water them.

Then one morning Dad was contacted by the Kolonel. He came home early, too upset and confused to carry on working. He didn't even want a drink, just cups of tea and lots of cigarettes until he started his story.

The Kolonel had rung in person, his voice almost sad as he said, 'I had hoped to have no further dealings with you.'

Dad said the Kolonel couldn't bring himself to use his name, stopping short each time he was about to say it. He called him Mr MacGregor once.

'I am asking you to come to my office to answer some further questions. This is a professional courtesy. I could have sent Viljoen and a van. You understand?'

Dad was about to tell him to piss off, then realised Windsor's trial would start soon and they might want to pump him for more information. He didn't want to make it worse for Windsor, so he went around.

He was shown into the Kolonel's room and there was Viljoen, walking up and down in front of the window, ignoring Dad. The Kolonel's office servant dropped his eyes and tiptoed out, clicking the door shut behind him. The Kolonel was behind his desk and gestured for Harry Mac to sit in the chair opposite. Behind Dad, Viljoen continued to pace.

Dad jerked a thumb over his shoulder. 'Does he have to do that?'

The Kolonel snapped something and Viljoen came and stood at the side of the desk, his face reddening.

'This interview is not being recorded,' the Kolonel said.

Sure, and pigs don't fly, thought Dad, smiling at his own joke.

'Nor is it a laughing matter. I must warn you, you could face arrest, depending on the course of this conversation.'

Dad decided to cut to the point. 'I've already told you everything I know about Windsor Dlamini. It's all there in my statement. Cut out the bully-boy act, I've got a newspaper to publish.'

The Kolonel and the sergeant exchanged glances. Viljoen leant forward, the tips of his fingers white on the desktop. Dad had no doubt the sergeant thought talking was a waste of time.

The Kolonel turned back to Dad. 'What can you tell us of the activities of Dr Solomon Lieberman?'

'Oh shit!' That was Mom, grabbing Dad's hand across the kitchen table. 'Oh, no, Harry Mac. Oh no, please, no.'

Dad nodded. He hadn't lit a single cigarette since starting the story. He was as shocked as we were, he told us, and had sat in the Kolonel's office, trying to straighten his thoughts.

The Special Branch had snatched the Liebermans in the night.

But why all of them? Then he thought, Hang on, this is Sol we're talking about, Sol who didn't want to get involved, who only wanted to bear witness. No, they were trying to get at *him*. It was him, Harry Mac, they wanted.

The Kolonel sat watching and Viljoen leant over him, fingers pressing into the desk.

Dad managed to control himself and spoke carefully. 'I have no idea what you're talking about.'

'And yet you are paying their servant's wages. Who is supplying that money?'

'Jesus, Loftus!' Dad couldn't help himself. 'Don't you have friends, neighbours? It's called common decency.' He turned to Viljoen. 'I suggest you add that to the curriculum at police college.'

Viljoen gripped the edge of the desk and leant into Dad's face, hissing, 'You will address the officer as Kolonel Engelbrecht, and watch your tongue.' He raised his fist and a finger quivered under Dad's nose, 'Your day is done, *Engelsman*.'

At this point of the story, Mom was wringing Dad's hand. 'Harry Mac, please tell me you didn't do anything stupid. *Ag*, man, this is just terrible—terrible. Please tell me.'

Dad shook his head wearily. 'No, I didn't do anything stupid. But oh boy, I wanted to snap that finger. Oh boy. I'll tell you what stopped me: I saw Loftus watching, calm as you like, and I remembered the rugby scrums. He wanted me to snap that finger.'

Mom got up and went to the fridge. She came back with a can of beer and a full glass of Drostein for herself. Dad hadn't moved so she opened his beer and pushed it across the table. Lion Lager. *Laager*, *lager* and lager. Sol might have found that funny. I don't know.

Dad carried on as though the beer wasn't there. 'And it got me here.' He ground his knuckles into his chest, scrunching the hair. 'Right here. I've never felt more alone in my life. Something in here was shaken loose. Deep in here.'

I'd never heard Dad talk like this. Raw. I wanted to look away, but he hadn't finished. 'I've always believed in basic decency. That young German officer at Tobruk, he could have just shot me and saved himself a lot of trouble. But he dragged me out of my desert hole, bandaged my ankle and gave me water. It seemed the normal thing to do.

'But there in Loftus's tastefully panelled room, in my own town, not far from my family, all conventions of decency had been abandoned. And I thought of all the Essies lying next to their husbands in the *kayas*, fearing the late-night fist on the door; of the Windsors having their injuries treated until they are well enough to be tortured and hanged; and of Sol's parents herded onto trains for a one-way journey.

'That is where we all come to when there is no higher power left to appeal to, neither physical, legal nor moral.'

He stopped grinding his knuckles into his chest, swallowed most of the beer and went back to his story.

The Kolonel had straightened the pad on his desk. 'Tell me what you know of Sarah Feinburg.'

Dad had never heard of her. 'Should I know her?'

'She left with the Liebermans on the night they disappeared.'

Mom and I both burst into the story. 'Disappeared?' We were talking over the top of each other. 'So the Security Branch didn't take them?'

Dad nodded. 'That's right. I nearly cheered. But then I realised they thought that I was involved somehow. I was glad I'd told the

Old Man where I was going, but what use would it be in these times? I had to find a way to get out of there.'

Dad told the Kolonel that as far as he could see Sol hadn't done anything wrong, so if there was nothing further, he, Harry Mac, was going back to his office.

There was a little smile on Dad's face when he told us this.

'Well, as I got up to go I pointed at Viljoen and said to Loftus: "And if this baboon tries to stop me he'll be whistling 'Sarie Marais' through broken teeth."'

Mom nodded. 'Good. Almost wish he'd tried.'

But Dad wasn't in the clear yet. The Kolonel stopped him with a raised hand. 'Sarah Feinburg is the wife of Joe Feinburg, the communist who fled the country last year. She has moved here to Pietermaritzburg and we suspect she is in contact with subversive organisations. It suited us to allow her to live openly, but she is also emotionally unstable, and for her own good, we admitted her to Town Hill hospital ahead of the prime minister's visit. You appreciate that, for security reasons, she was kept in a locked ward. Just over a week ago, your friend Dr Lieberman was seen entering the hospital late at night. He had not been called in, but told the duty nurse he wanted to check on a patient. The next morning, when the staff went to unlock the ward, Mrs Feinburg was gone. And your friend did not turn up for work that day, nor has he been seen since.'

Dad had shrugged and stood up, looking towards the door. 'So what's that got to do with me?'

That was Viljoen's moment. In an instant he was out of his chair and blocking the door. 'This, *Engelsman*, this has to do with you.' He shook a sheet of writing paper in Dad's face triumphantly.

'If you take your fat fingers off it, I might be able to read it,' Dad said.

Viljoen placed the paper on the desk and stepped back. The

Kolonel hadn't moved, sitting with his fingertips touching like a praying mantis.

Dad broke off the story and rubbed his face. He looked at Mom and then at me. 'Tom, it was a letter to you from Millie. She must have sent it the day after they fled. The envelope was pinned to the letter and I saw the postmark—Ponta de Ouro, just over the border in Moçambique. Sol must have driven through the night up into Zululand and crossed the border on a back road somewhere near Kosi Bay.'

'Have you got the letter, Dad?' I felt hot and cold at the same time but all I could think of was getting my hands on that letter.

He shook his head and closed his eyes. 'It wasn't long. I remember it.' And he recited:

'Dear Tom-Tom,

Sorry about this. I guess you'll read about it in the papers. I've worked out how long it should take for this letter to reach your house. So at 8 pm three days from now, visit the Milky Way. Laika will be passing through.

Stay hep. Signing off from Nowheresville,

Millie.'

Mom glanced at me and frowned at Dad. 'Yes? So what?'

Dad rubbed his face again and shook his head. 'Well that's exactly what I said to Viljoen. But he wanted to know who "Laika" was. Said it was a Russian name. He also wanted the address of this "Milky Way". It was obvious to him that Sol was communicating with me in code through the children.'

'Oh, Harry Mac, surely they're not serious? The Kolonel isn't stupid. What did he do?'

'Turned his back and walked to the window.'

And Dad said that's when he couldn't help himself and started laughing.

He picked up the story again, smiling at the recollection.

'Oh, you dumb fucking idiots.' Dad slapped the desk. (When he was telling us this part, he didn't use that word, but the way he said the word 'silly' made it obvious.) 'And they put the security of the country in your hands?'

Viljoen stepped towards Dad, who turned to face him. The Kolonel swung around and barked, stopping both men.

When Mom heard this bit I expected she would be anxious, but there was a light in her eyes. 'And then?'

Dad finished his beer. 'Loftus didn't believe that crap about the letter. No, it was pure intimidation, a little demonstration to me that he could twist anything to his purpose. Also, that he had creatures like Viljoen he could unleash at will. Men who believed Hitler was planning a comeback.'

Dad said the Kolonel's tone changed. He sat, crossed his legs and started chatting like they were colleagues. He told Dad that Sol was suspected of being a member of the Communist Party, with connections to the ANC. He had been under surveillance for some time, but they hadn't moved on him yet.

'Something is brewing,' the Kolonel said. 'Something big—and we were hoping he might lead us to whatever it is.' He was looking intently at Dad. 'So for the sake of your country, the safety of your family, all our families, if you know anything about Solomon Lieberman's activities, it is your duty to tell us.'

The Kolonel let that sink in, especially the bit about the safety of Harry Mac's family, then continued quietly, 'You English think we are stupid, but don't underestimate us. The silly radio station, your car parked on the highway near the fugitive Mandela . . . We could ruin your life, but listen well. You are nothing to us, *hoor jy my*?

235

Nothing. Not worth the effort. Sorry if that bruises your ego. You are a beetle under the wheels of the wagon.'

Dad held his gaze and said nothing.

The Kolonel continued, 'You of all people should understand what's at stake. You're a battler, like the Afrikaner, your family living off dog bones in the Depression. Yes, we know that, too. Despise us, but you will benefit when our work is done. Forget Hitler. The *volksgeist* I believe in is that of the Afrikaner. Our round-up of undesirables and terrorists is on schedule. Peace is beckoning. Why would you slap away its hand?'

Viljoen had been drumming his fingers against his thigh throughout the Kolonel's speech. He stepped towards Dad with an ugly smile.

'And just so you know, your son's little *Joodse* girlfriend has given away their location. How do you feel about that, *ne?*'

Dad had indeed thought about it. But he'd seen the postmark. There was nothing at Ponta de Ouro. The border town was a staging post, not a destination. And the Special Branch would already have guessed the fugitives had headed for Moçambique. The other nearest options were Swaziland and Basutoland, and both were too small to hide in, and were virtually provinces of South Africa anyway.

The Kolonel waved airily. 'It's no secret where terrorists run to.'

Dad had had enough. He stood and walked to the door. Behind him Viljoen complained, '*Sommer* letting him go?'

The Kolonel: 'He's not going anywhere.'

Dad turned. 'I don't know who I despise more: the one too stupid to think for himself or the one smart enough to know better. I'll leave you to argue which is which.'

Dad had finished his story and the three of us sat there in the kitchen. I wondered what Mom and Dad were feeling.

Dad, I thought, had lost his closest friend and was maybe hurt to learn that Sol had a secret life. Despite all his talk about not getting involved, Sol, the man with no roots, was quietly risking everything he had. Meanwhile, up the lane lived noisy, thundering Harry Mac, desperate to make a difference but being told by Windsor that it was not his fight. And now Sol was gone and the Kolonel called Dad a beetle under the wheels of the wagon. Poor Dad. I wished I could talk to Sol about it, but I would have to work these things out myself now.

Mom was more difficult to read. She didn't really like Sandra Lieberman, but she would have felt for a woman having to uproot her family and abandon everything. A woman who craved a better life, who hated what she had been born into.

'I wonder how much Sandra knew,' Mom said. 'I suspect not much. She would have been horrified and probably wanted to stay behind.'

Dad shook his head. He was really into the beers and smokes now and it wasn't even lunchtime yet. 'No way. The Special Branch would have dragged her in, for sure. Look at that poor Sarah Feinburg. Locked in a mental hospital. Like something out of Russia.'

Me? I felt hollow. Like I had nothing inside me to feel with.

'Dad, did you see when the letter was posted?'

He had, and we worked it out. I'd missed my date with Laika in the Milky Way.

29

MOM AND DAD DISCUSSED WHAT MIGHT HAPPEN TO
the Liebermans' house and to Betty. Dad said he would talk to an
estate agent and see if the property could be sold and the money held
in trust in the hope one day of getting it to Sol and Sandra, wherever
they found refuge. The only family they knew of was Sandra's
brother, and they had no address for him in America.

They also agreed to pay Betty two months' wages, write her a
reference and take her down to the Bantu Registration Office in
town. She was still young enough to land a job, particularly with a
good reference. Next morning, Mom and I walked down the lane to
tell Betty what had happened. We found her sitting on the verandah
steps, sobbing into a dusting cloth.

'Betty?' Mom touched her on the shoulder.

'Oh, missus,' she said, taking Mom's hand and leading us into
the house.

The Special Branch had done a thorough job. Every fitted carpet
had been ripped up, bookshelves emptied, paintings pulled off the

walls, their linings slit open. In the bedrooms, mattresses had been slashed and the contents of the wardrobes and chests of drawers emptied onto the floor. The kitchen drawers had been pulled out and up-ended, and the fridge and freezer were standing open, already starting to stink in the heat.

Mom looked for somewhere to talk with Betty, but we couldn't bring ourselves to sit on the furniture whose stuffing bulged out like the guts of dogs on the side of the road.

We went back to the verandah and, still holding her hand, Mom explained to Betty what had happened. Betty nodded dully. She hadn't expected to see the Liebermans again, but she couldn't believe that white people's property could be treated in this way.

While Mom talked with Betty, I walked down into the garden. Underneath the verandah were stacked Sol's crates of bottled ginger beer. The nearest ones were smashed but the police must have lost interest; nearby, a garden fork stuck out of the vegetable patch, which had been dug out, the soil scattered about. Next door, across the low hedge, Mrs Vincent was kneeling before a flower bed in her wide-brimmed straw hat, turning over the soil with a hand fork.

Outside here in the garden, the day was too normal, like the way life carried on around the *spookhuis*.

I tried to will Sol to step out of his rondavel, lope along the shady path under the cool blue canopy of the jacaranda, loose grin on his face, calling for Millie to fetch a cold bottle from the fridge. But the rondavel window hung askew on its hinges and the glass was cracked. That wasn't a search. That was anger.

Something white caught my eye in the bed of agapanthus that circled the rondavel. I pushed the leaves apart and pulled out a piece of jawbone. It was part of the eland skull, Sol's *memento mori*. The skull had been smashed and then tossed out the window. I gathered the pieces and laid them on the lawn, wondering if I could glue them back together with my Airfix kit.

'Young Tom? Tom MacGregor.'

I jerked my head up at Mrs Vincent's voice. She was standing at the hedge, holding something in her hand. I left the skull fragments and went over.

She didn't smile but held out a folded brown paper packet. 'Do forgive me, but with everything that's happened, it slipped my mind. Dr Lieberman asked me to give this to you.' She said in her matter-of-fact teacher radio voice, 'He obviously didn't want anyone to know they were leaving.' But he'd told Mrs Vincent. She knew Sol's secrets.

I looked inside the packet. It was Sol's copy of *If This Is a Man*.

Mrs Vincent watched me, unsmiling, but her voice softened. 'He said you'd like it.'

I thanked her, then asked, 'Did Millie leave me anything?'

She shook her head, lifted a hand and went back to her flower bed.

●

Over dinner, Dad sprang another surprise. He'd rung an agent and found out that, despite what the Liebermans had always said, they didn't own the house. It belonged to Edgar Lambert down the lane.

'Well, I never!' said Mom. 'Why would they say they owned it? That's Sandra for you.'

But I thought I knew why. Like the Van Deventers, the Liebermans had only been perching in the lane, not really belonging, and ready to move.

'What'll happen to all their furniture and their things?' Mom asked.

'I imagine the state will seize them,' said Dad. 'Sol will find that hard to take, his possessions funding the apartheid machine.'

'Well, we'll see about that! We'll let Betty take what she needs and Tom and I will go and pack whatever we can into boxes and take it down to PADMRO. Sol would like that. Maybe the furniture, too.'

'Oi-yoi-yoi!' Dad held up a hand. 'You might get away with a few pots and pans for your malnutrition charity, but be careful what you give to Betty. You want her to end up in jail for theft?'

But there were times when Mom just smiled and you knew she wasn't taking any notice of you.

So next morning, with Essie's help, we carted tea chests down the lane. We'd just stepped inside the gate when Mom stiffened. 'Uh-oh.'

An old Zulu man in a greatcoat got up from his stool on the verandah and lifted his cap to us. He held a *knobkerrie* in one hand. '*Sawubona, nkosikazi.*'

'*Sawubona, khehla.* Can we go in?'

The nightwatchman smiled and ducked his head. 'I'm sorry, madam. Police.'

And that was that. Mom gave the tea chests to Betty for her own belongings, and while she packed I walked through the garden, circling the Lieberman house, so familiar and now so strange. I just couldn't imagine not sitting on that verandah again drinking ginger beer and listening to Sol, seeing Millie roll her eyes and hearing Mom's voice calling me up the lane for dinner. Would they ever be allowed to come home? What would become of their house? Another *spookhuis* in the lane? Another house of shame?

When Betty was ready, we loaded her stuff into the back of our station wagon and drove her downtown to the African bus terminus. We stored her metal bed and wardrobe in our garage for when she came back from her *kraal* after Christmas to look for a new job.

That evening I lay on the lawn, just on sunset. I wasn't waiting for Laika to pass over. I wanted to see the evening star at the exact moment when it blinked on. That was when it was most powerful, and I had my own way of giving my wishes their best chance of coming true, a way even Millie didn't know: I made a deal with the stars—offered something in exchange.

I lay facing the silhouette of Swartkop, where the evening star came up. What would I offer to get Millie back? All sorts of silly ideas came and went through my head as the sky faded and bird formations started gliding overhead. I set my family aside. They were never part of my deals. But it had to be something big.

Then I knew. The leg. No, not the bad one. The stars could have the good one. I would allow the good leg to go bad if I could have Millie back.

I was staring into the leftover white-orange glow of the sunset, waiting for the star, when Millie's voice came to me, 'You're joking Tom-Tom! I happen to like that leg. Get real, banana peel.' I shut her out and there it was, a pinprick of light. And I made my deal.

•

I was asleep when the phone rang, and rang and rang. I rolled over, groggy, and switched on the lamp. 11.30 pm. Millie? I sat up and felt my leg, but it was the same. Then I heard Mom's bare feet running through the house. Late-night calls frightened her; had done ever since the police rang to say her only brother had been killed in a motorbike accident. She never spoke of it, but would start to shake if the newspaper rang late.

My feet were just swinging over the side of the bed when I heard her squeal, 'Little Harry! Everything okay?'

I slumped back on the bed and kicked out with my good leg. It was silly to expect the wish to come true so quickly. I lay and listened to Mom's girly giggle and Dad's sleepy grumbling when he came out of the bedroom. I got up then and sat with him, both of us shirtless, our hair sticking up all over the place. I snuggled into his animal warmth and was dozing off when he moved to take his turn on the phone.

Mom's smile had been replaced with a puzzled look as she handed over the receiver. 'Australia, for God's sake,' she said, walking out of the room.

When it was my turn, I could hardly hear Little Harry over the music and shouts.

'Gunna watch Mike Hailwood on the weekend.' He was slurring.

'Where are you? Did you hear about the Liebermans?'

'Fuck that shit. Now you know why I left. Why don't you come over? It's cold and everyone smells damp.'

'Why's Mom going on about Australia?'

'Don't forget to send batteries!' He laughed and hung up.

Dad and I went through to the dining room, where Mom was bent over the atlas.

'There it is,' she said, jabbing at the page. 'Sydney. Right over on the other side. Good heavens. Just look.' She sat back shaking her head. '*Ag*, Australia is so far away it isn't even on the same page as us.'

'What's going on?' I said, ratty and tired.

Dad rubbed his face. 'Little Harry had a fight with an Australian in Earls Court and then got drunk with him afterwards in his flat. That's where he is now. The Aussie says Sydney is the place to be: plenty of work, cheeky girls and everyone lives at the beach and gets drunk every day. The Aussie said if Little Harry gave him five pounds he could use his phone, so he called us.'

But Mom couldn't see the attraction. 'Why Australia? If he wants to live in a desert, why doesn't he come home and move to the Kalahari?'

'Australia's not all desert.'

'Oh no? And when were you last there, Captain Cook? I've seen *A Town Like Alice*. I know what a desert looks like.'

Dad had to retreat in the face of that.

Mom smoothed the pages of the atlas and ran a finger from

England to Australia. 'So far. How will he ever get there?' Then she brightened again. 'Oh well, he'll have to stop here on the way over and we'll see him again.'

I looked up at Dad and his sleepy smile faded. Mom had forgotten Little Harry could not come home without facing the police.

Mom closed the atlas and beamed at us. Dad ruffled her hair and lumbered off to bed.

30

Our beach holiday was due to start immediately after Verwoerd's visit was out of the way. I didn't care about Verwoerd anymore and I didn't want to go on holiday, but Mom said if I was going to mope, it would better to do it at the beach. 'There's lots of other kids down there, Tom. You mustn't be so fixed on one friend, it's not healthy. Anyway, you'll see Millie again when things quieten down.'

I know she meant well, but it was just words. I checked my good leg as I did every day now. It felt strong.

Each evening after work, Dad got me to drag bits of our caravan gear out of the garage. We checked the canvas awning for tears and rot, counted pegs, untangled guy ropes, cleaned the gas stove and checked the lamp, mantles and torches. Dad took me into town and we bought a new folding table and canvas waterbag, plus a stretcher for me because he thought it was time I slept outside under the awning.

A few days after Little Harry's call, Dad rang from work in the late afternoon and spoke to Mom. She put the phone down, her back to me, and said, 'Get your shoes on. Dad has to work late and he wants us to come and sit with him and have toasted sandwiches together.'

Dad wasn't in his office when we got there, but Miss Hammond told us to go in. Mom settled at the window and opened her magazine while I went to the black Remington in the corner and fed in a sheet of paper. I'd been two-finger tapping for years and Mom, who was a trained secretary, told me I'd be ruined if ever I had to learn touch-typing. But I'd watched the reporters and most of them used two fingers and I wanted to fly across the keys like they did.

Dad came into the office carrying sheets of torn-off telex messages, a lit cigarette in his mouth. He closed the door and sat heavily behind the desk. He took a final drag and stubbed out the cigarette. 'You'd better listen.'

Mom lowered her magazine and I turned from the typewriter. He flattened the curls out of the telexes, looked up at us and coughed through the smoke.

'About an hour ago we got a snap telex from the Reuters bureau in Nairobi. They'd been tipped off about some sort of military action in Moçambique. That's not news because there's a guerrilla war there, but the war is in the north, and this happened way down south in the capital, Lourenço Marques itself. And around the same time as the Reuters alert, underground ANC operatives have been ringing South African newspapers, accusing our government of involvement. It's all pretty garbled at the moment, but Ken Brady has calls in to the defence minister's office, and we're standing by the telex.'

A tap on the door and Bobby Naidoo, the telex operator, brought in a fresh message. He flashed me a grin and left. Dad scanned the telex before crumpling it and tossing it into the bin. 'Just repeating the alert.'

I went over to look at the telexes on his desk. 'Are we going to war, Dad?'

'No.' He looked surprised. 'Nothing like that.'

Then Mom, quietly, 'The Liebermans?'

'Well, I can't see why. The government wouldn't take such a risk for a minor player like Sol.'

'But?'

'But they're drunk with power. And there might be something bigger happening. The Kolonel said something was brewing.'

He took off his reading glasses and pinched the bridge of his nose. He spoke with eyes closed. 'They're rounding people up all over the country and now they're starting to look across the borders. The Liebermans aren't the only fugitives and they may find themselves swimming with some big fish in Moçambique. There's talk of guerrilla training camps, of safe houses.'

Dad shuffled papers and smoked and we all waited, but nothing more came through, so after a while Mom suggested she and I take a walk through town and look at the Christmas decorations and then pick up some toasted sandwiches on the way back. Dad grunted and went through to the newsroom for a conference with the chief subeditor, the print foreman and the circulation manager.

Mom and I left the building and crossed through the public gardens. We avoided talking about what Dad had told us, as if putting our fear into words might make it come true.

Church Street was strung with coloured lights and decorations and the pavements were full of families browsing the windows.

'Hell, you know I haven't even thought about Christmas presents,' Mom said. 'I think we'll wait until we get to the beach and get them at Umhlali, hey?'

I nodded, then realised I was holding her hand, but I couldn't pull away in case she got upset. So we walked the block while I kept watch for classmates.

We stopped at the Greek tearoom on the corner near the newspaper building, bought sandwiches and carried them up to the editorial department. Dad's office was empty but from down the corridor a buzz radiated like heat from the newsroom. I knew that sound from other times when Dad had brought me into the paper when big stories were breaking—a passenger train derailment, and once when a young lioness escaped from the Lion Park and people from outlying suburbs were ringing in with sightings in their gardens.

Mom and I decided not to wait for Dad and were eating our sandwiches when he burst in, talking loudly to someone behind him. When he was in newspaper mode, he noticed nothing else. He snatched a page outline off his desk and handed it to the chief sub, talking him through it and jabbing the sheet. The chief sub nodded to us and hurried out.

Dad tore open the greasy wrapping Mom held out, crammed half the sandwich in his mouth, shook out a cigarette and lit up while chewing.

'Reuters say there was an explosion and gunfire in a suburban house in LM in the early hours of this morning. Neighbours saw armed men wearing balaclavas run from the house, jump in a car and drive off. They said one of the men shouted something in Afrikaans to the driver.'

He swallowed and drank from a cup of tea on his desk. 'Lourenço Marques police have sealed the building and are searching for the car.'

Mom put down her food and started wiping her hands on a paper napkin. 'Who was in the house?'

He shook his head. Ken Brady was waiting on a South African government announcement expected any minute. He picked up the remaining half of his sandwich and left the room.

I looked at Mom, but she turned away and carried on cleaning her hands.

It was a different Harry Mac who walked slowly into the room a few minutes later, holding a telex in his hand. He sat in the chair under the window and read without looking up, his voice flat.

'From the office of the Minister for Foreign Affairs, Eric Louw:

A communique from our embassy in Lourenço Marques has advised that a gun battle between terrorist factions of the ANC and PAC has resulted in the deaths of twelve people in a house in the capital.

The embassy communiqué revealed that the house had served as the headquarters for criminals and terrorists who had fled to escape justice in South Africa. It is believed that the wanted communist Theuns Malan was among the dead.'

Dad hesitated then continued.

'Other wanted communists believed to have been in the house are Thabo Sizswayo, Zinzi Kumalo, Sarah Feinburg and Solomon Lieberman. There are no known survivors.

The incident demonstrates the need for vigilance by our security forces. Our enemies are armed and ruthless. They are even prepared to eliminate their own kind in the manner of communist-style purges. Moreover, they killed innocent women and children in the house.

As to accusations by the ANC that the South African government was responsible for the deaths, we say it is an insult to a country that stands as a model of stability and justice. It is typical of the devious nature of these organisations that they attempt to shift blame for their own internal bloodletting.'

Dad let the message drop onto his lap. 'They got them,' he said. 'They got them.'

Dad and Mom spoke quietly to each other. There was nothing for it but for Mom and I to go home and let him put the paper to bed.

But when I tried to stand up, I found I couldn't walk. It had nothing to do with my legs; it was just that with nothing left to feel, my body had given up. I was a Christmas beetle husk blowing across the crazy paving.

'Sorry, Dad,' I said as he lifted me over his shoulder and carried me downstairs to the car. His rhino stench was stifling.

•

I lay in bed facing the ceiling. Mom hovered, asking if I needed anything. She brought a glass of water and headache pills, but I told her not to worry, I would be all right in the morning. Dad understood better. He'd driven us home and carried me inside. And when Mom had finished fretting over me he came in and sat on the bed for ages, saying nothing. It was nice having him there in our own silence. It could go on forever as far as I was concerned.

He eventually patted my leg and said he had to get back to the paper. He kissed me on the forehead and left, turning off the light on his way out.

I waited until I heard the car drive away then opened the drawer in my bedside table. I'd cleaned the knife after Umfolozi and when I pulled it from the sheath it glistened with oil. I threw back the sheet and looked at my legs. The good one had to do most of the work and was muscly and strong. So the best thing to do would be to cut through the tendon at the back. The knife was sharp and it wouldn't take much, then the stars would have their offering and I'd have Millie. Millie. I started to shiver and she was there, sitting on the window sill, giving me the full frog mouth. I blinked her away and pushed the point of the knife into the skin behind my ankle bone. I gasped and heard Millie speaking in her 'don't-be-thick' voice. She was explaining to Titch the idiocy of his brick-throwing: 'Doesn't work like that.' The voice was kind of dry, in the back of her throat, and really did make you feel stupid. Then she turned to me and pointed at the leg and the knife. 'You too.'

'But I made a deal,' I shouted back at her. I scrambled to my knees, knife still in hand and leant out the window, straining up at the night sky. 'Didn't I? We had a deal.'

My words floated up to an empty sky, the evening star long gone.

I fell back to the bed. Mom had once taken me to a play called *The Monkey's Paw*, in which a family wished their son back from the dead. But this was no play and the stars were deaf. Millie was gone forever. What had happened in Lourenço Marques was real, just as what had happened to Sol's parents was real, and no amount of wishing would bring any of them back.

I threw the knife to the bottom of the bed, where it glinted in the light from the streetlamp. I looked down at the pinprick of blood on my ankle, pulled up the sheet and lay there, unable to stop shivering.

•

I wasn't all right in the morning. I could move my arms and legs but something stopped me from getting up. I was nice to Mom but she knew it was better to leave me alone, popping her head around the door every now and then to give me a smile.

I stayed like that for three days. Every morning when I woke I checked my good leg, just in case, then ate a bit of toast and drank tea, keeping an eye on the open window in case the frog mouth reappeared, challenging me to get up.

I read the paper and listened to the radio news. Reuters reported that villagers outside Lourenço Marques had heard a helicopter flying low over the bush on the night of the attack. About an hour later they heard it again, flying back in the direction of South Africa.

My mind was a fog of questions. What if it had been the same helicopter that had landed next to the school just before the republic? The smiling soldier who helped me up to sit inside—did he pull the trigger that killed Sol and Sandra and Millie? What would Little Harry have done if he'd still been in the army and they'd told him to get in that helicopter?

The radio kept repeating that the incident was an internal power struggle, and condemned the ANC and PAC for bringing violence to a peaceful suburb in a friendly neighbouring country.

Verwoerd made a speech in which he told us to be grateful for the peace his government had established while the rest of the continent was in turmoil and the world faced a growing communist threat: Russia had just exploded the largest nuclear bomb ever, their tanks were lining up against the Americans behind the new Berlin Wall, and America was forced to send military advisers to Vietnam to counter the rolling Red juggernaut.

Vorster came on after him and said the country was entering a new era of calm, despite the communist threat. Everything was normal, he said.

The final item on the news was the hanging of the Nazi war criminal Adolf Eichmann, known as the Head Butcher of the Holocaust.

31

THE DAY OF VERWOERD'S VISIT WAS BRIGHT AND HOT. It was the Dingaan's Day public holiday and cars streamed towards the coast. Downtown, the roads had been sealed off around the Church of the Vow, where the prime minister would attend a special morning service. We all knew the church, now a Voortrekker museum, from school excursions. After the service he would lay a wreath at the statue of the martyred hero Piet Retief. In the afternoon there would be *volkspele* at Jan Smuts Stadium, the ladies in their Dutch bonnets and long dresses swirling to the accordion. But the main event was the public meeting in the city hall that night.

I woke early and pushed down the sheet. I swung my legs to the floor and tested them out. I was shaky after three days on my back, but I would be all right. Today, I needed to be strong. I walked around a bit to get my balance back and went through to the dining room.

Mom was at the table drinking tea, while Dad read the paper.

They looked up and smiled. Dad said, 'About bloody time. Hey, boykie, you'll like this. They've caught the Panga Man.'

'Why would I like that?' It came out sharper than I meant, and their heads lifted again.

'Because,' said Dad, drawing it out, 'wait for this: he was an office servant at Special Branch HQ.' He shook with laughter. 'He was that creeping Jesus I saw, tiptoeing and serving tea to the Kolonel. He was under their fat, hairy noses the whole time.'

I didn't care about the Panga Man. I grunted and sat at the table, reached for a piece of toast and buttered it.

'So, what are you going to do today, my little man?'

It hurt to see Mom trying so hard to lift my spirits, and a part of me felt mean that I couldn't respond. I watched them while I ate and drank my tea. All the horrible things that had happened to us and our friends had brought Mom and Dad closer. They talked more to each other and Dad was less inclined to go off on his own and drink. Of course he drank and smoked as much as ever, and Mom was starting to nag him about the phlegmy cough we heard every morning when he got up, but there hadn't been a silence in ages. Sometimes when I watched them they seemed to huddle together. I wondered if they were frightened.

I shrugged in answer to Mom's question and said nothing.

I knew what I was going to do, but I wasn't about to tell them.

'Oh dear,' she said. 'My poopie-boy is growing up. He's learning not to speak to his mother, just like Little Harry. Boys!' She prodded Dad in the arm. 'You should have taken that rubber band off.'

This was a family joke. When Dad had been a court reporter years ago, he covered a paternity trial where a man said he could not be the father of the girl child because he had tied a rubber band around his left testicle. And everyone knew that was how you prevented girl babies.

I got up from the table and left them cackling to each other.

Despite the public holiday, Dad still had to work and I lay around and counted down the hours until he'd be home. The heat built steadily until around four when a black storm rode in on a roll of thunder and lightning flashes. The rain was a solid sheet, flooding the verandah and sending Mom and Essie and me scuttling around the house with rolled-up towels to jam under the doors. Within minutes the storm had moved on and steam curled off the lane as the sun returned hot and sticky.

Dad came home early because of the political meeting, had dinner, changed clothes and when he came out I was ready for him.

I heard him grab the car keys, say goodbye to Mom and call out, 'Boykie, where are you? I'm off now!'

His footsteps went through to my room. 'Where the hell is that child? *Ag*, I can't wait. I'll see you later.'

He walked through the lounge and stopped when he saw me blocking the front door. 'What do you think you're doing?'

He had on a suit instead of the trouble-making jacket, and a notebook stuck out of a trouser pocket. He carried the suit jacket over his arm and his fresh shirt already had dark circles around the armpits.

I had also changed and was wearing my school blazer. My caliper straps were so tight my leg was stiff.

The light came on in his eyes. 'Oh, no! Oh no you're not.'

I gripped the doorframe, braced my leg and said nothing.

'Tom, don't be silly. It's no place for kids.' His eyes flicked to the clock above the radiogram and he held out his arm to push past me. 'C'mon, boykie, I'll be late. I'll tell you all about it later.'

It was Mom who came to my rescue. She appeared next to him, frowning, 'What's the problem? Oh. Well, why don't you take him? It's only a political meeting. Boring as hell.'

The circles spread under Dad's arms and rhino was definitely leaking out. 'What if there's trouble?'

'Trouble? *Ag*, for pity's sake, you dragged him out to Plessislaer in the middle of the night among all those wild natives and police. You nearly got yourself shot, and you're worried about this? Maybe having Tom there will remind you to behave yourself.'

Dad's shoulders drooped and I knew I'd won.

'Jesus wept! Get in the car. But you keep your trap shut, or . . .' He tapped his fist against my block.

He wasn't even doing the black eyebrow thing, so I smiled and walked stiff-legged out of the house, reminding myself to loosen the straps later.

•

In the hours following the storm, flying ants had been streaming out of the ground in their fatal mating flight. Shed wings lay thick under the streetlamps and each passing car stirred up a shimmering tornado that rose to the light and then spiralled back down to the road. Sol had described to us what this was all about; the males latched onto a female and then died during the mating, literally bursting. I could still see Sol's face when he got to that last part and I couldn't help smiling.

The last time I'd driven down this road at night with Sol and Millie, a dry Berg wind had been blowing and Sol was taking us on a mystery tour. It had been the night of the Gandhi story, of the little man thrown off the train and huddling with his thoughts in the waiting room through the freezing night.

Sol said Gandhi had gone through three stages that night— revenge, then flight, before finally arriving at non-violent resistance.

What stage had Sol been at when the masked South African soldiers threw hand grenades into the bedroom of their Lourenço Marques safe house and raked them with machine-gun fire?

Dad was talking to me, but I hadn't been listening. 'Sorry?'

'I said why did you want to come so badly?'

'To see you kill Verwoerd.'

The car swerved and screeched and someone flashed their lights and hooted. Dad pulled over to the side of the road near the hedge between the tennis courts and the Voortrekker cemetery.

He turned on me, one elbow on the back of the seat and one on the wheel.

'What are you talking about? Are you fucking stark-staring mad?!'

The air in the car was unbreathable. I wound down my window. I was scared but there was no stopping now.

'I heard you, Dad. I heard you in the lounge with Haas Cockroft. The Group. The plot.'

He held his hand to his mouth and looked through the windscreen. 'Holy Mother of God, Tom!' He opened the door and jumped out, lurching up and down the pavement, hitting himself on the side of the head with the heel of his hand.

He stopped at my window and leant both hands on the sill. 'How could you want that?'

I held his eye. 'Do it, Dad.'

He flung himself away again, moaning and pacing. He came back, slumped against the car and lit a cigarette.

'Come here, Tom.'

I got out and stood facing him. His face was ghastly in the yellow light of the streetlamp.

'Is this what you've been thinking all along, that I was part of an assassination plot?'

'Weren't you?'

He threw the cigarette over his shoulder and gathered me in with one long arm. My face was squashed against his belly and I felt the howl uncoil deep within him before it erupted into the night above my head. He was trying to say things but the howl kept overpowering the words. I heard 'child' and 'sick, sad country'. And as he rocked and held me, my own tears flooded out, spreading across his shirtfront and mixing with the rhino stain.

I don't know how long we clung to each other there on the side of the road with the evening traffic going by and the flying-ant wings glittering around us. I remember a car pulling up and then accelerating away, and through my head was running one of Sol's stories about how we become beasts when we enter the *lager*.

When Dad pulled away he fumbled for a hankie, blew his nose and handed it to me. I found a dry corner and did the same. He hoisted me onto the front fender of the car and took my hands in his. He rubbed a thumb over the scar on my wrist, his mouth working as he leant in.

'Tom, I was never part of that plan, okay?'

A few weeks ago that was what I wanted to hear most in the whole wide world, but all I felt now was stubborn disappointment.

'But did you ever consider it?'

My eyes were locked on his and for a sickening moment his face dissolved into that of a child. He backed off, dragging his eyes away, turned and placed his palms on the roof, pressing his forehead against the metal.

'I lost a friend too, boykie. Killing Verwoerd won't bring Sol or Millie back.'

But he didn't answer my question.

He gave a dry, bitter laugh and lifted his head, staring out into the road. 'Funny, hey? I've been the one roaring and shaking my fist, while Sol was Mr Hands-off, supposedly the one to bear witness. Now it turns out Sol was the action man all along; he just didn't make a fuss about it. Since his death, I've thought it over. I've spent my life trying to find where I fit in; bellowing from the sidelines, desperate for someone to throw me the ball. But you know, boykie, what Sol said was true. It can be enough to bear witness and tell the truth. And who better than a journalist, hey? We all do belong, all have roles to play.'

He heaved himself off the car. '*Kom, Wagter*, let's go or the game will be over.'

•

The massive red-brick city hall was the pride of the town: the biggest brick building housing the biggest pipe organ in the southern hemisphere. The Vienna Boys' Choir sang here, great orchestras had filled the vaulted roof with sound, and now a crowd of another sort was pushing its way through the frosted-glass doors. Uniformed police had formed a cordon around the entrance and others were inside, stationed at each doorway, slowing the crowd's entry. And it seemed everywhere you looked you met the hard stare of thick-set men in tight suits.

Inside the lobby, about thirty young men in jeans stood next to the curved staircase, smoking and scowling. The sleeves of their T-shirts were rolled up to their shoulders and they gripped the banister, flexing their arms.

'Railway men,' said Dad. 'Waiting for the students to cause trouble. Come on, up this way—we'll never get a seat downstairs.'

We climbed the staircase and walked along a corridor, entering the auditorium through glass doors and finding ourselves on the mezzanine balcony, side-on to the stage. The main table was draped with the national flag and flanked by vases of proteas. We took our seats and looked around the hall. Heat rose in waves from the packed rows, reminding me of the sweating hall at Plessislaer where we had heard the lawyer Mandela speak.

The front rows were reserved for National Party members and guests, and the press were seated at a table to one side. Despite his opposition to the government, Dad had received a formal invitation and should have been down there among the town dignitaries.

On the same level as us, but at the back of the hall, fifty or sixty university students had draped a banner reading FREE ALL POLITICAL PRISONERS over the balcony and were arguing with police who were trying to get them to remove it. From where we sat, it looked half-hearted and the students were laughing and shouting slogans at the police.

Down on the ground floor, it was difficult to make out anyone in the crowd. There were uniforms and medals in the front row, among them the tall frame of the Kolonel.

Just below us a face turned upward and a hand lifted in greeting. Dad grunted and nodded. It was Haas Cockroft, sitting at the end of a row near an exit, rubbing his arm where the cast had been, his knee jiggling. Alongside him were two men from the paper who I knew were members of The Group, Mr Albrightsen and Mr O'Neill. I couldn't see Mr Farrar among them.

'Dad, d'you think they'll do something?'

He snorted. 'All talk, boykie. It's too late for "God Save the Queen", and judging by the number of policemen around, I'd say the fire hoses are safe.' He turned away from Haas and The Group. 'But if there is any sort of nonsense, you get down behind this wall, do you understand?'

There were two policemen guarding the door near Haas. He would have to go past them if he wanted to get to the light switches. I wondered if one of The Group was carrying the hand grenade Haas had rolled on our dining table. Maybe Mr Farrar, who I couldn't see anywhere in the hall.

A cheer went up and most of the crowd stood and applauded when the official party walked onto the stage, Verwoerd taking his seat at the table with a smile and a wave. At the back of the hall, the students set up a chant, which was drowned out by boos and cheers.

Verwoerd looked up at the students, smiled and gave a slight bow.

This was supposed to be the moment when Haas went for the lights, but he was still there, knee jiggling. Maybe they had another plan. Dad didn't seem interested and never once looked down at Haas.

A boring man who I took to be the local party head welcomed the crowd in Afrikaans, droning on before introducing the provincial administrator, who spoke in English and Afrikaans about destiny and the significance of the Day of the Vow to all South Africans. I had rested my head on my arms on the railing and closed my eyes until I heard the administrator introduce Africa's greatest leader and the man with the courage to do what others in the free world only dared think.

Verwoerd came to the microphone, acknowledged the applause and waited for the crowd to settle and the students to finish their chant.

When he spoke, it was the same smiley voice I'd heard on the radio. But he was even more friendly in person, speaking English in a cultivated, high-pitched voice that again reminded me of my Uncle Ian.

He started by saying how happy he was to be in Pietermaritzburg, 'one of our earliest Voortrekker towns and capital of the first Boer republic, Natalia'.

I had expected him to thump the lectern and threaten our enemies, but he spoke calmly of what a good friend South Africa was of the West and how it was a model of peaceful coexistence for people of different racial groups.

Everything he said sounded like a hand outstretched in welcome. He said the white man in Africa had brought with him a civilising process and ideals which were helping African nations to achieve their independence. And he wanted that same independence for the Africans living in South Africa, too. He wanted them to prosper under democratic systems, which his government was committed to helping them achieve. But the black South Africans would have to do it in their own separate democracies, not as part of the republic.

'If an Italian works in France, he votes in Italy. And so it will be for the Africans who choose to work in South Africa. They will have the vote back in their own country,' he said.

The applause rattled like hail against the decorated plaster ceiling above our heads. He held his hand out for quiet and beamed down at the press table. He said there had been sensational reporting in the press, but dismissed it with a wave of the hand. 'It will pass.' And with a kindly smile he added that there had to be restrictions 'to protect the orderly masses of all races seeking peace and order'.

Murmurs of approval and a few chuckles rippled through the crowd, and next to me, Dad was shaking his head. 'He's a clever old bugger. He can make it sound like the rest of the world should take its lead from the Nats.'

And that's exactly what Verwoerd did next. He went around the world, pointing out the racial practices of America, Canada, India, Australia and so on. He paused to let that point sink in, and in the brief silence a voice shaky with emotion rose from the front of the hall.

'*Verraaier!*'

Traitor.

Verwoerd didn't even look up from his notes, but smiled and inclined his head.

'*Jy het die volk verraai.*' The voice was stronger now and out of the front row, from among the party officials, stepped a small, wiry man with close-cropped grey hair, pointing at Verwoerd.

'Dad! It's Mr de Wet.'

But Dad had already recognised our neighbour.

Police moved forward to restrain Mr de Wet, but the prime minister stayed them with a hand. He addressed Mr de Wet in English, no doubt for the sake of the press.

'In what way, my old friend, have I betrayed the people?'

Mr de Wet struggled for words and then in broken English said, 'You promised to deliver the Afrikaner *volk* from British injustice and to ensure our survival. But you have brought nothing but death and lies. Before the Lord, you have lied and betrayed our principles!'

Verwoerd's smile was fixed now and he coughed and picked up his notes.

As another party member stood up from the crowd to end the embarrassment, Mr de Wet reached into his pocket.

'He's got a gun!' someone screamed. And as Dad shoved my head down behind the balcony wall I saw thick arms and hands clawing at little Mr de Wet.

I ducked away from Dad and peeped over the balcony to see the grey crew-cut head sinking under a scrum of police and party officials that rolled towards an exit. A final thin '*Verraier!*' wailed through the doors before they slammed shut.

Folding wooden chairs slapped around the hall as people jumped up for a look, and a line of police cordoned off the stage.

Dad grabbed my arm. 'Just sit. It's okay. It's over. Just wait, it'll settle.'

He yanked the notebook out of his pocket and started scribbling. Below us, Ken Brady and the paper's photographer had their heads together. They looked up at Dad and tried to call out to him over the hubbub. I tapped him on the arm and he looked down then pointed at the exit. Follow the action. Get the story. Get the pictures.

A party official had the microphone. He was waving police off the stage and asking people to resume their seats. Verwoerd hadn't moved. He stood at the lectern, head bowed, while behind him an African in overalls swept up proteas spilt across the stage.

The noise died down and Verwoerd continued speaking as if nothing had happened. I looked across to the back of the hall; the students' seats were now empty. They knew the railway men would want some sort of revenge.

'For the tendency in Africa for nations to become independent, and at the same time to do justice to all, does not only mean being just to the black man of Africa, but also to be just to the white man of Africa.' And here Verwoerd paused and with a gentle smile gestured towards where Mr de Wet had sat.

'The white man came to Africa, perhaps to trade, in some cases, perhaps to bring the gospel; but the white man has remained to stay. And particularly we in this southernmost portion of Africa have such a stake here that this is our only motherland, we have nowhere else to go.'

Dad closed his notebook. 'Okay, let's get to the office. I'll find someone to run you home.'

'Did he have a gun?'

Dad shrugged. 'Unlikely. But it'll be hard to get the truth straight away. The government will have a good think about what they announce tonight. Come on.'

At the bottom of the stairs the railway men milled about, looking like they wanted to break something. A group of policemen was talking with them, trying to persuade them to go home.

We walked around the corner to the newspaper building, where Dad called everyone into the newsroom to pull apart and redesign the coverage. Early pages already plated up on the press would be dismantled and re-melted, and extra subs and printers were being called in for the remake. The Old Man had authorised the expensive exercise and he himself had just arrived, smoking a cigar and watching from a chair at the back of the newsroom, one slippered foot resting on a desk.

The Old Man caught my eye and crooked a finger at me. He was round and bald, and his eyes were always narrowed like he was squinting through smoke.

'Tom. You were there? Something to remember.'

His eyes ranged over the journalists bustling about their tasks, directed by Harry Mac standing in the centre of the room.

The Old Man grabbed a pad of copypaper and wrote something down. He pushed it across to me. 'Look it up. It's what they do. What we do.'

I fetched a dictionary off a nearby desk and found the entry, struggling with the pronunciation. *Schadenfreude.* Pleasure at the misfortunes of others.

Was that really what they were doing?

The newsroom had a similar air of excitement to the night of the Lourenço Marques raid. The reporters' and subs' faces shone like people at church.

I looked at the Old Man and he chuckled. You could never tell if he was serious or not.

He pulled on the cigar and blew a stream of smoke. 'Even if he'd shot him, it wouldn't change a thing. There's worse than Verwoerd waiting in the wings.' He chuckled again and I felt uncomfortable being around him.

Bobby Naidoo, the telex operator, walked into the room, saw me and held up a set of keys. 'Come, Tom, I'll take you home.'

I went to say goodbye to Dad and he patted me on the head like a dog and carried on talking to the print foreman. Bobby and I were out the door and walking down the corridor when he came hurrying after us.

'Boykie! Hey!'

He grabbed me by the shoulders. 'Sorry. Sorry. Everything okay?'

I nodded but I didn't know if I was all right. After I'd broken off my deal with the stars I'd wished secretly for a man to die. The man who'd killed Sol and Millie. The man with the smiley face who looked and sounded like Uncle Ian. Had that wish nearly come true?

Dad hugged me and went back to the newsroom.

The flying-ant wings had all blown away when Bobby drove me home, the long main road out of town deserted. Bobby was shocked by the incident and wanted to know every detail.

'Terrible business, terrible,' he said. 'Thank God it wasn't an Indian.'

I looked at him. 'An Indian?'

He nodded.

Dad always reckoned the Indians were a bit like the English-speakers, caught in the middle. The Nats didn't like them and wouldn't let them travel freely around the country. The poorer natives also didn't like the Indians, who owned the shops where the natives spent their money. There'd been quite a few flare-ups. It was only ten years since the last big riots when the natives burnt and looted Indian shops down in Durban, murdering and raping families. No one knew if the trouble would spread inland; then the police discovered a native mob gathering outside Pietermaritzburg. Mom's parents were alive then and their house was in a street where Indians were still allowed to live. My grandparents had sheltered an Indian family for two nights during the terror.

I looked across at Bobby behind the wheel. He would have been about my age when it happened. 'Don't worry,' I said. 'It was an Afrikaner, a member of the Nats. One of our neighbours.'

'Thank God. Terrible business.'

When we arrived at the entrance to the lane, it was blocked by a police van. Of course. Bobby slowed, eyes widening.

'It's okay, drop me here and I'll walk down. It's not far. It's fine.'

Bobby didn't argue and pulled away as soon as I was out of the car.

Up and down the lane, the house lights were on but everyone stayed behind closed doors. Everyone, of course, except Mom, who was waiting on the verandah and ran down the drive to meet me. She smothered me with kisses as though I'd survived some great disaster and half dragged me up the stairs. It was only then I realised I'd forgotten to loosen my caliper straps and Mom gasped when she knelt to undo them and saw the red weals where the buckles had bitten in.

While she rubbed my leg, I looked over her head and across the lane. A floodlight had been set up in the De Wets' front yard and all the lights were on in the house. There were police on the verandah, moving through the rooms, and stomping around Mr de Wet's neat garden. An ambulance was backed up in the drive, red light whipping, and I heard the doors close and the muffled shrieks of the *Bosmoedertjie* from inside the vehicle. I wondered if the police had trampled the Esmé Euvrard rose. The ambulance pulled away slowly and it felt like something was coming to an end in the lane.

32

DAD WAS STILL SNORING WHEN THE PAPER WAS delivered next morning, and Mom didn't bother to rouse him. We sat together at the table and read the reports.

Nearly half the front page was given over to a photo of the police scrum. Big men with twisted faces, clawing at the small figure of Mr de Wet, who looked more sad than anything. Next to it was a picture of Mr de Wet from his boxing days.

I felt sick. And ashamed.

I moved away from Mom and sat with my head in my hands, shaking.

She put a hand on my arm and carried on reading. When she got to Dad's account on the editorial page, she looked over. 'Do you want me to read Dad's piece to you?'

I shook my head.

Mom folded the paper and clasped her fingers. 'God, it's so awful. Everything. Mr de Wet, of all people.'

'What'll happen to Mr de Wet?' I had nearly said, 'What'll

happen to me?'

She shrugged and tapped the paper. 'Someone from the government says here that Karel de Wet was *a hero of the nation, distraught with grief after his only son was crippled while defending our country against terrorists.*'

'They'll say he's mad.'

We turned at the sound of Dad's voice, thick with sleep. He held on to the doorframe and coughed, clutching the front of his dressing gown, chest heaving. He slumped at the table, still clearing his throat, while Mom poured him a cup of tea. He reached for his cigarettes on the table, but with her free hand Mom slid them out of reach.

'Declared insane. You watch,' said Dad. 'It's not in the order of things that a sane white man, let alone a party member, would . . . well, whatever he was planning to do.'

'What about the *Bosmoedertjie*, Dad? I saw them take him away in an ambulance.'

'I dunno, poor bugger. Maybe they'll put them together.' He drank his tea and started reading the paper.

I looked at him and wondered if he was also thinking: Town Hill hospital.

Outside, it was another sparkling day. A hoopoe hooted in the Liebermans' jacaranda and the lazy drone of a lawnmower drifted across the hedges from down the lane. Next door, Titch switched on his radio and started moving weights around.

How could it all be so normal? Surely something had to have changed—there should be a dark shadow over the day or a distant rumbling. But there was nothing. Mr Lambert's shoe scraped past the house on his way to buy the morning paper, and nearby, two servants called out, laughing across a fence. In our backyard, Essie was hanging up the washing.

'Oh, shit!' Dad said, rising and looking towards the back door. 'A report came through last night and got lost in all the hullabaloo.

Windsor and the others they rounded up might not go to the gallows. Because he didn't actually commit an act of terrorism, they're talking of a life sentence in the new prison at Robben Island. I have to go and tell Essie.'

Mom followed him through the kitchen, leaving me staring out at the normal day beyond the verandah and the flowering hibiscus.

•

That night, Dad took a late call from the paper, Mom standing anxiously at his side. A bomb had exploded in Durban, and others at Port Elizabeth and Johannesburg. Details were sketchy and it was so late the paper could only fit in a stop-press item in red ink on the back page.

We had to wait for the radio news in the morning to learn more about it. The Durban bomb had been planted outside the pass office. In Port Elizabeth, an electricity substation was blown up, and in Johannesburg the target was a military drill hall. There were no injuries.

The SABC ran it as the second item, after reporting Dr Verwoerd's speech about South Africa being an example of democracy and a friend to the West. No mention was made of Mr de Wet.

Vorster came on after the bombing story to growl that these were isolated incidents which would not deter the government from its path of self-determination for all races, and those who had perpetrated these acts would be rounded up and face the full force of the law.

It was a different story, though, when Dad came home for lunch. He showed us a poster which had appeared on city streets throughout the country.

It announced the start of the armed struggle by the ANC, headed up by a new unit, *Umkhonto we Sizwe*. The Spear of the Nation.

The poster read: *The time comes in the life of any people when there remain two choices: to submit or fight. That time has now come to South Africa. We will not submit but will fight back with all means at our disposal in defence of our rights, our people and our freedom.*

'This is it,' said Dad. 'It's starting.'

There was my dark shadow, the distant rumble.

•

That afternoon I went to the *spookhuis*. There was no secret anymore, but the shame was thick and there was a feeling of something trapped. After each visit now, when I left, I thought I felt fingers trailing in my clothing, like when you brush past a *wag-'n-bietjie* bush. Two more empty houses in the lane now, the Liebermans' and the De Wets'. Would they become *spookhuise* too? I didn't think I could stand it. I sat in the window where Millie and I had watched the coastal storms a year earlier. The sun was setting and my eyes followed the line of shadow as it crept up over Hesketh, flitted across the ridges towards the Valley of a Thousand Hills and then slowly darkened the slopes of Table Mountain until the last shaft of golden light slipped off the top and out to sea.

•

Next morning at breakfast, Dad had a new look on his face: sad and tired. Mom picked up on it straight away and asked what was wrong. He pushed the paper towards her. Down the side of the front page ran a story under the headline: THERE WAS NO GUN.

Police had revealed the contents of Mr de Wet's pockets after arresting him. All they found was his membership card for the National Party. It had been torn in half. Mr de Wet had not been planning to kill Verwoerd. He had just wanted to throw his torn membership card at his leader's feet.

The story went on to say that Mr de Wet was being held in protective custody because police feared he might harm himself. I looked at Dad. Town Hill. He didn't say anything, just got up and went and sat in the car, waiting for Mom to drive him to work.

Dad postponed our holiday at the beach because he couldn't leave the paper while so much was going on. He said he was sure we would make it to the caravan by Christmas Day. Mom didn't like that. She said she needed to get out of the lane or she'd scream. So she set a date for about a week away and told Dad that she and I would be leaving on that day and he could come down by rickshaw for all she cared. We'd stay at the hotel until he arrived. He grumbled and hmphed but you could see he liked the idea of a deadline.

Essie was waiting for us to leave so she could get a bus to the family *kraal* at Kranskop for her own holiday, but she wasn't looking forward to her first Christmas without her son.

We had all thought Essie would be relieved to learn that Windsor would probably escape hanging, but the news had made little difference to how she felt.

'It doesn't matter, master,' she said to Dad. 'He is gone now. My boy is gone.'

·

The pattern of hot days and stormy afternoons continued and our pool became a magnet for my classmates, who wouldn't have visited otherwise. I didn't mind. They dive-bombed and ducked each other, then plonked in the shade and sucked Kool-Aid ice blocks. Mostly, I sat on the side and watched. One afternoon, Mom drove a bunch of us in to see *The Guns of Navarone* and she became a bit short with me for not being excited enough. She told me I should thank my lucky stars that I had friends, a pool and a mother to fetch and carry them to the bioscope.

'There are kids all over the world who would kill for what you've got.'

Of course she was right, but there were also kids who would kill for what I'd lost. I don't know; that sounded like something out of a film. And as for lucky stars, well. Everything was so mixed up and my mind wouldn't settle.

Dad had been thinking carefully about the political upheavals and for once was restrained in his leading articles. He said things were happening so fast he wanted to get his head around it all.

So it was a few days before he came out with this:

And so it begins. A new phase in the struggle for African liberation exploded into the national consciousness this week with the announcement of the armed struggle.

The government's own bloody hand, revealed last year in the State of Emergency, has triggered its opponents into a policy of meeting violence with violence.

The ANC bombing campaign also marks a shift that will only sink in during the uncertain times ahead. No longer are white people dominating the debate over political rights for black people. We could say the high point of resistance by white South Africans against apartheid has passed. The agenda of resistance is now being set by black South Africans. And they will continue to do so, no matter what the Nats throw at them, until the day comes when apartheid is nothing more than a squalid chapter in a history book. Until the thugs who run the Special Branch face some unknowable future justice, some Nuremburg of their own.

But this new phase has also spawned a disturbing omen for the future. By jailing, murdering, exiling and forcing underground our best black political minds, this government is stifling a generation of black leaders who are familiar with and aspire to democracy, even though they are denied it. There is even something polite about this armed resistance: the ANC leadership has specifically stated that its bombing campaign is designed to avoid harm to people.

Who will be the heirs apparent of these lost leaders when, one day, black majority rule becomes inevitable either through the ballot box or at the point of a gun? Will those future black leaders aspire to the same ideals as their silenced elders, or will they grab what they can for themselves because they have been warped in the white-hot moral vacuum of apartheid?

Some in this country are already referring to this decade as the Silent Sixties. What term will be applied to the decades after this?

In the words of the poet: 'And what rough beast, its hour come round at last, / slouches towards Bethlehem to be born?'

My first impulse was to walk down the lane and talk to Sol about it, but then my stomach lurched. I closed my eyes and saw his face and heard his voice. 'Watch and listen, Tomka.' But Sol didn't just want me to be an empty witness. He wanted me to work things out for myself.

•

Dad's leader must have got something out of his system because three days before Christmas he said he was ready for the beach.

On the day he finished up at work, Mom and I started folding bedding, packing suitcases and filling boxes with everything we needed for a month at the caravan. We didn't dare start loading the station wagon, though, because whatever we did would be wrong as far as Dad was concerned. While I was packing, I remembered there had been something else in the packet Sol had left me: a blank notebook and a pen. I put them in my bag for the beach.

When Bobby Naidoo dropped Dad off around the middle of the day we were carrying luggage out to the garage and lining it up. He stopped at the gate, collected the mail and went inside with just a glance at Mom and me.

'Oi! Come here, you two.'

He was yelling at us from inside the house, and Mom, holding a box of pots and pans, shook her hair back and raised her eyebrows at me.

'Come here yourself,' she called back, stacking the box next to the car.

'No, I mean it, come here.'

So we trooped back inside and found him sitting at the dining table with a new, unreadable face. Mom's annoyed expression turned to worry.

'Harry Mac?'

He started to speak and it turned into a long cough. All the while he held his hand palm down on a letter in front of him as though it might blow away. When he'd finished coughing, he tapped the letter.

'Just thought I'd better let you know the Special Branch has sent me a Christmas present. They're suing me.'

'What?' Mom sat down at the table. 'What for?'

He shrugged. 'Don't worry. I'd rather they got at me through the courts than . . . you know. I think my last leader tipped it for them. They're saying I've defamed the head of the Special Branch by comparing him with Nazi war criminals. They're right. I've defamed them all, even though it's true.'

'But what will happen?'

'Don't worry. They'll win and the paper will be fined. But that's all. It'll give them an excuse to go harder next time. The Old Man doesn't like it but says he can live with it, for now.'

'Harry Mac, I don't understand why you're smiling about this!'

'Because there are worse things in life than being sued by a bunch of apes. And besides, I've finally got under their skin.' And that really was it. Harry Mac needed this. He needed someone to take notice. The beetle was chewing at the wheel of the wagon.

But there'd been something else at work in his face ever since we walked in and now it spread into a big cheesy grin. He pulled his other hand out from under the table and flicked an envelope across to me. 'Oh, by the way, I found this in the letterbox too.'

I reached for the envelope but snatched my hand back like it was a snake.

The envelope was addressed to *Tom-Tom MacGregor.*

I stared at it and then up at Dad, a roaring in my head.

'It's postmarked Lourenço Marques, boykie.' The teasing had gone out of his voice. 'And it's dated only three days ago.'

I kept on staring until Mom leant across and slit the envelope open with her finger, took out a single sheet of paper and handed it to me.

Dear Tom-Tom,

I'm not in the mood for being clever so I just want you to know I'm OK. Well sort of.

Three of us survived—a baby, a woman and me.

Some day I'll write and tell you about it. Not now.

The hospital has a flat roof where a nurse wheels me up each day to get some air. We're on a hill overlooking the harbour and the nurse has pointed out American and Russian warships moored near each other.

The people who are looking after me have written to my uncle in America and we're waiting to hear from him. So maybe I'll get to see the States after all. How about that, Tom-Tom.

The nurse who wheels me around has agreed to bring me up here each night for the next week at 7.30 pm.

Will you be there?

Millie

I dropped the letter on the table and while Mom and Dad watched me with open mouths, I jumped up and hopped around the kitchen on my good leg. It was fine.

•

I lay curled on my bed, back to the door. Mom came and sat for a while, her hand on my hip, then left me alone. I cried when she left, sobbing into the balled-up blanket. Eventually I drifted off, curious about what lay in wait. But when my eyes closed there was nothing there. The walls had gone. Flash and Dale had escaped.

It was dark when I woke and a cooling breeze blew in the window. Voices drifted towards me from the other side of the house. They must have put off the beach trip until tomorrow. I looked at my watch, checked my leg was still steady then walked through to the main bedroom, towards the sound of Dad's chuckle. The door was partly open and in the wing mirror of Mom's dressing table something flashed. I stayed in the dark and watched the reflection.

Dad lay propped up in bed, arms behind his head, laughing like bubbles popping. At his feet was an open flat box with the tissue paper folded back, and in the space between the bed and the dressing table was Mom, arms out, head back, the swing skirt lifting around her bare legs as she floated. Turning. Spinning.

•

The sweetness of the mown lawn rose around my body and the grass blades scraped the scar on my wrist. I'd turned the volume up on the radiogram and left the door open so the sounds of my new record swelled over the dark garden. I'd heard the new single only a few days before and begged Mom to buy it for me. 'Telstar', space music, new music, unlike anything I'd heard before. I'd put the turntable on repeat tonight so I had plenty of time before Mom or Dad got sick of the tune and turned it off.

I went out into the lane and did what I had to do then came back and snuggled into the grass, listening to the sounds of the lane creep back between each play of 'Telstar'; the tick of beetles on screens, Titch's murmuring radio, and the trill of crickets that drills into your head until your brain could burst.

Above, the sky was clear, the stars sharp, watching me, waiting. I'd tried to break off the wish a few days ago, but a deal's a deal and they'd given me Millie back. Now they needed something in return. They obviously didn't want the leg, that was mine to keep.

I'd thought about it while I lay on my bed that afternoon. Then it came to me. I would give them the Van Deventers, release the family from shame.

Little glowing boats were starting to drift above my face, settling on the grass all around, and the balloon of red light from up the lane grew brighter, silhouetting the hedges, flickering against the trees. The fire must have spread to a jacaranda now, billowing the flower tubes with flame and launching them into the night. A sound of glass exploding. It was going up fast.

I'd walked through every room, opening the windows and saying goodbye to the Van Deventers, mentioning each of them by name, saying sorry to Gillian for not trying to become her friend and to little Theo for not learning his name. And when I walked out of the *spookhuis* for the last time, I left the front door open. No more secrets in the lane.

In the distance I heard a siren and, somewhere behind me, Mom's voice was calling my name.

I settled back and scanned the stars, waiting.

There, a bright dot passing over.

I reached out for Millie's hand and we rose together, gaining speed as we flew towards the Milky Way.

Historical Notes

Here is the background to some of the events that informed this book:

Verwoerd assassination attempts: In 1960, Verwoerd was shot and wounded by farmer David Pratt, who was declared mentally unfit to stand trial and who later committed suicide in a mental hospital. Six years later, Verwoerd was stabbed to death in the House of Assembly by parliamentary messenger Dimitri Tsafendas. Tsafendas was found not guilty by reason of insanity and died in a mental hospital. Although the incident in this novel is fictitious, the premise at the start of the story is based on fact: the author's father, a newspaper editor, was briefed by plotters of a hare-brained assassination attempt that never materialised and was never made public.

Nelson Mandela: The All-In Africa conference took place as described in Pietermaritzburg. It was Mandela's last public appearance for nearly thirty years and he went underground soon after. Mandela's capture took place outside Pietermaritzburg, as described (the tyre-changing incident is fiction). The timeframe for Mandela's period on the run has been condensed.

S.S. *Stuttgart* refugee ship: The ship sailed from Bremen in 1936 with more than five hundred German-Jewish refugees. They were met with protests by pro-Nazi Greyshirts at Cape Town.

Mahatma Gandhi: He was thrown off the train at Pietermaritzburg station when white passengers objected to his presence. It is said that he formulated his policy of non-violent resistance while sitting out the night in the waiting room.

Boer War concentration camp: The Pietermaritzburg camp was one of the first established by the British army, as described. Nearly two hundred inmates, mostly women and children, died of diseases in the camp.

Freedom Radio: A little-known feature of anti-apartheid resistance in Pietermaritzburg. The book's description of police methods to locate it, and the doctoring of the detection van's antenna, are based on fact.

The Group: Sometimes referred to as the Horticulturists. Not much is known about this protest group's membership. They disrupted a few public meetings but were largely ineffective.

The South African Border War: Sometimes referred to as the Forgotten War, this shadowy conflict began in confusion and misinformation in the mid 1960s and continued in the same fashion for more than twenty years. The start of the war has been brought forward in the book's timeframe.

Cross-border raids by South African agents: As the armed struggle intensified, South Africa began a policy of 'hot pursuit' into neighbouring countries, assassinating activists who had fled there.

Start of the armed struggle: The ANC's new military wing, *Umkhonto we Sizwe*, launched its bombing campaign on the Afrikaners' sacred day, Dingaan's Day, 16 December 1961. The bombings in three cities were designed to avoid human casualties.

Operation Rhino: One of the world's great conservation projects, which rescued the southern white rhino from the brink of extinction. The author's father was present at some of the trapping expeditions and brought back stories and photographs which informed this book.

The Panga Man: Phineas Tshitaundzi, the real-life Panga Man, operated around Pretoria but became a nationwide bogeyman in the late 1950s. When arrested, he was found to be a cleaner working in the South African Police detective branch, where artists' impressions of his face were displayed. He was hanged in 1960.

MOTH Shellhole: the Memorable Order of Tin Hats is an organisation of ex-servicemen; its branches across South Africa are called Shellholes.

Acknowledgements

Many people helped this book through to publication. Particular thanks go to Marele Day, a wonderful writer and an extraordinary mentor and friend.

The Northern Rivers Writers' Centre (NRWC) residential mentorship gave the book its first impetus, and I'd like to make a special mention of Chris Hanley, chair of the NRWC. His vision in founding the centre and the Byron Bay Writers Festival has inspired many a writing career in the region. My mentorship led to a NSW Litlink Varuna fellowship, and the unpublished manuscript award. Thanks to all the fine people at Varuna, and to consulting editor Jody Lee, whose calm and clear eye provided direction at a critical time.

At Allen & Unwin, it's difficult to express the depth of my gratitude to Annette Barlow for supporting the manuscript in its early forms, and keeping faith with it all the way through. Thanks also to the dedicated team I worked with at A&U, and the culture of mutual respect they engender: Tom Gilliatt, Ann Lennox, Henrietta

Ashton, to Ali Lavau for her meticulous, wise and sympathetic editing and to Jennifer Hamilton for her detailed proofread.

Thanks to Eben Venter for correcting my rusty Afrikaans, and to Enoch Cele for fixing my even rustier Zulu. Editor T.B. 'Jack' Frost generously gave permission to use material from *Natalia*, the historical journal of the Natal Society Foundation. Angela Quintal, editor of the *Witness* (formerly the *Natal Witness*) offered access to the Pietermaritzburg newspaper's archives. Thank you to Kathy L'Amour for permission to quote from her husband Louis L'Amour's book, *The Walking Drum*. Re-reading Ian Player's *Translocation of White Rhinoceros in South Africa* reminded me of my father's happiest times in the African bush with the great conservationist. The quotation at the front of the book is by kind permission of Martin Langford.

And of course, thanks to my family for their support, interest and advice: David and Viv Eldridge, Rosalyn and Forrest Hill and Eileen Eldridge, all of whom lived through the times depicted in this book. To the next generation, Mandy and Mark Hill, Christie Eldridge, Heather Eldridge, Claire and Thomas Rapson, Lenny Stewart, Felix Eldridge, Amy Eldridge, Andrew and Bronwyn Hill, and David and Jodi Hill: you understand what it is to live in an open society. To my grandchildren, Alice Hill, Fletcher Hill and Charlie Rapson, may you always be blessed with the freedom to speak your mind. Two posthumous mentions: Harry, who lay at my feet, licked my toes and farted while I wrote, and Penny, who draped herself across the wheels of my chair, forcing me to stay at my writing desk. RIP sweet dogs.

Final and most important thanks go to Brenda Shero for her intelligent insights, her constant support, and for her love.

About the author

Russell Eldridge was born and educated in Pietermaritzburg, South Africa, where he entered journalism on the *Natal Witness*. He later worked for the *Star* in Johannesburg before emigrating with his young family to Australia. He wrote for the *Sydney Morning Herald* before another move, this time to the Northern New South Wales countryside. He ended his full-time journalism career as editor of the *Northern Star*. He has achieved several honours, including a Walkley Awards commendation. Russell is a founding member of the Byron Bay Writers Festival, and lives at Ocean Shores with his partner, Brenda.